D0863176

Alice K. Boatwright

COLLATERAL DAMAGE

Collateral Damage © 2012 by Alice K. Boatwright

Standing Stone Books is a division of Standing Stone Studios, an organization dedicated to the promotion of the literary and visual arts.

Mailing addresses:
951 Comstock Avenue, Syracuse, New York 13210 U.S.A.
and
Jesserenstraat 58, 3850 Borgloon, Brussels, Belgium

Email: info@standingstonestudios.org

Web address: www.standingstonestudios.org

Standing Stone Books are available in both print and ebook formats.

This book is printed by Bookmobile, Minneapolis, Minnesota, and distributed by Small Press Distribution, Berkeley, California.

ISBN: 9780983617242

Library of Congress Control Number: 2001012345

Design by Adam Rozum

Standing Stone Books is a member of the Literary Council of Magazines and Presses.

[clmp]

Alice K. Boatwright

COLLATERAL DAMAGE

To Allegra —
It's wonderful to be
able to share my work
with you — after all
these years of admiring
yours!
love,
Alice

Standing Stone Books
Syracuse · Brussels

Collateral damage: Unintentional or incidental injury or damage to persons or objects that would not be lawful military targets in the circumstances ruling at the time. Such damage is not unlawful so long as it is not excessive in light of the overall military advantage anticipated from the attack.
—*Department of Defense Dictionary of Military and Associated Terms (JP1-02)*

"Let us, together, mend our errors and rebuild."
Tu Duc, Emperor of Vietnam, 1867

For Jim,
with love and thanks for our shared journey

About this book

The impetus to write this book goes back to a snowy day in 1968, when I received a letter from one of my high school friends telling me that he had attempted suicide rather than go to Vietnam. I was shocked and, at the same time, not shocked. My older brother had just been sent to fight in the war. My younger brother was worried about the draft. All the young men I knew were struggling with how to handle the first big decision of their adult lives—and it was a very big one—whether to follow the dictates of law or conscience and to face the consequences either way. We young women—their sisters, friends, and lovers—were on the sidelines of this moral conflict, but we were also deeply touched by it, and all of our lives were shaped by it.

I wrote the first version of "Getting Out" when I was a graduate student at Columbia University in 1970. At that time, the wars in South-East Asia and at home were raging, and young people were dying on both fronts. The second and third sections, set at key points in the post-war years, began as short stories. The idea of a "triptych" came about when a friend asked me what I wanted to write next, and I realized it was this book about the broad and lasting impact of the war.

Although the draft ended in the U.S. in 1973, each new war brings up the same questions: what is justified and when, who will fight and why, and will any good come out of it in the end?

Alice K. Boatwright
Paris, France
January 2012

COLLATERAL DAMAGE

Three novellas

1968: Getting Out

1968: Getting Out

1

First of all, I want to make it clear that my goal was not to wind up dead. I was only 20, and I hoped I was closer to the beginning of my life than the end. However, if you're going to attempt suicide, you have to narrow down your thinking to that one option and accept the possible consequences. Otherwise you won't do it.

I took enough Seconal to kill me. I knew that as I swallowed the pills, one by one, but I had also given myself a loophole. A parachute. No one knew what I was up to, but I timed everything carefully and made my bunkmate Thomas promise to get me up in the morning. It was a big risk, but I had to take it.

Back when I was still in college, Martha and I used to argue about the value of black and white thinking. She couldn't understand how I could be against the war and still have so much trouble deciding how to stay out of it.

"De-cis-io. It comes from the Latin verb 'to cut off'!" she'd say. "You have to take a stand, Toby. You're either against the war and you don't go, or you aren't and you do."

She made it sound easy, but then no one was ever going to come after her with a draft notice. The decision—in or out—was mine alone to make, and I still thought we had gone to school to learn to see shades of gray.

I joined the Navy because I hoped it would be a path between yes and no, but I turned out to be wrong. When I received orders to go to Vietnam, I knew I had to get out, one way or the other. That's what I wanted. That's what I believed was right.

Once the pills were down, of course, the plan was over. I was completely out of control. Thomas did manage to wake me, but staying conscious long enough to get to the infirmary proved harder than I expected. I walked like my legs were sandbags, and I couldn't see very well.

I remember a confusing blur of lights and voices. A doctor shouted at me "What have you done?" as he slapped my face over and over. Then he injected me with a drug that fought the Seconal, so my body felt like it was tearing apart: my heart racing forward and the rest falling backward into darkness.

I thought they would pump my stomach and kick me out the door as fast as they could, but they didn't. When the doctor was through with me, two corpsmen shoved me into the back of an ambulance. I had no idea where they were taking me, but the siren screamed that we'd better get there fast.

I blacked out a few times, but I remember one thing clearly: the moment we stopped at the gate and turned onto the public road. I couldn't actually see the guard salute, but I knew he was there, and then he was gone, and I remember thinking: Good.

I didn't receive a warm welcome at the hospital. One of the corpsmen stuck me in a wheelchair, and another one came along with some forms to fill out. This was still the Navy, after all. When I was unable to give him my name, rank, and serial number, he wrenched the dog tags up out of my middy and got the information for himself.

Finally they brought me upstairs to a ward secured by a door with a small barred window. Even in the state I was in, I knew what that meant. The speeding part of my brain wanted to turn and run, but I couldn't, so I barfed instead.

Inside the corpsmen from the ward took over. They threw me into a cold shower that felt like falling nails, and then gave me a pair of cotton pajamas, paper slippers, and a blue terrycloth robe. Other men in blue robes crowded around to watch as they brought me to a bed.

I was glad to lie down and close my eyes, but I couldn't sleep. I drifted between a dreamless darkness and a wakeful state where half words and images flicked through my brain too quickly to be understood.

I don't know how many hours or days passed that way. Sometimes I heard voices. A nasal voice saying: "All right, come on, let's go" like a traffic cop fending off gawkers at an accident. I understood that I was the accident, but then I was gone again. When real sleep finally came, I was exhausted and wished I would never wake up.

I didn't mean that though. I still wanted to live, but I couldn't believe that I was already faced with the same old problem. How to get from where I was to where I wanted to be. The buzzing fear that I would be sucked into the war was gone, but when a fly bangs and bangs against a window until it finally dies, the silence afterward isn't very satisfying.

2

I fucked up badly when I had to leave school, but that was nothing compared to this. I had risked my life to ditch Radioman 2nd Class Toby Woodruff and get back to being myself, Toby Woodruff—architecture student and itinerant house painter. But what had happened? I'd become a blue robe. In other words: a nothing. There were about 30 of us locked on a ward where fresh air seemed to stop short at the barred windows. The place smelled of sweat and dirty socks, and, even in the middle of the night, it was never quiet. Some robe was always jerking off. Having a bad dream. Thinking it was time to shout.

I decided not to talk, because I was sure if I even opened my mouth, I would get into more trouble. I needed time to cool off and figure out my position. Determine my next move.

I crawled into silence like a tent and zipped it shut. I had read quite a lot about yogis, and I figured if they could go for years without speaking, an ordinary guy ought to be able to last a few days—or however long I was going to be in that hospital. It wasn't like there was anyone around I wanted to talk to.

Yogis have one advantage though. They're not in the military, and they don't live on a crowded locked ward. I could sit cross-legged and silent on my bed for hours at a time; the nurses and corpsmen didn't give a shit if I talked or not. But no one was going to drop rice in a bowl at my feet to keep me alive. I was expected to get up on command, make my bed, line up for showers, march to the mess hall, take medication, and otherwise follow orders. Except for the drugs, I did what I was told.

There was no way I was going to take those drugs. Most of the guys on the ward were bug-eyed and drooled. They shuffled around like people with nowhere to go and all the time in the world to get there. I'd already consumed more than a lifetime's worth of downers in one night, so I did whatever I could to avoid swallowing any more meds.

My biggest fear was that the doctors would know that I wasn't crazy and send me to the brig as a faker. But the doctors who came by on rounds each day didn't ask to hear my story. They only said "How are you today, Woodruff?" and recorded my silence on their charts.

The blue robes ignored me once they found out that I didn't have any money or cigarettes. They had their own trips going on and couldn't be bothered with me. I studied them at first to pick up pointers on how to act, but there wasn't much I could use. The guy in the bed on my right was named Jerry Williams. He'd been a radioman like me, and I don't know what happened to him, but he sucked and chewed all day on a black sock that hung out of his mouth like a rotting tongue and, when he talked, it was in his own version of Morse code. On my other side was Bill Kleban, a tall broad-shouldered guy who threw off his pajamas every night and started each day with a long, loud yell.

I thought most of the robes had gone crazy from boredom. They hung out on their beds or at the tables down the middle of the ward—dozing, talking to themselves, or watching a TV that hung from the ceiling so no one could change the channel. You might think they would be entertaining, but they weren't. Just watching a guy on Thorazine try to roll a cigarette was enough for one day. A ward full of them, around the clock, was too much.

I closed my eyes and took myself off on hikes through the woods where I grew up in the Adirondacks. My brother Jack and I had a tree house in a sprawling maple overlooking Indian River. It had been a refuge for us, the place we went to plan our getaway to the outside world, and I made it my refuge then.

I might have gone on like that forever, if a robe named Russell O'Malley hadn't decided to take on my case. He parked himself at the foot of my bed one afternoon after lunch. I knew who he was because he spent every day playing cards with a big black guy named Alonzo Cooke at the table nearest my bed. I had listened to them talk for hours, but this was the first time he'd let on that he even knew I was there. He studied me like I was a picture on a wall, and he was a connoisseur, tipping his head this way and that, then taking a drag on his cigarette. I stared back at him and hoped he would go away.

A lot of the blue robes skittered off if you made eye contact with them, but not Russell. Russell's face had been burned in an explosion on his ship, and what he had left was a tuft of red hair sticking out of the top of his head and a mask of scar tissue with eye, nose, and mouth holes. He dared you to look away from his angry blue eyes, and, as he studied my face, he exhaled smoke from his little nose holes.

I kept my eyes on his, and our Mexican standoff continued until he stubbed out the cigarette in an ashtray on the table behind him. Alonzo was there, watching me with his calm, dark eyes as he cascaded a deck of cards back and forth from one hand to the other.

"So—Woodruff," Russell finally said, after looking at the name card on my bed. "Alonzo and I have been discussing you, and we think you need our help. But first we have to find out if you qualify, and we have made a bet on that. Alon says you tried to off yourself the night before you were supposed to ship out for Nam, and you did such an outstanding job that you are still alive, but a vegetable. That's why you sit here all day long like a pumpkin on a fence.

Or should I say a squash?" He drew the word out and slid into the final shhh.

"Me, I don't think you look like a suicide. And you don't look like a vegetable either. There's something crafty in your face. That's why I bet Alon two packs of cigarettes that I could get you to talk.

"I figure your problem is that you're bored, so that's where we come in. We want to invite you to join our gin game. This will give you something to do, something to look forward to. Something to live for, you might even say. We live for gin, don't we, Alon?" he said, turning back to his friend, who nodded slowly.

If I had been talking I would have said that a gin game in a nut house was not my idea of something to look forward to. But I wasn't, so I didn't.

"He doesn't look pleased, does he?" Russell said to Alonzo, then to me: "Maybe my theory is wrong. Maybe you are a vegetable. Or even worse. A rock.

"You know the difference between a vegetable and a rock? A vegetable rots of its own free will, but a rock has to be changed from the outside. Ground down. Smashed." Then he laughed, showing a set of big white plastic teeth.

He went back to his table after that, but in the basement corridor outside the mess hall that night, he came up behind me and said: "Hey there, Rocky. Have you thought any more about what I said? About the gin game? We play for cigarettes, you know."

I think he could see he'd hit a target with that, because he grinned, his lipless mouth pulling away from those teeth. I hadn't had a smoke since the night before I OD'd. But did I want one enough to play gin with Russell? That was the question.

He came back the next day, but this time he didn't say anything about playing cards. Instead he talked about his career in the Navy. The ships he'd been on. The battles they'd been in. The medals he'd won but sent back, because medals were a crock of shit. The whole time he talked he smoked one cigarette after another, lighting the fresh one off the butt of the one before, and he blew so much smoke over me I might as well have been smoking myself.

"Maybe you don't want to hear all this," he said at last. "Maybe it reminds you of all the great times you're missing by being here." Then he laughed, a horsy tooth-clacking laugh that hardly moved his scarred face, and left.

He may have hoped I'd be sorry he was gone, but I wasn't. I didn't want anything to do with the ward or anyone on it. I might liked to have a cigarette, but all I really wanted was to get out of there. Get my discharge, go back to school, get on with my life.

When I got this second chance, I was determined that I would not fuck up again, and I had developed a whole list of don'ts to help me steer a better course in the future.

Don't drink.

Don't take drugs.

Don't skip classes.

Don't get involved in politics.

Don't look back.

I repeated this over and over to myself, as I waited like a yogi—under my tree or, more accurately, on my bed—for something to happen. And, I suppose like a yogi, I had to accept what came my way, and that was Russell. Russell wasn't waiting. He didn't want to lose his bet. So he kept on coming around and talking at me.

I don't know why he singled me out for attention. He claimed that his table was an exclusive club and only patients handpicked by him got to sit there. If that were true (which I doubted), it didn't say anything good about either of us. Other than Alonzo, who seemed OK, the only other robes who sat regularly at that table were Williams and another guy who read all the time. Russell called Williams "Sock" and the other guy "Book." He talked at them too, so maybe he just liked to surround himself with people who didn't talk back.

Williams sat at the table and rocked back and forth, sucking on his sock, and muttering dit-dah, dit-dahs to himself. Book positioned himself as far from everyone else as he could and hunched over his book or magazine or whatever he had. I think he would have read upholstery labels if that was all there was. Every once in a while he'd come up for air, and I was surprised to notice that he must have once been a good-looking guy, but all the life had gone from his face, which had the color and texture of yellow clay. If he caught you looking at him, he immediately retreated to his book.

Alonzo was the only one who talked, but he had such a low voice that I could hardly ever make out what he was saying. Everything he did had a slow dignity and method about it, and you had to watch him for a while to realize that his actions were identical and repetitive. The way he settled his chair. The way he shuffled the cards. The position of the pad and pencil on the table.

I eavesdropped on a lot of conversations, and most of them made no sense at all. The blue robes were forgetful—they asked the same question over and over like "Got any smokes?" or "Is it time for lunch yet?" When they did try to say something more complicated, they got lost almost immediately. The fronts and backs of their sentences never seemed to match up.

Russell, at least, was a good storyteller. I didn't believe his stories, but they didn't sound crazy either. His rap was the sort of thing you'd hear from someone you were painting a house with or the guy next to you on a bus trip. I must have logged hundreds of hours listening to guys like him, and they weren't behind bars, so why was he? It made me wonder. And it worried me too.

When I didn't immediately fall in with his plan, he stepped up the campaign, stopping by on his way to the john or calling out to me from the table when he won a hand. But I was determined to resist him, and finally he gave up.

"I hate to lose a bet, Rocky," he said, blowing smoke in my face. "Especially with Alonzo. It makes him conceited. But you know this isn't just about him and me. You oughta get up off your ass. Sitting around all day is no way to live." Then he tossed a fresh pack of Luckies on my bed.

"This is for you. From Alon. He says it's your share of the winnings. Now don't be an asshole and pretend you don't want it, because I know you do. But if you want any more, you're going to have to play cards to get them. You don't have to talk, but you do have to play."

I looked from Russell to the shiny pack with its red bull's eye and for a moment I could taste that first cigarette. So sweet. So sharp. But there was no way I could take that pack. If I smoked those cigarettes, I would want more. Then more. And then more. So I got up from my bed and walked away.

"Jesus, you're stubborn," I heard Russell say, but I didn't look back.

Unfortunately there was nowhere to go except the john. Even that wasn't private because there were no doors on the stalls, but was it better than the ward. I went to the stall furthest from the entrance and crouched on top of the toilet seat.

I thought about three strikes and you're out, and how many pitches I'd already let go by without even swinging. My father had wanted me to join his construction company, but I said no. I had to go to college. Then I blew that, and I had to join the service. Now I'd blown off the Navy too.

I should have been somewhere in Vietnam by then, hunched over my radio, hoping to get through the day without having to kill anyone or be killed myself. I told myself I had dropped out because I was against the war. That's what this was about. Some of the guys from boot camp and radio school were probably already wounded. Maybe even dead. I couldn't sit around in pajamas smoking cigarettes and playing gin.

I stayed in the john until a corpsman named Basto came looking for me. His thick rectangular body filled the entrance to the stall and cast me into shadow. He must have been really angry that he was stuck on our ward. Tending the zit on the ass of the Navy instead of Marines just back from the war. Disapproval radiated from him like a bad case of B.O., but it was nothing compared to what I felt myself.

"It's time for mess, Woodruff," he said in a surly voice.

I let him march me down the ward, and I didn't look at Russell and Alonzo, but I did notice that the cigarettes were gone from my bed, and I was glad.

Russell stopped coming around after that. Instead he sat at the table playing cards and talking loudly to Alonzo about how people change. "Some people, like me, have to be set on fire," he said. "But even the ones who stand still are changing, whether they know it or not."

I tried not to listen. There is a zone beyond boredom. Every yogi must learn that.

A couple of days later, Russell developed a bad headache and, after a doctor came to give him an injection, he lay inert for hours with a night mask pulled over his eyes.

At dinner I took my usual place as far from everyone else as possible, and I was contemplating the task of eating a plate of gray Swedish meatballs when Alonzo appeared opposite me and sat down. He had a tray full of food, but he didn't dig into it right away. He watched me begin to eat and rubbed at his upper lip with fingers as thick as Tootsie Rolls. He looked like he was pulling at an invisible mustache.

Finally he said:

"He isn't fucking with you, you know. This ain't a place you can ride out of on a high horse. I'm not saying you crawl either. But you gotta walk. So you gotta think about it. What is the first step."

I thought he'd keep talking, but he didn't. He looked embarrassed like a person caught having a serious conversation with his dog. He picked up his fork and ate steadily, beginning at the left side of his tray and moving to the right. He finished exactly at the moment the corpsmen said: "All right, everybody, let's go."

I wasn't a dog though, and I did hear what he said. I thought about it as I sat on my bed. Yogic detachment had its place, but maybe a military nut ward wasn't it.

When I was about 14, I got so sick of my parents' arguments, I decided to move into the tree house. I planned to stay there forever—or at least all summer—and I was doing fine, until one morning I woke up and knew that I was going back. I had realized that if I wanted to leave home for good, I had to go to high school first.

So that's what happened at the hospital too. I began to face the fact that I couldn't get out of there, if I hadn't been there.

3

Long before I built the tree house, I started drawing floor plans, only I didn't know the term floor plan, so I thought of them as maps. Maps of houses. I drew them everywhere—on school papers, envelopes, whatever came to hand. No matter how big or small they were, they all had passages behind the walls, trap doors, and hidden rooms. The way I pictured them, they would look like ordinary houses, but they weren't.

When my mother discovered a cache of these drawings in my closet, she told everyone in the family about them. "Toby's going to grow up to be an architect," she informed anyone who would listen.

I was angry at first, but going public gave me the idea of drawing houses for specific people. I made a house for my father, for example, that consisted of a tool room, a garage, and a TV room. Jack's house had an indoor ski run, and my mother's was built around a huge garden.

To encourage me, my mother began to give me gifts: boxes of pencils, drafting tools, books about architects and their work. My father said I could look at all the books I wanted but, to make a living, I'd have to design practical houses, not Fallingwater. He gave me a job as a carpenter so I could learn what it took to actually build a house, but my mother liked feeding my dreams.

All through high school I had only one thought in mind—to go to college— and I made it happen. I chose Pittsburgh because I'd never been there, and I liked the gritty sound of it. What better place could there be to learn architecture than the city where steel is made?

Once I got there though, I lost my single-mindedness. My black and white thinking. I still wanted to be an architect, but I found out I wanted other things too and not all of them involved school.

I became friends with Peter Kropotkin in a drawing class my first year. He planned to be a sculptor, and he turned me on to Guinness and Gauloises, the blues and jazz, Rimbaud and *Ramparts*. We took long walks around the city to study the houses and buildings like geological strata, and at night we sat on a hillside to watch the Bessemer converters at U.S. Steel light up the sky like fireworks with explosions of sparks and flame. We called this communing with our muse.

We met Martha Reynolds a year later at a teach-in on the war. She came wearing a t-shirt and jeans spattered with fake blood and a straw Vietnamese farmer's hat with a sign on it that said "1 million dead." Her long dark hair hung in a single blood-spattered braid down her back. At the end of the meeting, she and Peter and I fell into conversation about the war, and within a few days it was hard to remember that there had ever been a time when I didn't know her.

At first we were just all friends. Hanging out on weekends and listening to music. She was the smartest girl I'd ever met, and I never expected her to fall in love with me, but she did.

"I spotted you at that teach-in," she told me one night when we went alone to watch the Bessemer converters. "You were listening so intently I knew I would like you. And besides you were wearing a denim jacket with stars on it."

"Peter's jacket," I pointed out.

"That doesn't matter. The point is it helped me to see you. Like when you suddenly see the pattern of a constellation in the sky." She was lying next to me on the grass, her face barely lit by moonlight, and I could have stayed there forever just looking at her.

I'd had girlfriends before. Soft warm girls and giggly girls and girls who wanted to be bad, but weren't sure how to go about it. None of them had prepared me for Martha. Martha was majoring in philosophy and could talk all night without getting tired. She had lived in France and had never cut her hair in her whole life. She didn't believe in eating animals, and she thought sex was part of everyday life like breathing.

"You are my North Star," I said, looking into her dark moonlit eyes, and I meant it, but that was back when I still thought I had an infallible sense of direction.

My dean knew better. He looked really upset when he called me in to tell me that my grades were too low to keep my scholarship. I would not be able to come back the next year.

"We wanted you to explore, Toby, not get lost," he said.

Well, lost is a relative term. College is supposed to broaden your horizons, and that's exactly what it did for me. Things that had once loomed large shrank to specks or disappeared.

4

Sitting on my bed, I felt safe, but safe isn't always safe. When you run to first base and get there before the ball, they yell "Safe!" But you can't just stay there. That isn't how the game works. You've got to keep moving if you want to make it home.

The night I finally went to sit at Russell's table, I felt like I was stealing a base. Neither he nor Alonzo said a word, but Russell set a pack of Luckies down in front of me and Alonzo dealt me a hand.

Williams stared at me for a few minutes, working his mouth in little circles as if building up to an outburst of dit-dah, dit-dahs, then got up, and went back to his bed. Book didn't leave, but he angled his chair so he could keep his back to all of us. I guess they weren't happy to see me there, but Russell grinned, showing his bright plastic teeth, and Alonzo created a fresh score sheet with three neat columns headed Russell, Alonzo, and Toby.

Russell was right about one thing. You don't have to talk to play gin. All I had to do was lay my cards down, and they could see for themselves what I had; I didn't have to say "Knock" or "Gin." Alonzo kept the score, methodically toting up our points after each hand.

Whoever won the hand got a cigarette from each of the others. The first time I won, Russell handed over a cigarette and said: "I knew you weren't really a vegetable, Rocko. You're too fucking watchful."

Alonzo laughed as he gave me my winnings. "He's going to be watching you cheat now."

"Yeah," said Russell, "but silence is consent."

If Russell cheated that night, I missed it. By the end of the evening, my throat was sore from smoking, but I still had 16 cigarettes, which I thought was pretty good for my first night. In fact, I felt rich.

"It's good you joined us," Alonzo said, as he stacked up the cards, pad, and pencil and turned them over to Russell for safekeeping. "We been needing a new player. Russell has about wore out my good nature."

I smiled, and, after taking out one last cigarette, I tucked the pack of Luckies carefully into my bathrobe pocket. Russell gave me a light off his cigarette, and I went back to my bed to enjoy my smoke.

If you can appreciate the difference between a guy with only a toothbrush to his name hunched on his bed imagining himself to be somewhere else and a guy stretched out blowing lazy smoke rings into the air, you'll understand the distance that I traveled in that day.

I decided to go back the next evening, and the evening after that, and then it was no longer a decision; I became one of the players at Russell's table. After a few days Sock stopped leaving every time I sat down and resumed his vigil over every movement within his eyes' reach. Book made a compromise. He leaned forward with his elbows on the table and his head in his hands so that he could create a small, enclosed world occupied only by what he was reading. A good solution to overcrowding, I thought.

I still spent most of the day sitting on my bed, but I wasn't a yogi anymore. I had reentered the world, and I had lost my purity, because now I had something other people wanted. Cigarettes. A person with possessions is a person with power—and a target for everyone without power. Robes who had never acknowledged my existence before turned up at my bed wanting to bum a smoke.

Having cigarettes also meant I had a need of my own. I had to have a light. Blue robes were not allowed to have matches, but, like the eternal flame, there was a cigarette burning somewhere on the ward all day long. If you had a cigarette going, you became a lighter for anyone who needed a light. That was the code.

I usually got my lights from Russell, who smoked constantly. For my part, I didn't mind giving a light to anyone who asked, but I only gave cigarettes to Williams. He was my neighbor, after all, and I thought he was worse off than everyone else with his nonsense language and drool-covered sock.

What I'd do is set a cigarette down on the table in front of him. He'd stare at it, rocking back and forth, and then, with a lightning move, pick it up, and stick it between his damp lips. This amount of activity called for a period of rocking before he was able to look around and see who had a light. Once his cigarette was lit, he smoked it in fast short tokes as if he were trying to get it all down before someone came along to grab it. Or maybe he was trying to beat the drool effect, because he drooled so much that the paper would get wet, and sometimes his cigarette disintegrated before he was halfway through, leaving shreds of tobacco on his chin.

One afternoon I was more bored than usual. It was hot July day and the TV droned with a soap opera that no one was watching. A lot of guys were sleeping in chairs at the tables or napping on their beds. I had a fresh pad of paper and a pencil in my pocket that Russell had given me "in case I ever felt inspired to write him a message." I had no intention of doing that, but I thought I might like to use it for drawing.

I was weighing the implications of being a blue robe who drew as well as played cards, when I noticed Williams staring at me intently from his bed. His round glassy eyes were fixed on me, and the black sock hung twitching from the corner of his mouth as he worked his lips in and out. Really it was disgusting.

I looked away, but he continued to stare as if intensity would communicate his message. He probably wanted a smoke, but I didn't want to give him one if it would encourage him to stare like that. I had often wondered if somewhere in Williams' scrambled brain he still knew Morse code, so I decided to test him. I took out my pad, wrote "Do you want a cigarette?" in code, and handed it to him.

I don't know if he understood it or not, but he took one look at the paper and bolted off of his bed, dit-dah, dit-dahing for all he was worth. He ended up chittering in a corner like a rabbit surrounded by dogs, and Basto had to get a doctor to give him a shot to calm him down.

I felt bad that my experiment had upset him, but I didn't think it was my fault. He was crazy after all. Someone didn't agree though, because I received a note of my own that night. As I got into bed, I put my hand under my pillow and found a scrap of paper there. I pulled it out and read in Morse code, "Watch who you mess with, draft dodger."

I couldn't decide which part of this message pissed me off more—the threat or the judgment. I had no idea who it was from and that bothered me too. I didn't care what the other robes thought of me, but I found myself looking at the people around me more carefully and wondering who they were.

To guys who freaked out in combat, I guess I could look like a draft dodger, but that term always made me think of someone who let a fast-moving ball go by. It was the light, quick action of someone who didn't want to get involved. Someone who sidestepped responsibility and missed the main event.

Nothing in my experience was like that. My friends and I spent hours discussing the issues. Trying to decide what was right. What was wrong. If anything, going into the military, the way I did, seemed like dodging the issues. Taking the easier, softer way by doing what you were told to do. Following the rules that said this is the way to be a man. A loyal American.

So in a way you could say the dilemma was over how you saw the ball. Was the ball the draft? Or was the ball the decision? And which one were you going to try to dodge?

5

I didn't start out against the war. I was raised hearing my father's stories about his adventures in the ski troops during World War II, and Jack and I acted out his battles on our own ski trails. When Dad wasn't home we'd go into his room and look at his white uniform, hanging ghostly under a plastic bag at the back of his closet.

He assured us that we'd have our chance too, and we believed him. Every generation of men in our family had fought in a war, as far back as anyone knew. For most of them, it was the only time they ever got the hell of out the woods.

The guys I grew up with were the same. They couldn't wait to sign up. Even the most inbred types wanted to go in the Army—they just couldn't get in.

The trouble with me was I had already gotten out of the woods. I had more information than the six o'clock news from Utica, New York. At the teach-in where I met Martha, I learned how Ho Chi Minh had tried to get help from Harry Truman at the end of World War II. Ho thought that the U.S. would want to support a new country that had declared independence using the very words of our own Declaration of Independence, but he got no reply. Instead we gave millions of dollars to the French, who were trying to take back their colonial possession. When the French were defeated, we refused to participate in the Geneva Convention that determined what should happen next and went in ourselves to police the newly divided country. We put a corrupt unpopular leader in power in the south, and then, when he got out of control, we let him be assassinated.

What can I say? I was raised on Wheaties and Wonder Bread. I wanted Americans to be white-clad heroes swooping down out of the mountains to right wrongs and defend freedom. What I heard made me angry. And it fitted right in with a lot of other things to be angry about like civil rights—an issue that had pretty much missed me until then. There were no blacks where I lived, but there were Indian tribes, and I knew what had happened to them was no heroic tale.

"You're just gobbling up that commie bullshit, aren't you," my father said when I tried to talk about the war with him. "Haven't you heard of Red China? Don't you know what happened to Eastern Europe? You think those people wouldn't give anything to have us come in and save them? Well, they would. And the Vietnamese would too, if they knew what was good for them, but half the time I don't think they do."

He had a point about the communists taking over countries. At least, I thought maybe he had a point, until he went off on that business about people not knowing what was good for them. That was his argument for everything that involved people not agreeing with him and doing what he wanted them to do; it was my practice to stop listening whenever the phrase came up.

I decided it was better not to discuss politics at home, and after that I confined my reports about college life to long-winded summaries of the courses I was taking in math and drafting and the history of architecture. My mother would try to look interested, but it didn't take long for them all to wish I would shut up and go back to Pittsburgh. Which I did.

Peter and Martha and I volunteered to pass out leaflets and help the anti-war movement in Pittsburgh, but there wasn't all that much going on there. I didn't really understand the magnitude of what we were dealing with until we drove to New York for a mobilization against the war in the spring of 1967.

As we walked from the car to Madison Avenue, we could tell the people who were on their way to the march too. Not that they were all wearing peace buttons or carrying banners, although many were. It was the expression on their faces, a lightness that passed from one to another like candles being lit.

But even that still didn't prepare us for the crowd. Some 300,000 people had showed up—more people than any of us had ever seen in one place in our lives. Madison Avenue was packed with people as far as you could see, and this wasn't the Macy's Thanksgiving Day Parade. It was a political statement from the American people to the government: "Stop the war now!"

Above the crowd floated homemade flags and banners that had slogans like "Another Mother for Peace," "Bring the Boys Home Now," and "No More Bombing." The marchers moved slowly like a glacier of hippies and dogs, men and women in business suits, elderly people in sturdy walking shoes, and whole families with children. I thought that many people ought to have the power to make anything happen.

We chanted as we walked—

"What do we want?"

"Peace!"

"When do we want it?"

"Now!"

—and the sound reverberated off the towering buildings to rise up into the blue sky.

At home I skied and hunted and I could spin my father's truck in six perfect doughnuts on an icy road, but I was always thinking about getting away, and that set me apart. My high school friends tolerated me like an eccentric cousin, but they didn't share my dreams. Even in my own family, I felt like I'd been randomly assigned a place to live among reasonably well-meaning people.

But that day in New York, I found the country I wanted to be part of. For the first time, I felt the exhilaration of giving myself up to become part of a greater whole that made me greater as well. Pressed against the moving crowd, I forgot where my body began and ended; my voice blended so fully with theirs that I could feel their voices vibrating in my chest.

In the Navy they tried to produce that sense of oneness with marching and pageantry, teamwork, sweat, and ritual. They wanted to convince you that, as part of a greater whole, you were fighting for democracy, freedom, and all that. I know this had worked for my father, but for me, it never rang true the way it did at that rally.

I told myself that attempting suicide to stay out of the war was a way to re-declare my allegiance to the America that I wanted to serve.

6

The day I met with John Barry for the first time, no one explained what was happening. A nurse named Pearson, who had soft hands and an apologetic manner, appeared at my bedside with a contraption like cloth handcuffs and marched me off the ward. I didn't know where he was taking me. The Brig. Shock treatments.

For some reason Pearson thought I was deaf, as well as dumb, so he guided me along by pointing and pulling on my bathrobe until we reached a corridor I hadn't seen before. We finally stopped outside a closed door with a folded piece of paper stuck in the sign holder that said "J. Barry, M.D." in ballpoint pen. Pearson knocked, and the door opened.

Dr. J. Barry stood in the doorway with half a sandwich in his hand, and I realized that I had seen him before on the ward doing rounds. He stood out among the doctors not only because he was younger, but also because, while they looked merged with their uniforms—gold buttons, epaulets, and all—he looked like a person with a life apart. Someone who had not yet been fully digested by the Navy. He welcomed me to his office with a wave of his sandwich, and, when he smiled, a fleck of tuna fish on the corner of his mouth fell off.

"Hey, Toby. Come on in," he said, as if we were friends and I had dropped by for a beer on a summer afternoon. On his desk, along with a mountain of file folders, stood a portable radio tuned to a Phillies game and the rest of his lunch

—a bottle of Coke, a bag of potato chips, and a package of Hostess cupcakes.

Pearson took off my handcuffs and gave me a tap on the back, as if to urge me through the door. Dr. Barry pointed to the chair in front of his desk, and, although he continued to smile, I saw him lock the door behind me.

I sat on a wooden chair with my hands sweating onto my knees, while Dr. Barry flicked off his radio and sat down. On the ward he'd made a few attempts to talk to me, but usually he took notes as if I were an interesting specimen.

Now he leaned forward with his hands folded on the desk and, still smiling, said: "So, here you are." His expression was clearly meant to invite confidence.

When I didn't say anything, he continued the conversation on his own. "I've read up on you," he said, fingering a worn folder. "For six months you appeared to be doing very well, and then overnight"—he snapped his fingers—"you ingested so much Seconal that it was touch and go for quite a while to keep your heart beating. Do you remember that?"

I looked at my knees. I remembered the shots into my neck and the sudden rush of my heartbeat.

"Do you remember why you did that?" Dr. Barry asked.

I didn't look up.

I don't like doctors under any circumstances, and I definitely did not like this one. Way too much depended on what he thought. What he did. There was a long silence then his chair creaked as he leaned back.

"You know, Toby," he said. "Some guys don't really like the service. They think they made a mistake when they enlisted, and they'd like to get out. So they have an accident. They shoot themselves in the toe or something. Nothing life-threatening, preferably nothing too painful. Sometimes it works for them— they do get out—and sometimes they get sent back to duty with one less toe. I don't worry about them. They may not be good at their jobs, and they might be a pain in the ass to their officers, but those aren't my kind of problems.

"At the other end of the spectrum are the guys who want out so badly they put the gun in their mouths and blow their brains out. We never get a chance to find out what was going on with them, but you can be sure it wasn't good.

"Then there's the guy who goes for the middle road. He shoots himself in the stomach, makes a real mess of himself. Nearly dies. Suffers a lot. Maybe he recovers. Maybe he doesn't. He's the question mark to me. What would you think he was trying to say?" Dr. Barry waited for me to speak and, when I didn't, he leaned forward and opened his desk drawer. He got out a pack of Marlboros and took one himself, before sliding the pack across to me.

"Cigarette?" he said.

I still refused to look up. I could see where he was headed, and I didn't like it.

"All right," he continued. "Forget the guy with the gun. Let's look at people who don't talk. Is that interesting to you?

"When I have a patient who doesn't talk, there are a few conclusions I can draw. He might have had a stroke, for example, or a tremendous shock that caused a psychotic break. He might be catatonic. Or then again, he might just be pigheaded—trying to make some kind of point—or he might even be scared.

"It's my guess that the first three don't apply to your case. I could be wrong, but I don't think I am. And it's OK with me if you don't want to talk. It doesn't mean shit as far as my life's concerned. I go home at night. Drink a couple of beers. Take my girlfriend out. Walk my dog. Sleep in my own bed. I'm not the one who is on a locked ward is what I'm saying. You are."

"You came very close to dying from that overdose. Do you understand that? In my experience, people who try that hard to kill themselves, try it again, and I don't like losing patients. That's why I'm a shrink instead of a surgeon. The death rate is usually lower.

"I also don't like losing bright guys who could have a decent life ahead of them, but I can't do a fucking thing for you if you won't talk to me. You've got to play ball, and I'm the only one on your team right now."

Dr. Barry got up and went to the window.

"Let me set you straight on a couple of things about your situation. This interview is just preliminary. I'm supposed to check you out. Next week you'll go before the doctors' committee, and they'll discuss your case based on what I tell them and what you tell them. They don't have a lot of time, so they're going to pretty much accept whatever you give them. If you're unresponsive, they'll play you that way. Depressed. Maybe dangerous. A nuisance to himself and others. Lock him up. On the other hand, if you show that you're coming around, making progress, they might throw some bennies your way like hospital privileges. They're not going to let you out of here, so don't imagine that.

"Depending on what they think, you'll be here for a very long time or a not very long time. They'll also make a recommendation to the Medical Board, which will decide whether you were always crazy and shouldn't have been in the Navy in the first place or not. That will affect your benefits later.

"The Navy would like to know where you got all that Seconal. Personally I don't give a shit about that. I'd like to know why you took it, but we aren't here to do psychoanalysis, so don't build up any false expectations. When we talk about treatment here, we are talking about drugs."

He turned away from the window and looked down at me. "Nice beach weather today. You like the beach?" he asked. "I really love a day at the beach. I like to surf."

I crossed my arms and looked up to see if he really expected me to believe that. I guess he did, because he smiled and suddenly crouched down as if he were riding a wave.

I must have looked surprised, because he laughed and stood up again.

"Well," he said, "I think we're finished for today. But let me summarize what I want you to think about: Are you going to trust me? Are you going to talk to the doctors' committee? Will you be here short or long?

"You've been here what?" He went back to his desk and consulted my file. "Three weeks? Let me tell you, you'd better relax."

I couldn't help frowning when I heard this.

"Relax," Dr. Barry repeated.

"Take some cigarettes," he said, as he went to the door to get Pearson. "And, by the way, you can call me Barry. My first name is John, but I hate it. So boring." He flashed me a smile that suggested we had spent a very enjoyable time together and were parting good friends.

"Tuesday," he said, as Pearson put me back in restraints. "Today is Thursday. We go before the committee on Tuesday. Got it?" And then he shut his door.

7

I guess I should have been happy that my performance was so convincing—that I had not been consigned to the toe-shooting category of losers—but I wasn't. It was definitely contradictory, but I didn't appreciate Barry's suggestion that I might actually be crazy at all.

I retreated to my bed to meditate on how I could convince this doctors' committee to let me go. I had to persuade them that although I had nearly done myself in, I was not violent or a danger to others, and I wasn't going to try to kill myself again. Barry was dead wrong about that.

It was obvious that I was going to have to start talking. The problem was, when you haven't been talking for a while, it's hard to know how to go back. What word to say first. Do you start speaking in full sentences? Or do you break in slowly with a word here and there?

Martha and I had fights that ended up with our not speaking, but she could never keep it up as long as I could. She'd say, "If we don't talk, how are we ever going to resolve anything?" She was a great believer in resolutions—a kind of Hegelian dialectic of relationships that ended with her view and my view becoming our view. She also believed in honesty, and one of the rules in our relationship was that we never lie. That was hard for me. In my family, lies penetrated the fabric of our communication down to the level of "How are you? I'm fine." I wasn't accustomed to truth telling, and silence, I had found, was an excellent way to avoid lying.

So beyond the question of when to speak lay the question what to say. How could I explain myself without getting caught by either lies or the truth?

I went round and round on these issues without making any progress, until I became so restless, I couldn't sit on my bed any more. Instead I paced up and down in the john, stood by the window counting the cars in the hospital parking lot, and even tried watching TV with the robes.

"I don't know what bug you've got up your ass, Rocky, but you're a wreck," said Russell, and I would have laughed, but I couldn't.

Then, on Sunday, while we were waiting in the corridor outside the mess before lunch, a new guy on the ward named Donny Cullihan tried to steal Williams' sock.

At first Williams didn't even notice. He was leaning against the wall with his eyes fixed on some middle distance, and for once he wasn't sucking on the sock, he'd put it in his pocket. Maybe, like me, he was anticipating lunch. Sunday lunch was usually the best meal of the week.

Cullihan stood between Williams and me. He was a small guy with mean little eyes and a lot of tattoos, who reportedly had cracked up on his third tour of duty. I would have considered him as the likely author of my anonymous note, except that sneaky wasn't his style. He preferred an audience for his meanness.

That's why I noticed he was after Williams' sock. He made a big deal of it. He rolled his eyes toward the sock, reached toward it, and tweaked it part way out of the pocket. Really the guy was good. If he weren't such a show-off, he could have had a career as a pickpocket.

A couple of other robes were watching this show, but Williams was oblivious to what was going on, and the corpsmen were down at the front of the line, trying to figure out how long we were going to be kept in the hall.

I thought for sure Williams would catch on—he normally had the radar of a hunted animal—but he didn't, so Cullihan became more and more bold, and the sock advanced out of the pocket inch by inch.

I hated to think what a scene Williams would create if Cullihan took his sock or it fell on the floor. The emotional mayhem. The impact on how long it would take for us to get fed. So, at the moment when Cullihan was poised to make the final tweak, I grabbed his wrist, squeezed it hard, and said: "Don't."

The word popped out of my mouth, surprising me almost as much as it surprised him.

"Son of a bitch!" he said, and he looked at me as if I'd suddenly materialized from outer space. "Why are you messing with me?" He jerked his hand away and pressed his chest out, ready to fight.

"You know," I said.

"No, I do not know," said Cullihan.

At the sound of our voices, Williams finally came out of his trance. He glanced at Cullihan, eyes wide, and his hand went immediately to the sock dangling from his pocket. He snatched it up, stuffed it in his mouth, and began to whimper and bounce on his feet like a little kid who has to pee.

Pearson turned at that moment and started toward us. "What's going on?" he asked, putting a calming hand on Williams' shoulder. He looked from Cullihan to me.

"Nothin'," said Cullihan in a sulky voice.

I shrugged, but Russell, who had his own brand of radar, had heard me speak.

During the gin game that night, he went on and on about it, as if this were a miracle he had somehow brought about himself.

"I knew you could do it, Rocky. I always know the real score. You were never a vegetable. Now come on, let's hear you talk. Say gin. Say Russell. Say hurry up and deal."

"Leave him alone," Alonzo said finally. "Some folks only talk when they have something to say."

"Right," I said, and Russell let out a big hoarse laugh.

After that, it got easier.

8

The day I met with the doctors' committee started off badly. The weather was muggy and hot, and Bill would not stop howling. He clutched the window bars in his fists, threw back his head, and let loose a series of yells that could have lifted paint.

Everyone was used to his morning yell, but this went on too long. It set off an agitation that ricocheted around the ward. Williams began to chitter on his bed, and robes who usually stared numbly at the TV all day paced around as if they were trying to escape the sound. Russell shouted "Shut up! Shut the fuck up!" with every scream.

Bill was tall and probably weighed as much as Basto and Pearson put together, so they had a hard time subduing him. Bill screamed, his face sweating and contorted as Basto held him from behind like a pit bull. Bill strained to hold onto the window bars, but Pearson pried his fingers loose. The instant his grip began to give way, Pearson yanked his bathrobe into a kind of straitjacket, and they marched him, still howling, down to a small padded room known as the Quiet Room.

In the aftermath, everyone on the ward was quiet, but jumpy. Basto said to Russell: "You'd better calm down or you'll end up in the Quiet Room too."

"Go fuck yourself!" Russell said, and he would have lunged at Basto if Alonzo hadn't stepped in between them.

On the way down to the mess hall—a longer and more jittery trip than usual—Russell said "I've had it with this place," and slammed his fist repeatedly against the wall.

I filled a tray of food, but, when I sat down and looked at it, I couldn't eat the rubbery yellow eggs and toast that was soggy from the steam table. Instead I lit a new cigarette off the butt of each one I finished and drank black coffee to try to clear my head.

Russell scowled, looking from me, to Alonzo, to the bowl of oatmeal on his tray, and didn't eat anything either; but Alonzo, as usual, made his way from right to left through a pile of pancakes as if nothing had happened. When he stopped for breath, he noticed I wasn't eating and said: "You should eat, Toby. This is a big day for you."

"He's right, Rocky," Russell said, stabbing his spoon into his cereal. "The less I eat, the sooner I get out of here. For you it's not so simple. You've got to talk your way out."

"Or something," I said.

"Oh, the doctors' committee ain't bad," said Alonzo. "Just be sure you know the date. They always ask if you know that."

"The date!" said Russell. "What the fuck good is knowing that? They ought to ask how you stay sane without ever having one fucking minute to yourself. That's what they ought to ask."

"You're right about that," I said.

"Of course, I'm right. I'm always fucking right. You went to college, didn't you? Did you ever read Sartre? He's the guy who said 'Hell is other people.' I'll bet you didn't think I'd know something like that. A stupid shit like me.

But I know lots of things. The world ends, not with a bang, but a whimper. Right? Well, you can see that here every day. Christ, I'm the living whimper that should have gone out with a bang.

"Want to know where I learned that stuff? From the wall of a shitter in Nam. There are all kinds of guys in Nam. College kids like you. Smarter than you. Lots of them dead now. Or here," he added, waving at the tables reserved for amputees. "So what's that all about? What's the meaning of their lives? You should ask those doctors that. I don't know why they want to ask you questions anyway. If you had any answers about anything, you wouldn't be locked up here."

He was right about that too.

By the time Basto dropped me off for the doctors' meeting, my pajamas were damp with sweat. He left me in a sort of waiting room with three metal chairs and a small table with an ashtray that was overflowing with butts. I sat there, smoking, with my mind completely blank, until an inner door opened and Barry appeared.

"How're you doing, Toby?" he asked. "Are you ready for this?"

I stubbed out my cigarette and wiped my hands on my robe. He looked worried that I didn't answer, but when I said: "Whatever," he grinned.

"Good man," he said. Then he held up his wrist so I could see that he wore a Mickey Mouse watch. "It'll take about one hour. That's all." Mickey's white-gloved hands read 11 a.m. On right side of the face there was also a little box that said: 14. "OK?" he said, and I nodded. "Let's go. They're waiting."

He held the door wide for me to go in before him. Inside I could see three white-uniformed doctors sitting in a row and a single chair placed opposite them. From the wall President Johnson looked down on us with his tiny eyes, pendulous nose, and Buddha-like earlobes. Not a reassuring presence.

I put my hands in the pockets of my bathrobe and tried to relax. I imagined the cigarette I would smoke when this was over. Then I took a slow deep breath and met the eyes of the first doctor to speak.

They wanted to know everything from my name, rank, and serial number, date of birth, and mother's maiden name to the name of the president. Lyndon Baines Johnson, I said, as if I could forget that with him staring down at me.

And the date. Alonzo was right. They asked if I knew the date, and I told them: July 14, 1968.

The factual questions were easy, but eventually they moved on to the stickier ones.

"Why did you take an overdose of Seconal?" asked a doctor whose uniform buttons strained across his belly. His eyes, behind thick military-issue glasses, looked round and blurry. "Did you know that the regular dose is only one pill? That to take more was dangerous?"

"Yes."

"So you deliberately took an overdose?"

"Yes."

"What were you thinking when you did that?"

I took so long to say anything that he repeated the question:

"Can you tell us you were thinking—feeling—when you took the pills?"

Out of the corner of my eye, I could see Barry watching me intently as he tapped his pen against his clipboard. Dit dah dit dit dah. If it was supposed to be a message in code, I couldn't read it.

I crossed my legs and resettled my left hand around the cigarette pack in my pocket. Where my fingers had been resting, the cellophane was slippery with sweat.

"I was thinking it was the best choice," I said at last.

"What were the other choices, as you saw it?"

"Unexpected death," I said, looking into the doctor's face. "That was the other choice. It was a planned death or an unexpected one. I thought it would be preferable to know when I was going to die."

I might have added that I thought killing myself to avoid fighting in an illegal war was more patriotic than dying in combat, but I didn't think they'd appreciate that.

A pale thin-lipped doctor looked up from my file and said, "You were about to ship out to Vietnam, so, when you say the other choice was an unexpected death, are you saying that you were afraid you would die in the war?"

I knew this was where they'd probably go. I mean I had to be the loser to be here. But I didn't like their thinking what I did was about fear.

"I wasn't afraid," I said. "I was angry."

The fourth doctor, who wore a heavy gold watch, said: "And what exactly were you angry about?"

"A lot of things," I said.

"Like what?"

"I was unhappy about a lot of things."

"Unhappy or angry?" asked the gold watch.

"Both."

"Lots of people are unhappy and angry. They don't try to kill themselves."

It wasn't a question, so I didn't say anything. The gold watch stared at me, and I stared back until Barry jumped in and asked:

"Have you ever tried to kill yourself before?"

"No," I said, turning to him.

"Do you think suicide is a good way to solve problems? I mean, you said you were choosing a planned death. But then here you are. What do you think about that?"

"How good does anyone feel about being here?"

"I'm asking you. How did you feel when you found yourself here?"

"Surprised." I said.

"Exactly," said Barry. "And were you glad to discover that you were still alive?"

"No. Not at first."

"But now."

"Now I'm locked up. It's not exactly living."

"But it's not being dead either. What do you think being dead would be like?"

"Dead is dead."

"So is this better?"

He was waiting, pen poised over clipboard, never moving his eyes from my face.

"Yes," I said, finally. "This is better."

After a moment, he shut his file. "Thank you. I think we've got enough for now." He stood up and waited for me to stand.

"We'll let you know in a few days what we've decided," he said as he escorted me back to the waiting corpsman. He didn't give any sign of what he thought about the interview, so I had nothing to do but go back to the ward and wonder how many days a few would be.

I wished I knew what conclusions they would draw from the fact that I could recognize the president. And if they liked my explanation of the expression "Don't cry over spilled milk." ("Wait for something better to cry over.")

Would they tell themselves that was my problem?

That I refused to accept that the milk had spilled?

I was in the Navy for six years or bust?

Or was the problem that I'd stepped out of line by trying to take my own life? Fate and the government were the only ones allowed to do that. Not guys like me.

9

Last year, before I had any idea where I was headed, Peter and I had a conversation about the draft. The semester was over, and he, Martha, and I had rented an apartment together for the summer. I had lined up some house painting jobs for us, and everything should have been perfect, but I had just lost my scholarship, so I was in no mood for celebrating. Without a student deferment, I knew I'd get drafted soon.

Peter listed off all the ways guys we knew had stayed out of the war, and one by one I vetoed them.

I couldn't get conscientious objector status, I said, because my draft board would turn me down flat. I'd been hunting with some of those men since I was eight years old. They'd never believe anything I said about being against war. Killing.

I couldn't hire a shrink to say I wasn't mentally or emotionally fit for service because a) I didn't have the money, b) I didn't believe in shrinks, and c) that wasn't honest. I was fit for service. I just didn't want to serve in this war.

I also could not, would not maim myself, starve myself, or go to my physical on drugs.

I would not tell the Army I was queer, and I definitely would not go to jail.

"I want to be the first person in my family to get a college degree, not the first person convicted of a felony," I said.

"You're a tough case, Toby," said Peter, lighting up a joint. The Army wasn't interested in him because he had bad knees, and he had fantasies about dropping out of college to become a draft counselor. "I'm not good enough to kill," he liked to say. "I want to help the guys who are."

He took a long toke and exhaled slowly. "You've only got one choice then, you know."

"What's that?" I said, although I knew what he was going to say.

"You'll have to go to Canada."

I laughed. "Right. I'm nineteen years old, I have three hundred dollars to my name, and I'm going to go to Canada—where I do not know a single person—for the rest of my life."

"I thought Martha had a high school friend living up there with her boyfriend."

"That'll be a big help," I said.

"Hey, that's how this whole country got started. When your brother turns eighteen, he can join you. Pretty soon you'll have a whole Canadian branch of the family. It'll be great."

"Except I don't want to be Canadian, or a landed alien, or whatever they call it. I want to be an American."

Peter frowned and passed me the joint.

"Looks like you'll be working for Uncle Sam then," he said.

But I didn't see how I could do that either. All that summer I scraped and painted houses, and, in my head, I floated back and forth between the parallel universes of law and conscience. Two sets of rights and wrongs. I imagined that if I examined every possibility closely, I would experience a moment of revelation that would point the way I should take.

My problem, Peter said, was that I didn't understand when to apply my principles and when not to. "That's what maturity means," he claimed, but he was only joking. We all believed principles should be absolute.

Martha thought we should move to Canada together like her friends. "We'll be refugees," she said, as if this were a good thing. Unlike me, she longed for the chance to demonstrate the courage of her convictions.

She went to the library and brought home a stack of books about Canada. At night she lay on our bed reading them, and every few minutes she would announce something like:

"Did you know that a lot of Loyalists fled to Canada after the American Revolution?"

Of course I didn't. You could fit what I knew about Canada on a postage stamp.

Montreal, she decided, was her favorite city, so she went around the apartment saying, "Bonjour, cheri," "D'accord," and "Oui, oui," until I reminded her that if I did go to Canada, which I did not plan to do, I certainly wouldn't move to French-speaking Canada.

"It sounds hard enough without throwing in the problem of language."

"Mais, non!" she said. "I will teach you to parle français," and then she kissed me.

Martha was a persuasive kisser, and she was persistent in arguing her case, but I still wouldn't commit myself.

Politically I had become incorrect from all perspectives. I was no longer a student protester. I was not "in" as in "Are you going in?" But I wasn't clearly out either, as in "Are you getting out?" I was absolutely nowhere.

Martha said maybe I wasn't really against the war otherwise I'd do anything to stay out of it.

"I would do 'anything'," I told her. "It's the specifics I have trouble with."

It was easy to be against the war when you were at home drinking with your friends or in a crowd shouting slogans or handing around petitions on campus. Taking action, alone, and facing the consequences, was much harder.

When I tried to explain this to Peter, he said: "That's true, but those guys over there pulling triggers and dropping napalm are alone too. They die alone, and, if they get home, they remember what they did alone. That's why you've got to decide. What are you going to do."

Fall came, and they went back to school, while I kept on painting houses and getting more and more depressed. My life was fucked. I had held off regret about school as long as I could—in the long run, wasn't it more important that I learn about life than math?—but it engulfed me then.

I was at home alone on a Sunday night in October when I decided to go to Canada. Martha was at the library, researching a paper on *Being and Nothingness*. Peter had been gone all day scavenging scrap metal for a sculpture he wanted to make.

I hadn't changed my mind about Canada being the right place for me. I just couldn't stand another minute of waiting to hear from my draft board. I figured if I left in the morning the whole issue would be settled by the end of the day. That's what I focused on.

I stuffed some clothes in a suitcase, and I packed my drafting instruments and a few books into a cardboard box. I couldn't take too much; after all, I didn't want to look like a refugee when I crossed the border.

I gassed up my car. I made myself some peanut butter sandwiches. And then I went to bed.

Martha came in late and slipped into bed next to me. Her fingers smelled like ink and her body was hot, full of the restless energy that comes from sitting still and thinking hard. I hated that I knew it was the last night and she didn't, but I couldn't tell her either.

I announced my plan the next morning, while we were all drinking coffee in the kitchen. Peter dropped the bread he was toasting on top of the stove into the flame. Martha, who had been trying to explain something about Sartre, stopped in mid-sentence and sat down. Coffee splashed on her white t-shirt.

"Jesus, Toby, when you finally make up your mind, you don't mess around," said Peter, and Martha began to cry.

"I thought we would go together," she said.

"I know. But I have to do this myself," I said. "If you still want to join me next summer, that would be great. You could both come. We can paint houses together up there. I mean, I guess they must need housepainters too, right?"

They agreed that this sounded good. After all, what else could they do? Nothing.

I left Pittsburgh that morning with the sight of my friends waving peace signs in my rear view mirror, and I really believed I was leaving the country forever. I don't know who shook more, my old VW or me, as I roared up the highway through Pennsylvania and New York.

The closest place to cross was Niagara Falls, but I went east around the lakes to more familiar territory, in case I was never coming back. The problem was, when I arrived at the border, I couldn't cross.

I spent a whole night in my car staring across the St. Lawrence River and thinking about school and all I had hoped to learn there, but didn't, and the things I'd learned instead. About politics and art, music and other people, love and sex, and war. Worse yet, I started to think about home. My mother's kitchen with its windows looking out into the woods. Waking up to the sound of my father's chainsaw. Skiing down slopes of fresh powder with Jack. My tree house.

In the morning I started the car to go, but I made a wrong turn out of the parking lot and found myself headed away from the border. I didn't turn back.

For three days I drove west, imagining I could change identities and disappear, somewhere out there. I had never seen the West before. This seemed like a good time to do it.

Outside of Omaha, I ran out of gas, and, by the time I reached a gas station with my gas can, I was tired and thirsty. I stopped in a bar for one beer, which turned into three or four, and then more. I played "For What It's Worth" over and over on the jukebox and wondered if I could spend the rest of my life in Nebraska. Or wherever the hell I was.

The next thing I knew I was in a naval recruiting office telling the very sober recruiter how I didn't want to leave the country.

"I'm against the war, *because* I'm an American," I said. "Uncle Sam needs people like me here!"

Lurid red-white-and-blue posters wavered on the walls around me as I tried to focus on the recruiter's face, and I thought I saw sympathy there. I even thought: Maybe he's against the war too. In those days you could never tell.

He told me I'd come to the right place. The Navy was hardly involved in the war—except for the Marines, it was mostly the Army and Air Force doing the work over there. Then he pulled out a big binder of ratings to show me all the noncombatant jobs I could choose from. If I joined up right then for four years of active duty and two years in the reserves, he could give me a delayed enlistment, and I wouldn't have to go to boot camp until after Christmas. And there would be the GI Bill to pay for my education when I got out.

What can I say?

I teetered for a few minutes between going back out on the road as a fugitive, six years in the Navy, or a future as a landed alien, unable ever to come back home.

I hadn't yet caught on to the fact that every future is one you can't go back from, so I signed. And who knows? Maybe the recruiter thought he was telling the truth, that I would be able to become a cartographer or drum major or clerk. Maybe he thought radiomen were noncombatants. After all you were there to perform a service—communication.

Unfortunately I had been most concerned about avoiding "jobs that required killing." It hadn't occurred to me to worry about "jobs that required being killed." This omission became clear only after I got to boot camp and learned that I was not likely to be sent to cartography school or any other interesting school of my own choosing. Only two ratings were open—corpsman and radioman—and that was because vacancies were continually being created in those areas on the frontlines of the war in Vietnam.

10

Alonzo thought it sounded like my interview went well, but Russell laughed and said nothing went well in that hospital.

"I mean, the point is, look what you're dealing with here. Military doctors. What kind of doctor would make a career in the Navy? Only an incompetent asshole, that's who."

It was after dinner, and Russell's mood had had not lightened much, even though he leaned back in his chair and blew smoke rings as if he were a country gentleman on his own back porch.

"If you expect anything from anyone here, you're bound to get fucked. Take it from me. They all give you that 'Trust me, I'm on your team' shit,' and that John Barry is the worst. Smiling and carrying on like he's one of the guys. Jesus H. Christ. He's a doctor. He's an officer. Do I need to say more?"

"Dr. Barry's only in because of the war," said Alonzo, shuffling the cards over and over. He liked the game to start right after we got back from the mess hall, but, if Russell wanted to talk, there was no point in dealing. He wouldn't pick up his cards or he'd pick them up and not look at them until he decided he was ready to play. "I think Dr. Barry's OK, but I like Dr. Sam better."

"Dr. Sam sent you home to live with an aunt who'd been dead two years as I recall."

A shadow passed over Alonzo's face as if he were struggling to remember something. "Not two years," he said. "I don't think it was two years. The milk was still in her refrigerator."

"All right, two months. Two days. Two hours. It doesn't make much difference, does it?"

"So what happened?" I asked.

"He came back, of course. Alon always comes back."

Alonzo smiled ruefully. "Russell needs me," he said. "I taught him how to play gin."

"You did?"

"Rocky, you ought to know by now that Alon never lies."

Alonzo grinned. "Trouble is, you can't believe anything Russell says. So where does that leave you?" We all laughed.

"Some things are worth telling the truth about and others aren't," said Russell. "When I woke up after my face got blown off, the corpsman in the field hospital said to me: 'You are one hell of a lucky guy' because the rest of the crew on my boat was toast."

"He meant you should be glad to be alive," said Alon. "You should always be glad to be alive."

"Is that true?" Russell asked me. "I don't think Rocky here is glad to be alive. He tried pretty hard to off himself, but he fucked up. Didn't do the job. Now he's stuck here where his troubles can begin anew.

"Me—I was only trying to do my job. Keep my head down. Then rat-tat-tat-tat, ka-boom! Game over for little Russ. No more job. No more wife and kids. No more home. No fucking skin. No fucking face."

"Hey man, don't say that," said Alonzo. He stopped shuffling and looked at Russell sadly. "You've got a face. We see your face. Don't we, Toby?"

Russell cut me off before I could say anything. "No sympathy, Rocky. That's not your role. Some things—untrue things—I let Alon here say because he's so crazy he believes them, and I don't want to upset him. His card playing really sucks when he's upset.

"But you and me—we are dead men who lived by accident. Between us there should be no B.S. That corpsman would have done me a lot more good if he'd admitted I was a piece of toast that popped up too soon.

"He should have called a spade a spade," he said, motioning for Alonzo to begin the game.

"Who're you calling a spade?" said Alonzo, but he was smiling and began to deal.

A few hands later, Russell went to the john, and, while we were sitting at the table alone, I said, "In the committee meeting today, Dr. Barry wanted me to admit I was glad to be alive. Like it was really important to him."

Alonzo said: "Sure it's important. But in the end, it don't matter. You really can't kill yourself, you know. If God wants you to live, you're going to live. I know. I tried three times myself when I was out there. I drank poison and it ran right through me. Nothing happened. It couldn't touch me. I tried to hang myself. Didn't do it right. I even jumped out a window. Didn't hurt me. Every time God was holding me in the palm of his hand."

"I don't believe in God," I said.

"It don't matter," said Alon. "God don't care what you believe."

"What are you two talking about?" Russell wanted to know when he came back,

"God," I said.

He looked surprised and suspicious. "That's a big topic. I'm sorry I missed it."

Alon rubbed his lip with his finger, the way he did when he was embarrassed. Russell sat down and leaned back with his arms crossed, regarding first Alonzo, then me. A moment of silence stretched between us. Then he said: "Deal."

11

Mail call was always a bad time of day on the ward. The moment when the outside world intruded. It would be hard to say who was more upset—the robes who got letters or the robes who didn't.

Russell received a fairly steady stream of official-looking documents that he cursed at, but real letters arrived for Book regularly three times a week. They came in long blue envelopes addressed in black ink, and they were the one thing that he never read. He put them, unopened, under his mattress, and there were so many that the bed had a kind of hump in the middle.

Williams didn't appear to notice events like mail call, but Alonzo did. His heavy round face grew tense with expectation when the mail came, and it would sag as the nurse's pile of letters and cards dwindled, and there was nothing for him.

"Do you have family, Alon?" I asked him. I was doodling on the pad that Russell had given me, while he restlessly shuffled the cards.

"I had an aunt," he said. "She used to send brownies, but she passed a long time ago now. Everybody else is gone, except two cousins, and I guess they don't remember me. Or they don't want to."

"That sucks. What about Russell? Does he really have a wife and kids?"

"Not any more he don't. What about you, Toby? Where are your people?"

"My people." I knew he meant my family, but I certainly didn't think of them that way. "They're in New York. Way upstate. But they're not too happy with me right now."

My mother had sent me a get-well card with a picture of a bear in a hospital bed with a thermometer in his mouth. I guess the drugstore in the village didn't have any cards depicting people in the nut house, so that was the best she could do. She had not added any message to the chirpy poem inside except "Mom." That was predictable. As was my father's silence. But I was disappointed that I hadn't heard from Jack, and I wondered if they had even told him where I was.

"That's too bad," Alon said. "Families ought to stick together."

"Yeah. Well, my parents are stuck, and they're together, but I don't think it has done either of them any good."

"Everybody needs somebody to stand by. That's what life is about."

"I guess," I said, but what I really believed was that everyone was alone, and they'd better get used to it.

"What's that?" he said, reaching out to take the pad I had been drawing on. My doodle had become a little sketch of his hands with cards flying up all around them like birds.

"Nothing," I said, but he looked excited.

"Is that me?" he asked.

"Yes," I said.

He studied the piece of paper like it was a mirror. "Ain't nobody ever drawn a picture of me before. Can I have it?"

"Sure," I said, and I carefully ripped off the sheet and gave it to him.

"This is better than a letter," he said, tucking the drawing into his pocket. "Being here, good news feels almost as bad as bad news."

Russell had been off the ward for a doctor's appointment. When he came back, he took his chair at the head of the table and went into a rant about the incompetent, unreliable doctors at the hospital. "They're lying bastard pricks every one," he said, and then he stopped. "What's up with you?" he said sharply to Alonzo. "You look like you were dealt a gin hand."

I thought Alon would show him the drawing, but he didn't. Instead he laughed and said: "How can I get a gin hand when you never shut up and play?"

12

I didn't expect to hear anything more from my family, and, as far as Peter and Martha knew I was in Vietnam, so I wouldn't hear from them. I did expect some word from the doctors' committee, but none came.

The days passed. I played cards. I slept. I smoked. And I waited. It was very hot—the kind of July heat that makes corn shoot up and tomatoes flower, but is very tough on human beings behind bars.

Pearson caught a bad summer cold and almost immediately gave it to Williams, who gave it to everyone else, so that it was hard to sleep with all the coughing, sneezing, and snorting that went on at night. Williams with a cold was even more gross than usual; his sock looked potent enough for germ warfare. He sat at the table in a miserable lump during the day, muttering dit-dahs to himself, a wad of Kleenex in each hand. His sneezes were huge, hitting the rest of us with tidal waves of germs. Book's cold protection scheme was to slouch so low in his chair he was practically under the table with his book in front of his face. He didn't get sick, but the rest of us did. Colds were especially hard on Russell because his nasal passages and sinuses were all fucked up.

"You ought to be on a regular ward," I told him, after listening to him struggle to breathe through one whole evening of gin.

His eyes were feverish, staring out of their misshapen sockets.

"Don't get me started on the you oughtas, Rocky. How many times have they promised me I was going to have surgery, Alon?"

Alonzo shook his head. "Too many."

"Exactly. Too many."

"So why don't you?" I asked.

"Because the freshly maimed are a higher priority than old unsolvable problems like me. I guess they figure I'm going to croak soon, so why waste the money? The VA doesn't run on its big heart, you know."

"But if you can't breathe—" I said.

"Oh, I can breathe enough to get by," he said, heaving himself up out of his chair. "But I'm done for tonight." He didn't seem to notice that we were in the middle of a hand or that he had left his winnings on the table. Alonzo watched him leave with a stricken expression. It was Russell who kept the cards, the pad, and the pencil in his pocket when they weren't being used. He had never walked away and left them before.

I began to stack up the cards. "I'll take them tonight," I said, "if you want me to." Book, who never appeared to notice what was going on at the table, paused in the middle of turning a page. Sock stopped rocking.

"Russell always takes them," Alonzo said.

"Yes, but he's gone to bed. I don't think he's feeling well, you know. He forgot."

Alonzo took the cards from me and began to shuffle them nervously. Finally he turned to Book. "You take them," he said, thrusting the deck of cards at him. Book looked surprised and I wondered what he would do. He hesitated for an instant and then swept the cards into his pocket and left the table.

"You—" Alonzo said to Sock. "You take the pencil." Sock's face crumpled like a Kleenex.

"Dit dit dit dah dit dah dit dit dah," he said, which apparently meant no because he scrambled out of his chair and headed for the john.

"OK," said Alon. "I keep the pencil. You take the pad."

"All right, Alon," I said. "That's a good plan."

He didn't say anything about the half dozen cigarettes Russell had won that were lying on the table, and I didn't either. I put the pad in my pocket and got up.

Alonzo seemed reluctant to leave the table. He twirled the pencil between his fingers uneasily. I had the feeling that someone had died and his possessions were being dispersed among the survivors. Finally he got up too, leaving the cigarettes behind for anyone who wanted them.

Russell's breathing slowly improved, but his mood didn't. He picked fights over little things with everyone, even Alonzo. I didn't care what he said to me, but his barbed remarks hurt Alon. Between his tirades and temper tantrums, it was hard to predict how long a card game would last. Even when he didn't disrupt the game, he cheated flagrantly, so that sometimes we couldn't even complete a hand, he had so many cards tucked up his sleeves.

He also cultivated a weird relationship with Donny Cullihan. Russell called him Pup, but the only puppy-like quality that Donny had was that he would shit on anyone, anywhere.

Pup was not allowed to sit at the table, but he had a kind of hanger-on status, which meant he hovered around while we played cards, bumming cigarettes from Russell—the only one who would give him any—and making remarks like: "You shoulda gotten rid of that two of clubs."

For some reason, Russell found this entertaining. He laughed at Cullihan's commentary and seemed oblivious to the fact that it upset Alonzo.

Alon did not believe in cheating. He held his cards close to his chest whenever Cullihan came near him, which only tempted Cullihan to try harder to see what he had.

"Get away from me," Alonzo said time after time, but Cullihan wouldn't quit until Russell said "Down, Pup." Then he'd come around for a cigarette, and Russell would give him one.

Book and Cullihan ignored each other, but Sock watched him with eager eyes. Cullihan had an American flag tattooed on his chest and Sock saluted whenever he caught a glimpse of it. Once Cullihan opened his pajamas to show off the way he could make the flag wave by flexing his pecs, and Sock was mesmerized. For a full five minutes, he didn't chitter or rock in his chair.

He had apparently forgotten that Cullihan tried to steal his sock, and would have if it weren't for me, but I hadn't. I could see in his face that he was still waiting for a chance to get me back, but for the time being he kept his distance, sniping at me from the far side of the table, with Russell between us.

"I bet you're a hippie," he said. "I can always smell a hippie. Even without the hair."

I ignored him. I didn't understand what Russell was after, and I didn't want to care. If playing cards became too much of a hassle, I'd quit. Sooner or later, I'd have to hear something from Barry. It wasn't much to look forward to, but I held onto it and I waited.

When Barry finally did turn up, he had a fresh sunburn and a peeling nose. He stood at the end of my bed, bouncing up and down on the balls of his feet, looking pleased with himself and the world.

"Sorry for the delay," he said. "I had some leave coming, and I went down to the Great Barrier Reef. Have you ever been there? The surfing is great."

"Bitchin," I said, and Barry laughed.

"Don't sweat the small stuff, Woodruff. Come and see me this afternoon at two. I'll fix it with Basto," he said, and then he was gone.

In the afternoon I found him in such a jovial mood that I suspected him of being stoned or drunk. I sniffed the air in his office carefully, but the windows were open and a stiff breeze ruffled the papers piled on the desk. A duffel bag full of bright-colored shorts and t-shirts lay on the floor, as if he had come to work directly from his trip. A row of seashells, including a huge conch shell, now decorated his desk.

"Nice, huh? I found it myself. In a store," he said, holding it up to his ear. "I've never understood why this works."

He offered me the shell, but I shook my head.

I didn't care about his vacation experiences. "I want to know what the story is," I said, trying not to sound irritated.

Finally Barry put down the shell, and his expression became more settled. "The story," he said. "OK. But why don't you tell me first."

"What do you mean?" I asked.

"Well, like what have you been doing? What did you think of the doctors' committee?"

"Nothing and not much," I said.

Barry laughed. "Those were supposed to be open-ended questions, but I guess those are good enough answers." He paused, scribbling something in my file. "Now let's try one that calls for a different kind of answer: How long have you been off your medication?"

I had been lighting a cigarette with Barry's lighter, and I looked up at him, taken aback.

He met my eyes straight on. "Hey, Toby, what kind of a doc would I be if I couldn't tell the difference between someone who's on Thorazine and someone who's not? So don't try to bullshit me."

I took a drag off my cigarette before answering. I could have said, "Not a very good one, since you didn't notice before," but before I hadn't been talking. I hadn't even been looking at him. I suppose that made a difference.

"There are various ways to avoid taking it," I said.

Barry tapped his pencil on the desk. For a few minutes he didn't say anything, just sat there, playing a pencil riff, and studying me. I continued to smoke my cigarette and look him right in the eye.

"I'll tell you what," he said at last. "If I write up that you haven't been taking your medication, it will reflect poorly on all of us—you, me, the staff on your ward. So why don't we do this. I'll prescribe something different, something nicer, like Valium, but you've got to promise to take it. What do you say?"

"I don't like drugs."

"Really? I'm surprised to hear you say that. But it doesn't matter what you like. That's the game here. Everybody's on something."

He wrote a note in the file, and I understood that the discussion was over. I had to do what he said or he'd put the corpsmen onto me.

"The other thing," said Barry, "is the doctors' recommendation. They think you're making good progress, and they're willing to give you hospital privileges as long as you continue to get better. That means you'll be able to leave the ward for a few hours each day. Go to occupational therapy. Visit the snack bar. That kind of thing."

"I don't see how going to a snack bar is going to make me better than I am now." I wanted to say why can't you just discharge me, but I held back.

Barry picked up the conch and turned it around and around. "The committee should review your case again in a month and then it goes to the Medical Board," he said.

"A month?"

"That's right. But sometimes they get behind and it takes longer. You've got to be prepared for that."

"But I thought—"

"Whatever you thought was wrong," said Barry. "Look, only a few weeks ago you came within an inch of killing yourself on the Navy's time. The Navy doesn't like that. It reduces the troops, lowers morale, and it's bad public relations. Ninety days is the usual observation period required after an incident like that. Didn't you know?" he asked.

His tone was sharp, inquisitive. We stared at each other for a long moment. His clear blue eyes were carefully neutral. I let him look into mine, and I put all my energy into showing him nothing but surprise.

"No, I didn't know," I said. "It wasn't like I sent away for a brochure before I came here. I intended to be dead."

I threw the sentence down like a gauntlet, and Barry drew back in his chair.

"And why do you think that was?"

"At the time it seemed like the best place to be."

"Since the other choice was Vietnam?"

I didn't answer. Barry lit a cigarette.

"We have a lot of guys in this hospital whose health has been destroyed by serving in the war. They may spend the rest of their lives here."

"I don't intend to be one of them," I said.

"Yes, well. You also intended to be dead, didn't you," said Barry.

I stood up, pushing my chair back sharply.

"OK, OK," said Barry, standing up too. "All I'm trying to tell you is to stay cool. You don't have all the answers. You don't even have any of the answers. So go slow. Got it?" He had followed me to the door and now put his hand on my shoulder.

"Take your meds and relax. Go have a milkshake. Make a wallet. Life is worth living even here."

"Thanks for the advice," I said and knocked on the door for the corpsman.

13

I couldn't decide if it was a disaster that Barry thought I was acting according to a plan or not. Every suicide attempt has some kind of plan behind it. If it doesn't, then your death is an accident. But he also seemed to think I had a plan for afterward, and that was different. That was getting close to the truth, and I didn't want him there. On the other hand, I didn't want him to think I was completely crazy either, so basically I had no idea how to play him.

There was a time in my life when I thought I knew all the answers. I treated high school like a downhill race, and I made every gate without tapping a single pole. Pittsburgh was a different story though. The dorm I moved into had more guys in it than the village I came from, and the work came at us fast and hard. Every day was a steep unfamiliar trail with icy conditions until I met Peter. He reminded me that you can't ski watching your feet. So I broke a few bones. That was how I had learned to race.

But I didn't go into the Navy looking for an opportunity to fuck up. I was sincere enough in hoping I'd finally stumbled on an acceptable alternative to Canada, jail, or the war.

Not everyone agreed with me about that though. Martha, for one, was furious.

"How could you do that?" she said, when I turned up in Pittsburgh a week after leaving. She had already hung a Canadian flag in her dorm room alongside a photograph of me looking dark and brooding in a leather motorcycle jacket.

I tried to explain that I'd found the "gray" answer I was looking for, and she should be happy for me.

"I'm getting a noncombatant job," I explained, but she didn't buy that.

"It's all part of the same thing," she said, ripping down the flag.

"Well, it's better than the infantry. Or going to jail."

"How can you say that? I don't believe you believe that."

"I believe there's a difference between going in the service and fighting in the war."

"To-by," she said, her eyes full of tears. "That is such bullshit!" Her dark braids snapped like whips as she moved around the room. I watched in amazement as she proceeded to eliminate all signs of my existence. Just in case

I didn't know how she felt.

"Look, Martha, I know you wanted us to go to Canada, but I couldn't do it. I don't like Canada. And I couldn't live knowing there was a line in the air that I couldn't cross. You would have been able to come back. I wouldn't, and that would have driven me crazy.

"I know this country is fucked up, but I want to live here. I want this to be my home. So I guess I'm one of those 'My country right or wrong' guys after all, huh."

This was supposed to be a joke, but she didn't laugh. She stopped crying and stared at me, her face hard and pale.

"Then you've gotten exactly what you wanted and that's all there is to it," she said, and, with that she left me, standing in her room, with my ripped-up photo at my feet.

Peter was surprised to see me back too. I found him at the sculpture studio, feeding car parts into an electric hammer that pounded them flat. "Whoa!" he said, when I told him how I'd gone from being enshrined to shredded in a matter of minutes. "Well, you know Martha. She did kind of throw herself into the war widow thing. She's been wearing black ever since you left."

"Too bad I came back from the dead to spoil it."

"No, I'm sure she didn't mean that. She was just caught off balance," he said. However, when I explained what I'd done, he looked at me as if I were a person he'd never seen before too.

"You're going in?" he asked, pulling a joint out of his shirt pocket.

"To the Navy," I said, stressing the word Navy.

"God, that's heavy." He lit the joint and took a toke. "I guess it makes sense, if Canada didn't work out. Jail would have been a lot shorter than six years though."

"Jail was never an option for me." He tried to pass me the joint, but I waved it away. He looked surprised by that too.

"You know I met a guy the other day who had his little fingers taped down flat to his palms. When I asked him what happened he said he wanted to find out what it was like to get along without them because if he got drafted he was going to cut them off."

"Jesus. Do you think he'll really do it?"

"I don't know. It's freaky what this situation makes people do," he said, and from the way he looked at me I knew that included me.

I thought at the very least my father would be impressed when I called and told him I'd enlisted, but his response was: "In what."

"The Navy," I said, and all he said back was: "What did you do that for?"

I had already run out of answers to that question, so all I said was "Let Mom know," and hung up.

In January, I went to boot camp at Great Lakes, where it snowed and snowed and snowed for six straight weeks. All around me the country was turning to shit, while I marched and cleaned my gun, waved my flag, and perfected my technique in folding underwear. I took my cues from the people around me and pretended the Tet Offensive was a complete surprise. I maintained my neutrality on the presidential election and students getting Clean for Gene.

I swallowed my shock when they assigned me to radio school and went to Bainbridge still hoping that maybe—just maybe—I would not be sent to Vietnam. There I learned Morse code and sat at my key taking and sending messages eight hours a day, saluted my superiors, and kept my mouth shut. When Martin Luther King Jr. and Bobby Kennedy were assassinated, I got drunk in private. But you have to draw a line somewhere, and when my orders came, I finally drew it.

Suicide wasn't my first thought. I tried talking to the base chaplain, but all he had to offer were some platitudes about doing my duty, for which advice I told him to go screw himself.

I went into Philadelphia to see a draft counselor too. When I entered the small frame house in Germantown that was the headquarters of No War, I imagined I was entering the underground railway. Somehow. Magically. The people at No War were going to issue me the password I needed to get out of the mess I was in.

My counselor, whose name was Dave, studied me in my white uniform with Quaker detachment. He looked like a man who had never raised a sweat in his life.

"Are you a conscientious objector?" he asked.

"No," I said. "I'm against this war. We don't have any business there."

"Even though you're in the service, you can still apply for a C.O.," he told me.

"I don't have time for that. I've already gotten my orders."

"There aren't too many choices then," he said, taking off his wire-rimmed glasses to wipe them. When he looked back up at me, his eyes were suddenly smaller. "You can tell them you're queer and get a dishonorable discharge. Or you can go AWOL and you'll go to jail if they catch you. Or you can do something crazy. You know, freak out. If you go that route you have a chance for an honorable discharge on medical grounds as mentally unfit for service. With that you still get benefits."

"I'm not thinking about benefits here. I'm trying to stay out of the war."

"I'm only trying to help you understand the pros and cons," he said, putting his glasses back on.

I stalked out of there, thinking he had been less than useless too. But I was wrong. He had told me exactly what I needed to know, and before I even got back to my barracks, I had laid out my basic plan.

Committing suicide isn't as easy as it looks. You think, well, there's only that thin membrane of a moment between life and death, but the effort it takes to go through is surprising. You have to really psych yourself up for it. In the end, it's best not to think at all. I suppose if I'd known that when I was sitting at the border, I would have ended up in Canada, but I didn't. The power of acting without thinking was something I learned from the Navy.

14

My hospital privileges were approved a couple of days after my meeting with Barry. I could leave the ward for three hours a day, and I had to attend occupational therapy three times a week.

"You're moving right up the food chain, Rocky," Russell said when he heard the news.

"Potato to tomato," I said, lighting a cigarette for Williams off of my own.

"Vegetable to fruit," Russell said. "You know what that means, Sock?"

Williams didn't like to be addressed directly. He puffed hard on his cigarette and got up from his chair.

"Some of us never make it to the fruit stage," Russell said, watching him shuffle off to the john.

"You're gettin' on good, Toby," said Alon. "You be careful though. You don't want to lose what you got."

"What do you mean?" I asked.

"You can get tempted out there. That's all I'm saying," and he wouldn't add anything more.

Later, on the way to mess, I asked Russell if he knew what Alonzo meant.

"Sure I know," he said. "I know everything about Alon. He has a thing for open doors. He wanders out. Last time he had hospital privileges, he lost them within a week because he went out some door and got half way across Philadelphia before they caught him."

"No shit. In his pajamas?"

"Oh, he got clothes. Some old lady gave him clothes and ten bucks. You'd be surprised how resourceful Alon can be."

"I'm blown away. So what about you? Did you run away too?"

"Nah. I'm toast, remember. A permanent vegetable."

"Toast is a grain, not a vegetable."

"If you say so, country boy. Anyway, they don't want me wandering around out there. They can't hide the amputees—they're too fucking many of them—but they can keep me under wraps. Don't want to scare the visitors, you know. It's bad PR. A cute young guy like you though—I wouldn't be surprised if they put you on a pedestal in the lobby. You're a regular poster child for the system."

"Right," I said. "That's me."

When Pearson finally let me off the ward by myself, the first thing I did was find a door to the outside and park myself there. I had no plans to escape, but I did want to see the world eye to eye, not from three flights up.

The door was locked, of course, and it only looked out onto a parking lot, but I liked watching the cars and people come and go. The people looked hot and preoccupied. Oblivious to the freedom they had. When I got out, I told myself, I would never again take for granted the freedom to go where I wanted. Spend my day however I chose.

I waited a long time, but no one actually came through my door. At one point a mess hall worker headed my way, but when she saw me looking through the glass, she turned and went back to her car. I don't know why—maybe I was less cute than Russell thought. Or maybe she had forgotten something. Finally I decided that looking out the door was like standing at the edge of the ocean on a summer's day and not being able to go in. It made me feel more shut in than ever, so I headed off to explore the hospital instead.

Any freedom to move around—even if it's within a building—is a big change from being locked up or marched along under guard. I climbed up and down stairs until I out of breath, rode elevators, drank from water coolers, and sat in toilet stalls where you could not only close, but also lock the door.

When I got back to the ward, Alonzo was waiting for me right by the door.

"How was it?" he wanted to know.

"Great," I said. "I didn't get run over or break any rules."

"Did you have a hamburger?"

"No, I went to the john."

Alon looked shocked, but Russell burst out laughing.

"Jesus, Rocky. That is pitiful. But poetic. I mean it. What does a man really long for? A place to have an uninterrupted solitary shit."

"Yeah, I really enjoyed it," I said. Then I promised Alon I would try the Snack Bar soon.

I didn't go right away though. I wanted to discover the boundaries of my territory first, and the hospital had more wings and floors than I thought. Each day I walked as far as I could before I hit a locked door and slowly the building around me expanded. It took on a whole new shape in my mind, and the parts I knew well—the ward, the mess hall, Barry's office—shrank by comparison.

I found more of the world inside the hospital than I expected too. There were places where I could watch secretaries in short skirts hurrying along with files under their arms, volunteers carrying flowers, and families and friends on their way to visit patients. I sat in the lounges, watching TV game shows and eavesdropping on conversations among people who were not insane.

I didn't talk about what I did with Russell and Alonzo. I figured they wouldn't understand why listening to a boy argue with his mother about when he'd get his homework done or watching a man snap his gum while he read the sports pages could make me so happy. But it was true. Those people were messengers who reminded me where I wanted to be. Out.

Sometimes I was aware that people were looking at me, and they didn't like what they saw. A blue robe. I didn't shuffle or drool or mutter or stare, but they saw something in my face that set me apart. Their bodies stiffened to define the space between us. Their eyes moved away quickly, and their voices lowered when I came near. Just in case I needed a reminder—which I didn't—they let me know that I was still in. Not even close to out.

I expected the library to be a kind of sanctuary, but it wasn't. It was a small windowless room, and the books—hardbacks that no one would ever read and slouching paperbacks—smelled like someone's basement. Each time I touched one, the librarian, who sat at a desk by the door, tensed as if I had put my hand up her skirt. I left empty-handed and didn't go back.

The Snack Bar, on the other hand, reminded me of home. It had a horseshoe-shaped counter with red-topped stools and booths like the ones in Vee Bee's Diner. There were glass cases for doughnuts, pies, and Danish and metal racks of candy, chips, and gum. The heavy greasy smell of a hot griddle mingled with the fragrance of coffee.

I sat down in one of the booths and a little sigh escaped from the plastic upholstery. I loved that sound, and I bounced on the seat a few times so I could hear it again.

Then the old man behind the counter said: "That seat ain't a trampoline, bud. Are you gonna order something or not?" He wore a white grease-spattered apron, and his arms were thick and tattooed with big blurry anchors. His cool blue eyes weren't friendly, but at least he looked at me.

"Black coffee," I said, "and apple pie with vanilla ice cream. Please."

"Coming up," said the man as if I were an ordinary customer.

The coffee was like black water and the pie was stale, but it came on a plate, and I was able to eat it alone in a booth with no one timing me.

A newspaper on the seat of one of other booths caught my eye as I was leaving. The thick black headline said Richard Nixon had won the Republican nomination for president.

Two thoughts bolted through my brain at once and collided.

One was: How the fuck did that happen?

And the other was: I couldn't afford to let myself think about it.

Later, when this was over, things would be different. But for now, I had only one job, and that was to get out.

15

I found the trouble I could get into when I went to occupational therapy and met Dorothy. The first time I saw her she was on a stepstool taking a bag of ceramic tiles down off a shelf, and, before I even noticed her face, I saw her legs—pale and smooth from her feet all the way up to where they disappeared under a blue smock.

Every patient in the room was watching her, mesmerized, and she knew it. I guess she felt safe with the others because they were all in wheelchairs. When she saw me standing in the doorway, she tugged instinctively at her skirt and hopped down from the stool.

"You must be Toby Woodruff," she said. Her cheeks flushed and her smile was uncertain.

"Yes," I said, and, maybe surprise made me stare, because she tugged again at her smock and said: "Good," in a stiff voice.

I don't know what I expected, but it definitely wasn't Dorothy. She was about twenty-five, and she had smooth skin like bread dough, bright amber-colored eyes, and curly dark hair cut so close to her head it looked like fur. Her short hair and blue smock were modest, almost nun-like, but her legs were not.

She had quick intelligent eyes, and she didn't need time to figure me out. The robe said it all. "You can sit down here," she said, pointing to a bench by an empty table. "I'll be with you in a minute."

Then she took the bag of tiles over to the tables where the other patients sat. One guy about my age opened the bag with prosthetic hooks and began picking out red tiles. Two others, who had lost their legs, were painting ceramic bowls. An ashtray full of cigarettes smoldered on the table between them. Dorothy bent down to say something quietly to them, and they all looked at me.

When she came back, she told me I had a choice of doing mosaic work, painting a ceramic piece, or making a leather wallet. She talked like an elementary school teacher—slowly and in short sentences.

"I like to draw," I said.

Dorothy pursed her lips. "You can't draw here. This is occupational therapy, not an art class. Part of the point is learning to follow directions."

I laughed, and she didn't like that at all. The amber eyes assessed me. How difficult I might be. How crazy. She crossed her arms. They were as white as her legs and, no doubt, all that went between.

"OK," I said, "In that case, I'll make a wallet."

Dorothy looked relieved and smiled. Her teeth were small and even. She went to a cupboard and got out a packet with precut leather pieces, gimp, and a big plastic needle. "The instructions are all on that piece of paper. Why don't you look them over yourself first and let me know if you have any questions," she said, handing it to me. Then she went to back to the other table and sat down, while the patients picked up a conversation that sounded like it had all been said a million times before.

They reminisced about their sexual exploits in high school, while Dorothy mixed paint colors, picked up dropped tiles, and lit cigarettes. I listened too as I assembled my wallet. One of the guys with no legs described having sex with the same girl on the same day in the girls' bathroom at his high school, between the goal posts after a football game, and in the backseat of his Mustang. It sounded like horseshit to me, but Dorothy said: "Wow! I never would have made it to college if I'd hung out with guys like you!"

"Damn straight," said the amputee with the hooks, and Dorothy laughed. She had a high light laugh like a young girl.

"I never did it with same girl twice. I like to share the wealth," said one of the amputees.

"You mean they never made the same mistake twice," said another, and Dorothy laughed again.

"Oh you guys," she said and continued to flirt with them for the whole hour.

I understood that they were letting me know what they thought of blue robes, and I told myself it was just as well. I wasn't there to make friends. I finished the wallet before my time was up and, when I handed it to Dorothy, she said, "That was quick," and admired my neat sewing.

"I'm good at following directions," I said.

Her eyes flicked across mine before she said: "Next time you can try out the leather stamps, if you want. You use them to decorate the leather before you put the pieces together."

"That sounds great," I said, so the next time I came, she had the stamps out on the table, ready for me.

Dorothy still sat with the amputees, but I was aware of her watching me from the corner of her eye as I sat alone pounding a swirling pattern of stars across the front and back pieces of my second wallet. She examined my work at the end of the session, studying the way I arranged the pattern. "That's really very nice," she said, and she regarded me more closely.

During the gin game that night, Russell teased me about going to OT.

"You'll be a grain soon if you keep going to Oa-Tee," he said, lifting two cards off the draw pile. His cheating was part of the dynamic of the game; neither Alonzo nor I bothered to say anything about it. "So what did you make today, Rocky? An ashtray?"

"A wallet," I said. "I'm not advanced enough for tiles. I might sniff the glue."

"I made a wallet once," said Alonzo, sorting his cards. He liked to rearrange them completely after every draw. "I sent it to my aunt and she never used it. I found it in her desk drawer after she died. I think she was ashamed of it."

"No. She probably just wanted to keep it nice," I said.

"You think so?" said Alon.

"Definitely," said Russell, discarding the king of clubs.

"Dorothy says next time I can start a pair of moccasins."

"I made a pair of them once too. They were sharp."

"So sharp you wore them when you ran away," said Russell.

Alonzo looked at Russell as if he didn't know what he was talking about. Then he said: "I believe you're right. I did."

"So you really did escape, Alon?" I said.

"You think you're the only one ever wanted to leave here?"

"No, I don't. I think it's great that you got away."

"Didn't do him much good," said Russell.

"Yeah, they took them moccasins away, and I never got to make any more either."

"You're better off playing cards," said Russell. "That shit's just busy work. A card game has some strategy to it. Something to win. Something to lose. Like right now. You're both about to lose some cigarettes." Then he laid down his cards and said: "Gin."

I knew my leaving the ward pissed Russell off, but I wasn't going to fuck up to please him. I developed a daily routine that was a lot better than sitting around all day. I climbed stairs to build up my strength, put in some time observing the parking lot, and then went to the Snack Bar. After a few days, the old man, who was called Ernie, began to pour my black coffee as soon as I walked in.

I took my seat in the booth farthest from the door, drank my coffee, and daydreamed about how good life was going to be when I got back to Pittsburgh. I'd get a new apartment in Shadyside—maybe with Peter, maybe alone. I'd line up some carpentry or house painting for the fall and spend all day every day working outside. I felt like I needed to soak up a lot of sun and air before I could go back to any indoor occupation. In the spring I'd get back into school and, eventually, Martha would fall in love with me again. I had a variety of scenarios for that.

When I went back to the ward, I brought presents—chips for Alonzo. Cigarettes for Russell. A candy bar for Williams. A magazine for Book. Russell didn't approve of these gifts, and even as he pocketed the cigarettes, he scowled. "You know, Rocky, you're not doing anybody any favors by bringing all this crap onto the ward."

"Really," I said, opening a Snickers bar.

"It pollutes the place," he said, waving his hand at the door, "Makes people more dissatisfied. When they get one thing, they want two. So instead of the world seeming bigger, it seems smaller than ever. Then they start wanting to get out."

"What's wrong with that?"

Russell shrugged. "There's no future in it for me. What about you, Alon, you want to go back out there again?"

Alonzo concentrated on unwrapping a Mars bar and mumbled that he didn't know.

"You see? He doesn't want to go. You think getting out of here is the be all and end all. You think you'll leave here and never come back. But you don't know that. None of us thought we were coming to stay, but you wouldn't be the first to discover that life here is habit-forming."

"I can't imagine it," I said.

Russell laughed his hoarse hollow laugh. "Well, you know what they say:

What you can't imagine, you can't avoid."

"Russell is wrong about hospital privileges being bad," I told Alon when we were alone in the mess hall. Russell had stayed in bed with one of his headaches.

"Don't say that," said Alonzo. "What he says is right for him."

"But not for you." I persisted. "You could have more of a life, even if he doesn't want one."

"Huh. You sure have some funny ideas. Seems to me every person alive has the same amount of life."

"Well, I want more than this. And you could have more too."

"More what?"

"I mean you could be out there. Off the ward. We could have a burger together in the Snack Bar sometimes."

"Yeah, that would be nice," he said, but without conviction, and he looked away from me at something I couldn't see.

That night, I found another message under my pillow. In Morse code it said: "You're on thin ice." Was that a threat or a warning? I couldn't decide, but it didn't tell me anything I didn't already know, and I threw it under the bed.

16

I planned to make a pair of moccasins, but, before I started decorating them, I experimented with the circle and triangle leather stamps to make my design. Dorothy gave me pieces of cardboard and scrap leather to practice on, and I spent a couple of sessions fooling around, planning how to fit a pattern on the leather pieces.

Dorothy didn't tell me that I had stopped following directions, and she didn't try to make suggestions the way she did with the other patients. Every now and then, she came by to see what I was doing, and sometimes I'd look up and find her studying me from across the room.

When I had my design all worked out on the scraps, I laid it out in front of me on the table. Dorothy came over and stood looking over my shoulder at the overlapping patterns.

"That's beautiful, Toby," she said. She touched the pattern, her hand stopping close to where mine rested. "How did you make that?" she asked and listened gravely while I showed her the way the shapes intersected.

"You're very talented, you know," she said. Then she moved away, but I could still feel how close she had been, and I had trouble concentrating for the rest of the hour.

The day I finished sewing the pieces together, she urged me to put on the moccasins to see how they fit.

"Go on," she said. "Try them!"

"All right," I said, embarrassed.

On my feet, they felt stiff and scratchy, and I thought they looked like they belonged to someone else, but Dorothy thought they were great, and said: "Look, everybody! Look what Toby made!"

The other patients stopped what they were doing to see what she was making a fuss about, but they were not about to be impressed by a robe. A double amputee who was painting an ashtray said, "Nice work, fruitcake. Why don't you make a pair for me now?"

"Harry!" Dorothy said sharply, and then she blushed, obviously confused. "Really Toby, those are the nicest moccasins anyone has ever made here," she said and then she turned away from me and spent the rest of the session, sitting with Harry and talking quietly to him. I was shut out of her circle again.

I had moccasins now though, and that was a step up from slippers. I wore them whenever I left the ward and slowly they assumed the shape of my own feet. I liked looking down at them. They reminded me that I was going somewhere, and not only down the Indian trails in my head.

I started work on another pair right away. They were going to be a present for Alonzo, and I decided to decorate them with the sun, the moon, and the stars.

Dorothy kept her distance until one day when I arrived to find her in the OT room alone. A summer flu was going around, she said, getting out my materials. She handed them over in a detached way and began to clean up the supply shelves.

I went to work, but Dorothy on the stepstool distracted me. She was a lot more interesting than sewing moccasins. She worked in silence and maybe she was aware that I was watching because she kept dropping things and getting down to pick them up.

When a whole bag of leather pieces spilled to the floor, I went to help her. As I crouched down beside her, she angled her body away from mine, but our hands brushed against each other. We both pretended it was nothing—and it was nothing, unless you were a blue robe who'd been locked up for two months.

Dorothy quickly swept the scraps into the bag, and stood up. "Thanks," she said, when she'd put the bag back on the shelf.

"No problem," I said, going back to my table.

I thought she'd go back to cleaning, but she didn't. She lit a cigarette and came over to where I was working. She watched for a while, and then she said:

"Those are going to be too big for you."

"I know," I said.

"Who are they for then?"

"A guy who needs to point his feet toward the door."

"You think moccasins will help?"

"I don't know. Maybe."

She was silent, gazing around the empty room in a dissatisfied way. "Toby, can I ask you a question?"

"You just did."

"No, I mean a personal question." I glanced up at her face. She was on the other side of the table, but I was sure I could feel her breath.

"All right," I said.

She paused as if trying to think exactly what to say. "Why are you here? You seem really different from the other patients I've worked with."

I looked into those amber eyes and considered this bait, but self-protection— or was it the truth?—made me say: "Oh, I belong here all right. I tried to kill myself."

"Really?" she sounded surprised. "Why did you do that?"

"That's what everyone wants to know."

"Don't you know?"

"Yes."

"Can you talk about it?"

I set down the moccasin that I was sewing. She waited, glowing with sympathy and curiosity.

"I don't think you really want to know," I said.

"Yes, I do!" she replied, and her voice cracked.

I could have leaned across and kissed her then. I was close enough, and she had opened herself to it. I could see in her face that she'd started thinking of me as a guy, not a patient.

My desire to be a guy was almost greater than my desire to kiss her. I already knew what her lips would be like. How her pale skin would look in the dusty light of the storeroom.

But I wasn't a guy. I was a blue robe, and I knew what would happen if I got caught, so I picked up my sewing again, and said: "I wanted to end the war."

Dorothy's eyes widened. "To end the war? By killing yourself?"

I think she wanted to say "You're joking!" but she was afraid to.

I could see that whatever ideas she'd been developing about me conflicted with this new information. The struggle lasted only a few seconds, then she stood up and put her cigarette out. My brief life as a guy was over.

"Well, I'm glad you didn't succeed," she said primly. "I mean in killing yourself. Everyone would like the war to end. It has ruined so many lives."

From the way she looked at me, I could see that for her I had moved into the category of ruined, and I was surprised because I liked to think of myself as one of the ones who survived.

17

Russell was not happy that I gave Alonzo a new pair of moccasins, but Alon put them on his big square feet and walked up and down the ward, showing them to everybody. He wore them to the mess, and he would have worn them to bed if Basto had let him.

"I am a new man," he told me, admiring his feet. "Now I have more of a life too."

"What's with the sun, moon, and stars?" Russell asked me as we stood in line for dinner. His tray had a banana on it; I was eating Swedish meatballs again. "Are you trying to tell Alonzo you're in love with him?"

I laughed. "Nope. I'm trying to tell him he's at the top of the top of the food chain," I said.

"He's in outer space is more like it. And that's probably how far he'll go in those." Then he walked away and sat down to eat with Cullihan and Sock.

I didn't care. I liked having the opportunity to talk to Alonzo alone.

"Tell me about the time you ran away," I said.

"I don't really remember it," he said.

"Russell says you persuaded a woman to help you. She gave you clothes and money. You don't remember that?"

"How many times have I told you, you can't believe what Russell says?"

"So you didn't ever run away?"

"Russell is the one who ran away. He wanted to see his wife and kids."

"I thought you said Russell didn't have a wife and kids."

"He don't."

"But he did. At one time."

"Toby, sometimes people don't want to talk about the past. That's another thing you should know by now."

We tried to play gin that night, but everyone was in a bad mood. The cards slapped down on the table and no one talked much, except to say: "Your deal." "This game is doubled." and "Gin."

Cullihan hovered near the table, picking his nose, and grinning at Sock, who wriggled and blushed. Book didn't like tension. He slammed his book shut and left, right as Cullihan made his move.

"Hey, Rocky, got any candy?" he asked.

"No," I said, "and the name is Woodruff."

"But I saw you come back here with a shitload of stuff."

"That was for my friends."

"Your friends, huh?" He glanced at Russell, who was concentrating on his cards. "So—I guess I'm not one of your friends."

"No, you're not," I said.

Cullihan grabbed me by the bathrobe. "You're goddamn right, I'm not," he said. "My friends are dead. Their eyeballs blew right out of their heads. They drowned in water covered with fire. But they did their job—they didn't sit on their asses all day while the country went to hell."

"Let go of me," I said. Cullihan's eyes were light blue like flames. I tried to pull his hands off my robe, but his grip was amazingly strong for such a small guy.

"Let go," I said again.

"Not on your life, you hippie son of a bitch." He didn't speak loudly, but the energy in the ward changed like a sudden drop in the barometer. Then as Cullihan drew back to punch me, I caught his arm, Alonzo jumped up from the table to grab him from behind, and Basto came bellowing down the ward toward us. He shoved Alon aside and put Cullihan in a headlock so fast that he had him twisted down to the floor before he knew what had happened to him.

"What the fuck, get off me, you bastard!" he yelled.

"No chance," said Basto, who sat down on Cullihan's back holding his hands behind him. Cullihan beat his feet on the floor.

"Are you crazy? I didn't do anything!"

"You're right, you didn't. But it's no thanks to you."

Shipley, the nurse on duty, helped Basto get up and carry the twisting, shouting Cullihan down to the Quiet Room to cool off. For about a half an hour, we could hear the sound of scuffling and banging, then silence.

Basto made us go to bed early, but it didn't restore peace. In the middle of the night, Russell woke up yelling: "What's happening? Jesus fucking Christ! What's happening?" He thrashed around so much that he fell out of bed before

Shipley could get to him.

"It's all right now," I could hear Shipley, saying softly. "You're all right. You were only dreaming."

Russell must have woken up then, because I heard him say: "Leave me alone, you fucking idiot. I'm all right? Is that what you think? I'm all right!?! That is the biggest joke I've ever heard."

For the next two days, Russell stayed in bed with his night mask pulled over his eyes, and Alonzo began to fall apart. He sat at the table, staring at the lump of Russell on the bed, shuffling his cards over and over until I was sure they would disintegrate.

"Hey, Russell," I finally said to him, standing by the foot of his bed. "You can't stay in bed forever, you know."

"Don't get above yourself, poster boy," he said without moving a muscle, but that evening he did get up and come to the table. He looked thinner than ever, and his hands shook when he lit his cigarette off mine, but he said he was ready to play gin, so that's what we did.

I didn't see much of Barry because I wasn't on the ward when the doctors came on rounds, but I was doing everything I could to show that I had recovered. I even had been reassigned to light duty, mopping the floors on the ward.

I hoped he would notice that I was ready to go, so I was pleased that he said: "Nice mocs," when I arrived at his office for an appointment. He leaned over his desk to get a closer look. The shells had been moved to the bookcase, and the pile of papers on his desk was even taller than usual. His sunburn had turned to a golden tan. "Very nice," he said, sitting down again. "Usually they come out looking like they're made for two different people."

"Thanks. I'll make you a pair if you want," I said.

"Really? That would be great. It might be considered bribery though."

"No kidding. What can I bribe you to do?" I asked.

Barry laughed and passed across his cigarettes. "Sit down," he said. "We've got to talk."

I sat and smoked, while he hunted through his files.

"I've got some news for you," he said, not looking up.

"Good news?" I asked. My heartbeat quickened.

"I think so." At last he found the file he wanted and opened it. "The doctors' committee has scheduled you for Thursday. That's one good thing. Your reports look very good. You seem to be doing very well. What do you think?"

"I think I'm better," I said.

"They'll want to know more than that, of course," said Barry. "They'll expect you to be able to talk about what happened. Why you wanted to kill yourself. What insight you've gained."

"From being locked up?"

"From being kept alive."

"Oh."

"And—do you have any insights?"

"Well, I guess it was a pretty insane thing to do if that's what you want to know." I said this because I thought it was what he wanted to hear, but as it came out of my mouth, I also knew that I meant it.

Barry looked interested. "So if you had it to do over again, you wouldn't have done it?"

"I didn't say that."

"What did you say then?"

"The way I saw my situation. That can make you do insane things."

"So you think you were temporarily insane?"

I wasn't sure how to answer that, but finally I said, "Something like that."

"What do you think pushed you to that point?"

"I don't know. A lot of things."

"Like what?"

I didn't answer.

"At the doctors' committee session you said—" he looked down at the file, "'I thought a planned death would be better than an unexpected one.'"

"I did?"

"Don't you remember?"

"No."

"Most people, when they go into the military, are aware that they will be in dangerous situations. Didn't you realize that?"

"I thought I was going to get a noncombatant job. That didn't sound dangerous at all."

"So that's why you enlisted in the Navy?"

"Right."

"And instead you got orders to go to Vietnam as a radioman."

I said nothing. It wasn't a question.

"So are there other situations where you think it would be appropriate to kill yourself? Say you had a terminal illness. Or your house had burned down and you lost everything."

"I don't know. I've never been in those situations."

Barry made a note then leaned back in his chair. "I've said this before, but I'll say it again. I may not be much, but I'm all you've got. It would really help if you trusted me."

He turned and looked out the window. His elbows rested on the arms of his chair, and he pressed his fingertips together, straightening and bending his fingers, as he waited.

I lit a cigarette before I spoke. "This isn't a situation that fosters trust," I said. "I'm the one with everything to lose. You don't have anything at risk here."

"Is that what you think?" Barry asked. He swiveled his chair to face me again.

"Yes."

He gave me a long steady look, then said: "Why would I be here if helping people didn't matter to me?"

"I don't know. Why should your experience with the Navy make any more sense than mine?"

Barry's expression turned rueful. "Well, you do have a point there," he said, "because my other news is that I'm being transferred."

"Oh." I dipped my head down over my cigarette to hide my surprise.

"It won't happen for a few weeks, but I wanted to let you know."

"Oh," I said again. "Well, I hope you'll discharge me before you go."

Barry smiled. He was toying with the mountain of papers, trying to stack it more neatly. "It's not up to me, you know," he said. "All I can do is make a recommendation."

I got up and walked past his desk to the window. There were no bars here, only panes of glass, and the window was open to let in the summer air. Three flights below me was the parking lot. People were talking and waving. Getting in their cars and driving away like it was nothing.

I began to pace up and down in the small space of Barry's office.

"You know, it's not easy being here," I said. "It may not look like a lot is going on, but compared to this, being in the Navy was easy. This is the hardest thing I've ever done."

"Listen," said Barry, his voice low and calm. "I understand that. I'm trying to help. I'm not leaving yet, but I wanted you to know in advance so you'd be prepared."

"I don't want to be prepared," I said. "I want to get out of here. I'll do anything to get out of here."

"So how about telling the truth?"

"The truth? What the hell's that supposed to mean?"

Barry looked at me across the paper mountain.

"The truth is I tried to kill myself. I did it on purpose. I was willing to die rather than face my life. Now I'm facing it. Nothing happened the way I expected, and I'm dealing with it. Is that what you call insight? Sanity? The reasons behind why I wanted to kill myself don't seem like anyone's business but my own."

"You sound like a trained behaviorist."

"Well, I'm not. I'm just a guy who wanted to go to college and become an architect and make nice places for people to live. I loved my girlfriend and my friends, and I thought maybe I might be able to do some good in the world, but I screwed up and screwed up and screwed up, and I lost everything. So now I'm here, and I just don't want to screw up any more."

"OK," said Barry. "OK."

We were both silent for a few moments. I really wanted to go back to my bed. To be alone.

Barry began to make another note in his file. I was about to say I was leaving, when he stopped writing and looked up.

"You know," he said, "there's an old expression: I wanted the world to judge me by my intentions, but it judged me by my actions instead."

I rolled my eyes and leaned back in my chair, running my hands through my stubby hair. I really couldn't listen anymore.

"No, wait a minute. All I'm saying is you're right. Especially in the military, your actions are all that counts. If you disobey an order, no one cares about the reasons why. If you accidently do something heroic, even if you were trying to do something else altogether, you're still a hero."

"So?"

"As you say, the question of why you tried to kill yourself is not of interest to the Navy. The fact is that you did it. They don't really care why. I do."

"Yeah? Why?" I asked.

This time it was Barry who didn't answer. We stared at each other across the space between us. Then he said: "Why do you think?"

"I have no idea."

"Because I want you to know. You're the one who needs to know."

"I can't talk anymore today," I said. I got up.

"OK," said Barry, getting up too. "We'll quit for now."

18

"Why did you want to kill yourself?"

That question. Everywhere I went it popped up again. This time at the doctors' committee.

They stared at me like a jury, waiting for me to confess. I had tried to impress them with how well I got along on the ward and what I'd made in OT, but they weren't really buying any of that. They scribbled on their pads, looking bored, until that question came. Then their plastic chairs stopped squeaking restlessly and silence filled the room.

Barry said I needed to know why myself. Maybe he thought of it as insurance. I would have self-knowledge like an oil light that would come on and tell me: Pull over right now or the engine will blow. I didn't think that would work. In two months I hadn't come up with any reason that covered the whole story, and, if my oil light came on all the time, I knew from actual experience that I would ignore it. I wouldn't stop until the engine did blow, and I could name a couple of dead cars to prove it.

What I had started to understand was that I expected questions to have answers, and they didn't. And not only that—I thought I knew the answers, and I was wrong about that too. I had thought I could plan my life like a pair of moccasins that I could sew up and get the result pictured on the direction sheet.

So that's what I told the doctors.

I tried to kill myself because I had all the answers.

"I looked ahead, and everything in front of me was black," I said. "I couldn't see anything I wanted to be part of. Any way forward. I didn't believe any good could come from a bad situation, and I didn't believe anyone could help me—or that they would if they could."

"And now?" asked a doctor with thick round glasses. He leaned forward in his chair.

"Now I don't know anything. And that's OK. It's not my job to have the answers."

"What is your job, as you call it?" he pursued.

"I don't know yet. Maybe to show up."

"So by showing up do you mean that you don't think suicide is a good course of action?"

"Right."

"And if you look ahead now, what do you see?"

"Possibility," I said.

"How does that make you feel?"

"Curious."

"Not anxious?"

"Yes. But more curious."

"Are you saying that attempting suicide was a bad decision?"

I considered saying no, but I didn't want to have to explain why, so I said: "Yes."

A small sigh of satisfaction went up from the row of doctors, and I knew I had made the right choice. The doctor questioning me took off his glasses and rubbed them with a handkerchief.

"If you were to leave here now, what would you do?" he asked.

"All I want is a chance to finish school." I said.

After the interview Barry ushered me out to the hall. He had an expression on his face like he'd eaten a chocolate that had something unexpected inside. He didn't say anything though, so I had to decide for myself if I had convinced the doctors that I had been rehabilitated. That it was time to set me free.

Back on the ward I was surprised to find a group of women from a church organization had come to visit us poor blue robes. They passed out bags of candy, fruit, and used paperback books, and, in each bag they had also included a small American flag on a stick, but I didn't know why. It wasn't the Fourth of July.

In their bright-colored summer dresses, they stood out like wildflowers growing in a vacant lot. They tried to make conversation, but most of the robes took their bags and retreated to their beds to wolf down the food inside.

A few, like Russell and Cullihan, took the opportunity to perform. Russell grabbed each woman by the hand to thank her personally. He seemed to take pleasure in the fear that crossed their faces as they tried to be polite. When Cullihan saw the flags, he pulled open his pajamas so that he could show them his flag tattoo. Luckily Basto collared him before he got completely undressed. By the time the visitors had left, the robes were wired on candy. American flags festooned the bed frames and windowsills, so the place looked like a cemetery on Memorial Day.

All evening, Russell complained about do-gooders. "Why do they come here?" he wanted to know. "What do they think they're doing? Why would we want to see them here?"

Alonzo said, "They remind me of my aunt," and his expression was lonely and downcast.

Russell played a sloppy gin game, and, when he'd lost all his cigarettes, he put down his candy. I didn't get a good hand all evening, so Alon was the big winner. A pile of cigarettes and candy accumulated in front of him, and this attracted Cullihan like a fly to dead meat. He left off trying to intimidate some of the more withdrawn patients into giving him their goody bags and began to circle around the table.

"You've got gin, but except for those six cards," he said to Russell, looking at his hand.

"Buzz off, Pup," Russell said. "We're busy."

"I wanna watch," said Cullihan.

"Well, we don't want you to."

"It's free country. I can if I want."

"No you can't. Now beat it. You're being a fucking pain in the ass, and you know it."

Cullihan looked surprised. Russell had never spoken to him like that before.

"Ah c'mon. All I want is a couple of smokes. Some candy," he said, moving around to Alonzo's side of the table. "Can't I have one of those Hershey bars?"

"No, Pup, no," Russell said, but it was too late. He had encouraged Cullihan too often to be able to stop him now. Cullihan ignored Russell and made a lightning strike on Alonzo's pile. His hand darted down to scoop up a handful of M&Ms.

Quick as he was, Alonzo was quicker. He grabbed Cullihan's wrist and shook it until the candy clattered to the floor.

"Let go of me, you crazy nigger!" said Cullihan.

"I am not crazy!" said Alonzo, rising from his chair.

He still had Cullihan by the wrist and, standing, he towered over him. "I am the sun and the moon and the stars," he said, and then he thrust Cullihan away from him, so that he stumbled against the beds behind him and landed on the floor.

The robes at the other tables laughed.

Cullihan turned white, and he was ready to leap at Alonzo, when Basto came out of the john, escorting a robe who had thrown up all over himself.

"What's going on," he demanded.

"Nothin'," said Cullihan, scrambling to his feet. "I slipped."

"Right," said Alonzo. "I dropped some candy on the floor."

"Well, pick it up," said Basto, glowering at both of them until Cullihan went to his bed.

Alonzo swept up the M&Ms and set them back on the table. Only when all his winnings were tidy again, and he had picked up his cards and carefully rearranged them, did he turn to Russell and say: "What you see in him, Russell?

All I see is trouble." It was the first time I ever heard Alon come close to challenging him.

Russell acted as if he didn't notice. "I find Donny entertaining," he said. "Like fireworks."

"Hmph. Fireworks at least is pretty."

"But they can't hold a candle to the sun, the moon, and the stars. Now I believe it was your turn, champ."

Alonzo looked embarrassed, but pleased, and he grinned as he reached out to pull a card off the deck.

Late that night I woke up suddenly with the feeling that something was wrong. I looked around and noticed that Alonzo's bed was empty, and I wondered where he was. If his getting up had disturbed my sleep.

Then I noticed another thing. Cullihan was awake too.

I stayed very still and watched him get out of his bed. He paused, quickly surveyed the ward, and then began to move like a man trying to be invisible on an open plain. He almost looked like he was sleepwalking. If he were, what would happen when he bumped into Alon?

I sat up, once he was past me, and Cullihan didn't notice. He continued to creep from bunk to bunk.

Down in the corpsmen's booth, Shipley slept, his feet up on the desk. There was no sound except the soft rustlings and snoring of the robes. When Cullihan reached the end of the ward, the light from the john fell on his blue eyes and cold pale face.

As soon as he was out of sight, I followed him. I didn't have any plan except to make sure that if he did know Alon was down there and intended to surprise him, I would even up the score.

I saw Alon first. He stood at the far end of the john with his face to the wall. He was perfectly still, his forehead tipped against the tile, arms hanging at his sides, feet bare. Sorrow emanated from the loose folds of his robe, the tie dangling to the floor.

Cullihan was nowhere in sight, and, in the long moment that followed, I stood still, suspended in silence. I thought maybe I had been dreaming myself and should go back to bed. Then a shadow on the wall moved and Cullihan leapt out from a toilet stall into the light. Alon was so startled he didn't even have time to turn around before Cullihan had flung himself on him. His forehead hit the wall under the impact, and his knees buckled as Cullihan grabbed him around the throat. I ran toward them, even as I saw the glint of metal in

Cullihan's hand, and heard Alonzo grunt and then scream in pain.

I jumped on Cullihan's back and struggled to get hold of his arms, as Alonzo crumpled underneath us, blood spurting from a wound in his neck.

"You bastard! You fucking bastard!" someone shouted and it might have been me, because Cullihan had turned Alonzo's fall to his advantage and tossed me hard against the wall. It took me only a moment to regain my footing, but it was long enough for Cullihan to grab my shoulder and thrust something sharp into my stomach: Scissors, I saw, as they flashed into my body. Sewing scissors with gold birds on the handles like my mother used. They fitted Cullihan's small fingers perfectly.

I was too surprised by the pain to cry out, but I kicked Cullihan in the balls as hard as I could before I slipped to the floor. Blood leaked through my hands as I curled myself tight. Cullihan kicked and stabbed me again and again, and I thought he would never stop, but suddenly there was a roar of voices and commotion and then, as suddenly, silence.

19

When I woke again it was still night. Or rather a night. I was in a strange bed in a different part of the hospital. This was a ward where flowers and cards stood on the bedside tables and folding cloth dividers provided patients with privacy. My own bedside table held only a plastic pitcher of water and a cup.

I looked at it, but I couldn't reach it. My body was stiff with bandages from my armpits to my hips and my left wrist was attached to an IV. My mouth ached with dryness, but being thirsty was nothing. I was not dead.

I had no idea how much time had passed, but, as I drifted in and out of consciousness, I remembered Culliham kicking me and calling me a no-good fucking traitor, and someone's blood spreading across the cold gray tile.

I wondered where Alonzo was. If he was all right.

I wanted him nearby. In the next bed. Or the next.

But, even in my groggy state, I knew he wouldn't be there.

You couldn't grow up where I did and not be familiar with death. Killing. Not of people, of course, but of animals, fish, and birds. I knew the difference between a fatal wound and a miss. A mess. I was a mess—the result of Cullihan's rage at being surprised—but he had gone for Alonzo like a skilled hunter. An assassin.

Earlier—had it really been the same day?—I had been so satisfied with the idea that questions did not have answers. Now I couldn't help asking why.

Did Alonzo die for a handful of M&Ms? Or because he was black instead of white, big and strong instead of small and mean?

Would it have happened even if he hadn't let his guard down in the middle of the night?

Would it have happened if I hadn't showed up?

I really wanted a drink of water. I hoped a nurse would come around soon to check up on everyone. I could ask for a drink then. I could ask about Alonzo too.

I might be wrong. He might be there, down the ward, behind that folded screen, or even farther down in the shadows beyond my range of vision. In a couple of days, we might be up and around, playing gin again.

I had always liked playing cards with Alon. I liked his slow deliberate way of arranging his hand, and the seriousness with which he shuffled the deck. He gave himself to the job completely, and he never cheated.

He won his share of games anyway, like the straight man of a comedy team who gets his own laughs by not joking. To me that was the interesting thing. In a way, because of this, I had come to think of Alonzo as invulnerable to cheap tricks. But I had been wrong about that. In some situations integrity is no protection. Metal against flesh. Alonzo had shown his mettle and it was good and true, but Cullihan's metal had been fast and sharp.

And what about me?

All I could say was that I had gone to help, and it hadn't taken a three-syllabled de-cis-io for me to do it. I tried to hold that thought as I went to sleep, instead of the others that crowded in. Alon's last gagging breaths. The ease of the scissors cutting through my flesh. Cullihan's shocked blank expression.

I opened my eyes to find Barry standing by the bed bouncing up and down on the balls of his feet nervously. His jingling keys had awakened me.

"Oh good," he said. "I was starting to think you were going to sleep all day again."

"Have I slept all day?" I asked, turning my head to see blue sky framed by the window at the end of the ward.

"Two days," said Barry. "But that's good. The best thing for you."

"How long have you been here?"

"I've been checking up on you every now and then. I told you I became a shrink because of the low death rate. I don't like it when my patients nearly get killed. Especially the ones I'm doing a great job with like you." He tried to laugh then, but I could see the worry in his face. His tan had faded.

"I'm thirsty," I said, trying to lift my head.

Barry poured water from the pitcher into a cup with a bent straw and held it up to my mouth. I drank two cups and would have drunk more, but I was suddenly too tired.

"Where is Alonzo," I said, as my eyes began to close.

"You're going to be fine," said Barry. "You've got some holes in you, broken ribs, bruises, you know, but he missed the vital organs and that was really lucky."

"That's not what I asked you," I said, pulling myself back from sleep.

"I know." He fiddled with the water pitcher for a minute then said, "He died, Toby. They tried to help him, but it happens very fast if the carotid artery is cut."

"That's what I thought," I said and shut my eyes so I wouldn't have to see him anymore.

The next time I opened them, I was surprised to find a bouquet of yellow chrysanthemums by my bed. The card attached said, "Get well soon, Mom, Dad, and Jack."

"Take those flowers to the morgue," I told the first nurse I could get hold of. "I want them to go to Alonzo Cooke."

I think she started to say that they don't allow flowers in the morgue, but then she remembered which ward I came from and took the flowers away.

Slowly Barry told me more about what happened. That Alon had died before they could get him to surgery. That Cullihan had been arrested and taken to the brig. That Russell had created such a ruckus—calling the corpsmen negligent bastards and picking fights with the doctors—that he had been put in the Quiet Room and then moved to another ward.

I listened, but I didn't say a word. Every part of me hurt, and silence was the only cure I could think of.

For once, Barry didn't urge me to talk. He came to visit every day and sat by my bed for an hour or two in silence. I appreciated that. At first I slept a lot, but after a few days I was awake and I watched him sit there, calmly doing nothing. He had real yogi potential.

Finally I asked him, "What are you thinking about?"

He crossed his legs and looked at me, as if it were not surprising that I had started a conversation.

"Just then?" he said. "I was hoping my dog didn't get into the garbage. I'm afraid I left the door under the sink open. What are you thinking about?"

"Why he didn't kill me too."

"Ah. Well. I will learn the answer to my question when I get home tonight. You will never learn the answer to yours."

I shifted uncomfortably in my shell of bandages. "Alon told me you couldn't die unless God wanted you to. That's why the Seconal didn't kill me."

"Did you believe him?"

"No."

"But, if he believed it, maybe it helped him. Maybe it made it easier."

"Easier to be murdered?"

Barry shrugged. "Maybe."

"I don't know about that, but I do know I sure didn't help."

"Yes you did, Toby," he said. "You were there. You risked everything to be there. He knew that."

"It didn't make any difference," I said.

"You don't know that. You only know the outcome wasn't what you wanted. Those are two different things."

I groaned. There were moments when the pain flared, and my body felt like it was on fire burning from the inside out.

Barry patted my blanket and rang for a nurse. "The morphine will help, but it doesn't do the mental part. You have to do that."

"I need to sleep now," I said. I closed my eyes.

"OK, but listen, Toby, there's something I've been wanting to say."

"What," I said, without opening my eyes.

He paused. "Do you remember when I talked about people judging you by your actions, not your intentions? I just want you to know, off the record, you understand, that I think you should be proud of both. Your intentions and your actions. And I'm not only referring to the other night."

I reopened my eyes and looked at him. He was pulling on his upper lip to disguise his embarrassed smile. It was a gesture that reminded me of Alonzo. "Thanks," I said, and I turned my face away.

As I got better, Barry came less regularly, but I had new people to talk to. Everyone on the ward knew the story of the fight and wanted to hear the details firsthand. Anticipation made them friendly. They told me their war stories, life histories, and health problems. Their wives plumped up my pillows and loaned me their magazines, and I thanked them, but I never did talk about what happened.

During the day when the hospital routine bustled around me, I was able to go through the motions of recovery—shots, dressing changes, baths, meals, walks up and down the hall. I felt Alon's presence the whole time like an amputated limb, but I hid it from the doctors and nurses and did what I was told. It was at night that the fight replayed in my head most relentlessly. More than anything I wished that I could change it.

It was true I had gone to help, but why hadn't I called out right away? If I had, Alon would have turned around. He would have seen Cullihan come at him and that might have made all the difference.

I hadn't wanted to disturb him, but I'd gotten up because I thought something was going on and then I didn't call out. I went into the fight uselessly after it was too late.

As usual, it seemed, my timing was wrong. The pain I felt as I healed seemed less than I deserved. My life would go back to normal. Whatever that was. That was more than Alonzo, Russell, or Cullihan could hope for.

I had learned something about war though. When I assessed the risks of the jobs I might get, I had only considered the dangers of killing or being killed. I hadn't considered what it would be like to have to watch helplessly as someone you had come to love died.

20

They made me go back to my old ward in a wheelchair, which I thought was silly. I could walk perfectly well, but those were the rules. Basto peered out the barred window in the door at me and grinned. "You're back," he said, as if nothing would give him more satisfaction than to slam that door behind me again.

"I'm back," I said, feeling a weird mixture of relief, sadness, and revulsion.

If it were possible the ward looked dingier and more depressing than I remembered. The spaces occupied by Alonzo, Russell, Cullihan—and me—already seemed to have been filled by blue robes with blank faces.

Sock and Book were still there at what I thought of as Russell's table, but Book had taken over my chair. He now faced the window—not that he looked out of it. The first time Williams saw me, his eyes widened suddenly and he began to dit-dah, dit-dit-dah, then just as suddenly he stopped and gestured for a cigarette.

"I don't have any today," I said, but he kept on pulling at my sleeve and touching his lips with two fingers until I walked away.

I sat on my bed—not too comfortably, with my ribs taped—and considered my position. The way I figured it I should be getting out in 14 days. It surprised me that I felt simultaneously that I couldn't last that long and not ready to move at all.

I thought it would help to return to my old routine—start walking more, go to the Snack Bar, see Dorothy—but my first afternoon back, when I asked to leave, Basto grinned at me again and said Barry had cancelled my hospital privileges until further notice.

I was shocked. Barry had assured me that everyone understood the fight was not my fault.

"Are you sure about that?" I said. "That was an order from Dr. Barry?"

"None other than Dr. John the Surfer."

I was half-convinced that Basto was lying to piss me off, but I couldn't say that, so I glared at him and stomped off to the john.

Until I got there, I forgot where I was going.

The room was clean now, of course—as gloomy as it had ever been and stinking of Lysol. I walked slowly past the place where I had paused when I first saw Alonzo, past the spot where I'd been when Cullihan appeared, and reached the wall where Alon had been standing when I last saw him alive. It seemed like there ought to be something there to mark the place. Something beside my memory of his scream, the spurt of blood, and then the noise and confusion of the fight. But there was nothing. Any sign of what had happened had been carefully scrubbed away.

I touched the cool gray tiles and then tracing Alon's path slid down to sit on the floor with my back against the wall. I closed my eyes. I didn't believe in God, but I did believe in saying goodbye. No one was left but me to do it, and I was still there when Basto came to round everyone up for dinner.

After I'd survived the march to the mess hall, the wait in line, the Swedish meatballs, and the return march, I knew what being back on the ward was going to be like. Lonely and boring. I sat with Book and Sock in the mess hall, because it seemed like I'd inherited them and we understood each other's habits. Bill asked if he could see where I got stabbed and I said no, but other than that the robes didn't express any interest in me. I spent the evening on my bed, smoking, until Shipley came around with the night meds.

He handed me a paper cup containing several pills, including one large one I'd never seen before.

"What's that?" I said, pointing to it.

"Doctor's orders," he said.

"I've never seen one of those before."

Shipley shrugged. "It's what the chart that came with you ordered. Now be a good boy and don't cause trouble when we're all so glad to see you back."

"I want to see Dr. Barry," I said. "As soon as possible. Put that on the chart, why don't you."

"OK, but it's bedtime now. So take your meds and have a good night's sleep."

I took the cup and then hesitated.

"I'll wait here to make sure they go down nice and easy," Shipley said, and he didn't leave until I had taken all the pills.

"There you go." He patted me on the shoulder. "We're glad you're making a good recovery. Now get some sleep. Tomorrow you'll feel better."

I don't know what Barry gave me, but it knocked me right out. I didn't wake up until Basto rattled the frame of my bed in the morning. The first thing I said was "I want to see Barry," but he didn't care. He wanted me up, ready to march. All through the routine of meds, showers, and breakfast, I felt dizzy and stoned and, when I got back to my bed, intending to lie in wait for Barry, I dozed off.

"What happened?" I asked, when I woke up again.

"You missed him," said Basto.

"But I told you I had to see him."

"You were asleep. He didn't want to wake you. But he'll see you at two o'clock. So keep your pants on."

"Very funny."

At five of two, I was waiting at the corpsmen's station for Basto.

"I'm ready," I said.

"I see that," said Basto, setting down his newspaper.

Because I no longer had hospital privileges, I had to be in restraints when I left the ward. "This is ridiculous," I said, as Basto fastened my wrists together.

"You bet," he said. "But that's the rule." He gave my hands a little jerk, in case I didn't know exactly how much power he had over me, and I would have liked to kick him just once, but I didn't.

Barry's office was tidy for a change. The mountain of files on his desk had been reduced to a small stack. The shells from his trip to South Carolina were gone. He was at the window when I came in, his back to the room, but when he turned around he gave me a friendly smile.

"Hey, you look better," he said.

"Yeah, well, I don't feel better," I said. "What the hell is going on? Why did you take away my hospital privileges—and what's with the elephant tranquilizers?"

Barry started to laugh, but then he caught himself. "You still don't trust me," he said.

"You're goddamn right I don't."

"Toby, you need to rest. You're still recovering. A sleeping pill helps. OK? There's no plot here. You're getting paranoid."

"I'm not paranoid. You told me I'd be here ninety days. That means I should have thirteen days to go, but no one's told me a fucking thing. I want to know where I stand."

"Sit down," he said.

"I don't want to sit down. I want to get out of here. I haven't done a thing but sit on my ass and sleep for three months. How that's supposed to improve your mental health is beyond me. But don't tell me, I know—it doesn't matter. Drugs are all that count."

"The one I gave you doesn't seem to have had a lasting effect."

"I suppose you'll give me more then. Dope me up until I can't talk."

"You're the one who did that, Toby, not me. Is there anything else?" He had taken his seat at the desk. "Come on. You want to lay your bad trip on me, go ahead. I can take it. What else is on your mind?" Barry patted his chest with his open hand.

"My bad trip?" I said, shaking my head. "My bad trip! Boy, you are a mystery to me sometimes. One minute you're asking me to trust you and the next you're giving me some patronizing bullshit. I've really had it with this place."

"You're starting to sound like Russell."

"Russell! Well, maybe I am. I always wondered why he was here. It seemed to me he spoke the truth, and nobody wanted to hear it."

Barry looked a little surprised. "And do you still wonder why he's here now?"

"What do you mean?" Something in his tone stopped me dead.

"Think about it, Toby. Think about what happened."

I stared at him and he stared back.

"That was Cullihan," I insisted. "He hated Alonzo—and he hated me too."

"That was Pup."

I got up from my chair and went to the window. Just hearing that name made me feel sick. Down below the cars moved in and out of the parking lot as if the world were an orderly, logical place.

"I don't believe that," I said. "Russell and Alonzo were friends."

"Yes."

"So there's no way he would want to see him hurt." Even as I said this, memories of the tension I'd watched building between them surfaced.

"Really," said Barry. "That's what you think. People who love each other don't hurt each other."

I scowled at him.

"Did Russell ever tell you how he got burned?"

"There was an explosion on his ship."

"True. But what he probably didn't mention is that he also set fire to his own house with his wife and three children asleep in it, because he thought his wife was seeing someone else."

"No! Were they hurt?"

Barry shook his head. "Russell rescued them himself—and got badly burned in the process."

"So, he didn't get burned in the war?"

"The first time he did. This was the second time—when he wound up here."

"Wow," I said. I didn't want to believe it, but I also couldn't imagine Barry making something like that up. And how many times had Alon told me not to believe anything Russell said? How many times had he told me that himself? It must be true, but then the picture shifted to Russell, Alonzo, and me playing gin—and, for a minute, all the aches in my body fired at once.

"So what that means is that it was my fault," I said. "I came between them. I encouraged Alon to think about leaving. I knew Russell didn't like it, but I did it anyway."

"Whoa!" Barry looked alarmed. "Who appointed you Captain of the Universe?"

"But it's true. Russell said he would never leave, but I thought Alon could do it. I told him I thought he could have more of a life. Jesus. What a prediction that turned out to be."

"Toby, there were four people involved. The only actions you're responsible for are your own."

I sat back down in my chair. I wasn't sure I believed that, but I wanted to. More than anything.

Barry pushed his cigarettes toward me, and I took one.

"I can't believe Russell wanted Alonzo to get killed."

"No, I don't think he did. But people don't always want things in clear-cut ways. And they don't always choose the right tool for the job they want done. After all, you say you tried to kill yourself so you could live."

I couldn't believe he brought that up again now. "Why do you always bring that up? I don't want to talk about that any more. You could as easily say I tried to get killed so Alonzo could live."

"All right. Let's say that. What does that mean?"

"I don't know. All I know is I want to get out of here."

21

I told Barry all I wanted was to get out, but, in another example of life's perfect timing, when he reinstated my hospital privileges, I no longer wanted to do anything. I went back to sitting at the table with Sock and Book. Book sat in my old chair, reading as usual, with Williams next to him, and I sat at the end facing Russell's empty chair. No one took Alon's place.

We didn't talk. I sat there and brooded about whether or not I had walked into a problem or created it. Was I a brave guy who risked everything for his friend, or a jerk who tried to manipulate other people into thinking his way? Another version of the guy with all the answers.

Barry found me there when he came on rounds a couple of days later.

"Hey," he said, tapping his clipboard with his pen. "Aren't you supposed to be at occupational therapy right now?"

I scowled at him with my arms crossed.

"Toby," he said sharply. "Snap out of it. If you aren't there for every one of your scheduled times, it's going into the record that you're regressing. Maybe you should stay a few weeks longer to be sure you're all right."

This was the person I had to trust with my life. I got up and walked away.

I did what he said though. With all the speed and willingness of a guy walking through wet cement, I went to OT the next day. At least, I told myself, that way I wouldn't have to see his face with that what-the-fuck-are-you-doing-now expression on it.

When I walked in the door, Dorothy leapt up from a table full of other patients to greet me. For a minute I thought she was going to hug me, but she only blushed and said, "I'm so glad you're all right, Toby. We heard about what happened."

Then she stepped back into her OT role, adding, "I saved your project for you. It's right here, the way you left it."

The project was a half-finished pair of moccasins decorated with hearts, diamonds, clubs, and spades. I'd been making them for Russell.

"Thanks," I said. "But I don't think I can work on those anymore."

She started to ask why, but stopped herself. "All right. Do you want to do something else? Something different? A new pair?"

I didn't feel like making moccasins at all, but she handed me a kit and the leather stamps and one thing led to another. I spent an hour stamping a piece of cardboard until it was almost completely black.

At the end of the session, I looked at it and thought: this is something a crazy person would do. I didn't want Dorothy to see it, so I folded it up and stuck it in the trash.

That afternoon I sat on my bed and debated whether I was crazy or not. Was it a choice people made—to give up and be crazy? Or did it happen against their will. Without their will. This was a different conversation than the one about suicide. I never felt that was crazy. This sliding away from life was scarier. For the first time, I understood how it could become a habit.

I called up pictures from my old life:

My mother picking tomatoes wearing a faded New York State Fair scarf around her head.

My father on a construction site telling ten people what to do at once.

Jack jumping moguls on a sunny winter day.

Peter welding car parts together with Cream playing full blast.

And Martha leaning over me, her hair smelling like dry summer grass, as sparks from the Bessemer converters flew up in the air.

From the vantage point of the ward, it was hard to imagine ever being part of any of those lives again.

I didn't plan to ask Dorothy if I could be her assistant. The words came into my head the next day, while I was watching her clean up, and I said them before I could have second thoughts.

She looked surprised, but pleased. I had made no progress on the moccasins beyond taking the pieces out of the bag and arranging them on the table.

"All right," she said and handed me her broom.

My mother used to say that she never got tired of housework because the repetitive motions were soothing, and she liked to restore order. It didn't bother her that everything got messed up again. Order and disorder are two sides of the same thing, she said. Wishing there would be only order would be like wishing there would be only days. "Haven't you ever noticed, Toby, that plants grow in the night as well as the day? Both are essential."

So I swept and washed the floor and cleaned paintbrushes and put away supplies. At times my healing body ached, but I pushed myself to do whatever chores needed to be done. Dorothy and I made a plan to reorganize the shelves in the storeroom that took several days to carry out. By the time we were finished, whole hours could go by without my asking myself why I had lived and Alonzo had died. A good thing because, as I had already learned, I did not have the answer to any question—especially not why.

I still had the hots for Dorothy. Watching her scrub down a table, her sleeves rolled up over those smooth white arms, was the most exciting thing that had happened to me in months, and I definitely liked the excuse to be alone with her. But more than lusting after her, I felt better when I was around her.

Listening to her talk to her patients, I realized that the attraction was not only that she was pretty and friendly. What made her really irresistible was her capacity for acceptance. That was what she offered, and that was what we all needed the most. Maybe the fact that she was right that learning you had to sew Part A together before you could attach it to Part B helped too.

I enjoyed talking to her while we worked. She wasn't a nut or a doctor, and even though she could report what I said to Barry, I let my guard down a little, and she did too. I told her stories about my life, and she listened attentively as she always did. I talked about college and the Navy, the woods and my tree house, and how I had decided to become an architect because the answer to the world's problems was good shelter for everyone.

She laughed at that. "You sure think big, I'll say that for you, Toby."

"What do you mean?" I said, leaning on my broom.

"Don't you remember telling me that you were going to end the war by killing yourself?"

"Yes, I do." I expected her to tease me, but she didn't. She sat down at one of the tables and began to fiddle with a bowl of tiles, first stirring them with her fingers and then laying them in rows on the table.

"My fiancé was killed in Da Nang," she said. "That's why I came to work here. I thought if I could just help one guy who'd been in the war, maybe that would make me feel less lost. Less like my life—my dreams—were expendable."

"No one is expendable."

"Do you really believe that? When that guy tried to kill you, I thought what if you died here? What would that have been for?"

"Something I believed in anyway. Which is more than I can say for the war."

"What's that?"

"Helping a friend. At least that's what I thought I was doing."

She gave me a long look and took out a cigarette. "Curtis's mother says he died for freedom. She says he believed that, but I'm not so sure. I think he was scared. I think he didn't know what it was for."

"I'm sorry," I said.

"When you told me that about ending the war by killing yourself, I thought you really were crazy. But then I realized it wasn't any different for Curtis. He went out there and let his body stand for an idea, and he got shot for it. I love the amputees because they did that too. It's only fate that they didn't have to give their whole bodies. Only part. They are very special people to me. I try to help them see themselves that way. I would have been so happy to have Curtis come back—in any way, shape, or form. If you can keep the spirit whole, the body doesn't matter."

"Keeping the spirit whole isn't easy. In fact, it's probably harder."

"I know," she said, regarding me. "But I believe it can be healed even when the body can't."

"Through making tile ashtrays?"

She stubbed out her cigarette. "Yes," she said. "And sweeping."

22

Dorothy wasn't satisfied with just hearing stories about my past. She wanted to know what my plans were for the future. What I intended to do after I left the hospital.

"I'm going back to Pittsburgh," I said.

"But what about your family? Don't you think they'll want to see you? To know you're all right?"

I shrugged. "Not really. They know I'm all right. The hospital informed them."

She let that pass. "So what about your friends in Pittsburgh then? Do they know you're coming?"

"No," I admitted, "they don't."

"Why not?" she asked, and I couldn't come up with an answer, so every time she saw me, she asked if I had called them yet.

I got as far as the phone booth, but I felt superstitious. I didn't want to say I was getting out until I knew for sure that it was true. The story I had to tell wasn't worth hearing without that ending.

I hesitated for other reasons too. The closer I got to going back to my old life, the more I realized how far away I had been. The world outside didn't exist on my ward. I felt like a diver down so deep that the light from the surface can't penetrate. You know it's up there, but it's not so clear anymore which way is up. I wanted to reach the surface, and I didn't want to get the bends when I did, so I made myself start to read newspapers again.

After I'd finished helping Dorothy, I would go to the coffee shop and plow through whatever papers I could find. I read them straight through, cover to cover, even the ads.

That the war news was bad was no surprise, but what had happened at the Democratic Convention blew me away. I stared at the pictures for a long time: The mob of protesters faced by an even bigger mob of armed police and National Guardsmen. Kids throwing rocks. Getting beaten. The clouds of tear gas. Fires. Smashed windows. Arrests.

I couldn't get over the change from the peaceful marches of a year ago. In one photograph I saw a girl who reminded me of Martha, screaming as two cops dragged her toward a police van.

I sat studying this picture for so long that the edges of my sandwich started to curl, and Ernie said: "Everything OK there, bud?"

I said yes, but I left the sandwich and went to call Peter. I still didn't know what I would say, but I needed to hear his voice. I needed to know that he and Martha were all right.

No one answered at the number I called. I sat in the phone booth with my feet propped against the wall, kicking it with every ring, and saying: Shit. Shit. Shit. There was nothing else I could do.

But then, just like that, when I stepped out of that phone booth, the world reversed. I saw myself as part of the outside again. A guy in a robe, but not a blue robe. I hadn't even realized I'd become one until I wasn't any more.

Suddenly everything looked different. I noticed things that had been in front of me for months, like the trees that edged the parking lots and the lights of the city beyond. I became aware of the weather again, and I stopped eating food that disgusted me. Swedish meatballs.

The afternoon I received an unexpected request to see Barry, the weather was on my mind more than anything else. A heavy rain was falling—one of those late summer thunderstorms, where the rain pounds so hard you can't hear anything else—and I had settled myself to watch the show. The flashes of lightning against the turbulent sky, the tossing trees, the sheets of rain, and the fast-forming puddles. But Barry had summoned me, so I went.

When I arrived at his office, I found him watching the storm too.

"Hey, Tob," he said, and there was an excitement in his face that seemed greater than a good display of thunder and lightning could explain.

I joined him at his window just as lightning forked and re-forked across the sky. A tremendous clap of thunder followed almost instantly, rattling the glass.

Barry grinned. "Next to big surf, there's nothing I like more than a good thunderstorm."

New strikes slashed across the dark sky to the ground, illuminating the landscape with an eerie light. The crashing and booming that followed created so much satisfying noise that we didn't even try to talk.

When it subsided, Barry leaned against the window frame with his hands in his pockets and studied me.

"You look different," he said.

"I am different," I said. He raised one eyebrow and waited, but I didn't know how to explain it.

When I didn't say anything else, he said: "Don't you want to know why I asked you to see me?"

"Sure."

"The Medical Board's recommendation came today."

My eyes were on Barry's face, but lightning streaked across the sky in my peripheral vision. My heart boomed. "And?"

"They're giving you an honorable discharge as emotionally unfit for service."

"Really?" The blood rushed out of my head as if someone had pulled a plug, and I had to sit down fast. I slid against the wall to the floor. "You mean this is it?"

"This is it," said Barry, leaning down toward me. "Hey, are you all right? You're all white. You know I don't think you've really recovered yet."

"I'm fine," I claimed, but I had the whirlies, as if I were drunk. As if I had climbed a hundred flights of stairs fast and finally saw the last flight in front of me.

After a couple of minutes, my heart stopped pounding, and I realized that the thunder had moved off into the distance too. I opened my eyes.

"Did you really just tell me that I got my discharge?"

"I did," said Barry.

"You wouldn't kid me about that."

"Toby, I have never once lied to you. Now do you want me to help you get up? For someone who just got good news, you certainly look terrible."

"I don't want to get up," I said, closing my eyes again. "If I move, something else might happen. Something might change."

"OK," said Barry, "let me know when you're ready."

"You know what?" I said after awhile. "It's going to be my birthday next month. This will all be over by my birthday."

"How old are you going to be?"

"Twenty one."

"That's a good age," said Barry. "I'm glad you lived to see it."

"Me too," I said, looking up at him.

"No thanks to you, I might add."

For once, I didn't get mad. I laughed instead. "But I'm really getting out? Next week?"

"Yes," he said.

"I can't fucking believe it."

When I left Barry's office, I went to the nearest phone booth and dialed Peter's number. This time he answered on the first ring—as if he had been standing by the phone waiting for my call—but I heard disbelief in his voice when the operator asked if he would accept a collect call from Toby Woodruff.

As soon as she was off the line, he said: "Toby? Is that really you?"

"Yes, it's really me," I said, and my heart began to race again.

"Where are you calling from? Are you in Vietnam?"

"No," I said, and then I told him my story.

"Holy shit!" he kept saying, until I finished. Then there was a silence on the other end of the phone, and a trickle of sweat ran down my spine, as if I were waiting for a verdict.

"Jesus," he said at last. "I guess you think that was better than going to jail. Anyway it was shorter. And you didn't die. That's something."

"It wasn't that risky."

"Are you joking? Between overdosing and getting stabbed, it sounds pretty fucking risky to me, but it will be good to have you back. I'm sure plenty of guys will be interested in your experience."

"They will?"

"Sure. Things have gotten a lot worse since you left."

"I know. I've seen the papers. In fact I thought I saw a photo of Martha in Chicago. She was getting hit on the head by a cop."

"No kidding. That picture really got around."

"You mean it really was her?"

"No, but it might have been. She was there, and you know Martha. She charged right into the thick of everything, banners blazing. The irony was it was her sister who got hurt. And famous. Did you ever meet her? They look a lot alike."

"Martha took Maura to the convention?"

"Yeah, and it was a really bad scene. I mean Maura is fine. She's thrilled to be the only girl in her high school with a battle scar, but Martha feels terrible about what happened. She'll be happy about you though. I mean that you're OK."

"You mean that I'm getting out of the Navy."

"Well, you know, neither of us really understood that. What you were trying to accomplish."

"But you think she'll understand this?"

"Sure. She'll have you cast as some kind of incarcerated martyr to freedom in no time."

"Actually, I'm sort of hoping to forget the whole experience as soon as possible."

23

That last week Peter and I talked every day, and slowly my future took shape. I had a place to stay, a car to use and a lead on a housepainting job. When I considered that I first went to Pittsburgh imagining I'd become the next Frank Lloyd Wright, it wasn't much, but most of the time I was so happy at the prospect of having my own life back, I didn't care.

I couldn't bring myself to call Martha from the hospital, and I was glad I hadn't when Peter broke the news about her new boyfriend—an artist into radical political murals. "I'm really sorry I introduced them," he said. "But who knew that you would ever come back?"

"No one," I said and tried not to spend too much time planning my campaign to win her back.

I still had plenty of moments when I worried that my discharge would not come through after all. One night I dreamt that I was locked in the Quiet Room, pounding my fists against the door and shouting, "I just want to go home!" but no one would come, and no one would let me go. I woke up sweating and terrified until I was awake enough to be certain that I was still in my own bed.

Nothing so dramatic happened during the day. Hour by hour, the time of my departure approached. I had a physical and was pronounced to be recovering well from my injuries. I filled out forms, and the ties that bound me to the Navy unraveled one by one.

In OT, I finished my last pairs of moccasins, decorating them with care. One pair was for Dorothy, who'd asked me if I would make her some with the sun, the moon, and the stars on them. At first, I said I couldn't, but then I thought, what the hell. Alonzo never had a chance to walk away in his; Dorothy would.

The other pair was for Barry and had a pattern of curling waves. On my last afternoon, I went to his office and found him sitting at his desk reading the funnies. The desk was bare except for the newspaper and an overflowing ashtray.

"So you're leaving too?" I asked.

"Any day," he said cheerfully. "This place will see the last of us at about the same time. Only I'm going to San Diego. I still have two more years before I get out."

"There's great surfing in San Diego," I said.

"I know, and I'll be able to get a tan like George Hamilton."

"Maybe you'll be able to use these there," I said, setting his moccasins on the desk.

"Wow, surf mocs! These are great, Toby!" said Barry, who immediately slipped off his shoes, put on the moccasins, and then leaned back in his chair with his feet up on his desk so that he could admire them.

"I'll wear these all the time and remember the good times we had together. Me busting my ass to get you to talk to me, and you not talking. Me jumping through hoops to get you through the bureaucracy, and you not trusting me. Me trying to save your life, and you thinking I wanted to screw you every step of the way."

"Hey—I'm saying thank you."

"I know," he said. "I'm only teasing. You can take it, right? You're a hard-as-nails guy." He passed over his cigarettes, and I took one. "So, are you ready to go back out there?"

"That's one of the sillier questions you've ever asked me," I said.

"You might think so, but it's a serious one. Don't be surprised if you find it's not so easy to put this bit of your history behind you. You need to be prepared for that."

"You mean the ex-mental patient draft dodger thing."

"Exactly," he said.

"I'm not worried." I said, hoping I sounded confident. I wanted to say, I wasn't worried because I knew the truth, but I was no longer 100 percent sure that I did. Whatever I was, it wasn't quite as clear-cut as being a white-clad hero of the ski troops.

"I figured you'd say that. You've never believed anything I've said before, so there's no reason why you should start now. Are there any other last words we need to exchange?"

I looked around the room that would soon be occupied by someone who had never heard of either of us, and then at Barry with his feet on the desk.

"I couldn't have made it through this without you," I said. "I wouldn't want you to think I don't know that. I know I've been very lucky to have your help."

The tips of Barry's ears turned pink. "My pleasure, Woodruff. You're a good man. I hope you have a long and happy life." Then he swung his feet to the floor and leaned forward with his hands folded on his desk.

"So are we going to have a Lone Ranger ending here? You riding away in a swirl of dust with me saying 'Who was that masked man'?"

"I'm the guy in the blue robe, Barry, you're the man with the mask."

"Am I?" He looked at me for a long moment then he laughed. "Well, 'Hiyo, Silver!' then," he said. He stood up and held out his hand. "Fight the good fight."

I took his hand and shook it. "You too," I said, and he just smiled.

24

When I returned to the ward, I was surprised to find Russell, Book and Sock all sitting at their old places. Only Alon's and my chairs at the table were empty.

"So there you are," said Russell, barely glancing up from a hand of solitaire. "I heard you were still here. What the fuck is going on?" Since I last saw him, he had lost so much weight that his blue robe was wrapped in folds around him, and his eyes looked glassy and over-medicated.

"Actually I leave tomorrow, so I'm glad you're back," I said. "I hoped I would see you again."

Russell laughed, his hollow barking laugh. "Rocky, you are definitely the only person in the entire Navy who would say that. Maybe in the whole universe." He studied me, as if he were trying to decide whether I was telling the truth or not, then turned his attention back to his card game. "Anyway, here I am. I'm not that easy to get rid of."

"Where have you been?"

"Oh, they whisked me away for some surgery they were supposed to do years ago, probably to shut me up about their fucking negligence. It was all as good as a pisshole in the snow. I still can't breathe half the time."

"That's too bad."

"They tell me it's better than being dead." He slid the cards back into a pile and began to shuffle them. "So they're really letting you go?"

"Yup."

He shook his head. "You're one lucky dumb-ass kid. I hope you know that. I'm usually very good at picking losers."

"Nobody's right all of the time.

"Nobody and me," said Russell. "Don't kid yourself that getting out is the same as a happy ending. You should've learned that from Alon and me, if nothing else." He began to deal a hand of gin. "So, one last game for now?" he asked with his skeleton's grin, and I said OK.

After I let Russell clean me out of every cigarette I had, I felt as if some debt had been repaid, and I lay awake all night, fingering the toothbrush in my pocket, trying to focus on the idea that I had succeeded. In a few hours, I would be free, with the Navy and the war behind me. Instead I felt completely blank—rigid, not with fear, but uncertainty.

The next morning Pearson gave me back my sea bag and my own clothes, which no longer fit. The person who last wore them was bigger than I was. I had pared down to essentials in my time as a blue robe.

I thought about Alon as I put on my moccasins and walked out through the barred door of the ward for the last time. I didn't look back, but I also didn't hurry, and when I reached the door to the outside, I paused. This was the gray. The position in between.

I still wasn't sure if what I had done was good or bad, right or wrong. Which is worse: thinking without acting or acting without thinking? Maybe I would never know, so I did what was in front of me: opened the door and went out.

1982: If I Should Stay

1982: If I Should Stay

I. Wednesday

1

On the afternoon before Thanksgiving, Jane Carter sequestered herself in the kitchen to bake. Raz had helped her with the washing and chopping, but from there on she liked to be alone in a vortex of flour, butter, and sugar. Now the smell of cooked fruit and spices, sweet and rich with promise, permeated the house.

From the living room Raz could hear her humming over the soft knock-knock of her wooden spoon and the more staccato sound of her knife hitting the cutting board. He remembered the tune from grammar school. It was a Thanksgiving hymn that they sang every year. They stood in rows in the chilly gymnasium, waiting for the barrel-shaped principal to blow her pitch pipe, and then sang: "We gather together to ask the Lord's blessing. . ." The boys wore paper Indian headbands with paper feathers of faded red and yellow. The girls had sheets of white paper folded over their heads into prim Pilgrim hats. Raz had thought the paper feathers were ridiculous even then, and, when their childish voices screeched to a climax with "Lord, make us free!" he didn't feel the exhilaration that Jane says she felt. All it meant to him was that school was over and the holiday weekend had begun. He had the whole afternoon to himself to play outside in the long slanting light of a November day. At the end of the hymn, the children burst out of the school, their paper feathers flopping in the breeze. Pilgrim hats circling off into the air.

In the kitchen, the singing stopped. Raz heard the ca-thunk of the heavy oven door and then running water.

"Raz," Jane called, "What are you doing?"

He hated that question and willed himself to fall asleep instantly.

"You were going to check the oil. Did you?" Jane stood in the doorway still wearing the long white apron she used to cover her clothes when she baked. Her left cheek was smudged with flour.

Raz blinked slowly, making her disappear, bringing back the moment of release from school. The freshness of the cold air. When he opened his eyes again, she was still there. His wife. They had known each other since third grade, when her family moved to Brettville.

Back then she had been a small shy girl with tousled chestnut curls, and she had never grown very tall, but she was a teacher herself now and sometimes forgot that he was not one of her students. "Did you?" she repeated, her voice rising a step in pitch.

Raz folded his book shut and rolled up into a sitting position. The holiday was over.

"No," he said. "I didn't. But I'll do it now." He began putting on his boots and, looking over his extended arm at her tense face, he added, "Relax, Jane. We'll get there."

They were going to spend Thanksgiving with Jane's family at her parents' home. Unlike Raz, who thought family relationships could thrive on phone calls and the odd postcard, Jane still seemed to believe there was a bosom where they should all be joined. A sort of familial beanbag chair in which all members could cozily recline.

Raz used to respond to this notion by getting drunk—from which vantage point he imagined that he was viewing the proceedings with detachment. Today he was sober, as bare as the trees that clawed at the windowpanes.

He rose from the couch, tucking his wool shirt more firmly into his jeans, and scrutinized the weather. The wind had picked up since early morning, and the sky was covered with low thick clouds, dimpled like a mattress.

"It looks like snow," he said.

Jane turned to the window. "Damn," she said.

They had a three-hour drive ahead of them—first over two-lane roads that dipped and snaked through small towns, woods, and farm country, then up the interstate that raced across the suburbs and through Syracuse.

Raz stretched. "It'll be all right." He picked up his jacket from a hook on the wall by the door and put it on. "Why don't you finish packing and make some sandwiches. Then we can eat them if we get hungry on the way."

Jane nodded.

"I hope Charlie's paying attention to the weather," she said. Charlie was

Jane's younger brother. He owned a bookstore in Vermont and was planning to drive up that night after the store closed. "I don't know why he couldn't have found someone else to take over today. It seems so ridiculous for him to have to drive all that way at night."

Raz shrugged. Everyone raised the same question each year, but Charlie never varied his plans. Raz thought he liked to arrive as late as he could without appearing to be late. The alternative—driving up on Thanksgiving in time for dinner—would be too obvious. It surprised him that Jane didn't get that. Maybe it was because her approach was to be as early as possible. She still thought if she could do it right, find the right position, the beanbag would be comfortable.

Jane's older brother, Tom, owned a house nearby, but he had recently moved back into their parents' basement, where he had a sort of apartment that he'd lived in when he came home to recover from the war. Why he would want to go back there was the piece Raz didn't get.

"Make some sandwiches," he repeated. "We'll get off as soon as your stuff is out of the oven."

He opened the door and stepped out into the wind. The air smelled like snow—icy and wet. Raz stood on the back steps, lifted his nose into the wind like a dog, and breathed deeply. The cold drove down into his lungs. He stretched, letting it all the way in, and then shivered.

The grass crunched softly underfoot as he crossed the yard to the car. It was a '74 Plymouth Duster with over 100,000 miles on it. His father had given it to him when he moved to Florida. Jane wished they could get a new car, but Raz couldn't see any reason to replace this one as long as it ran. Besides, the Duster was like a piece of history. It wasn't often that an American carmaker accidently built a car that would last. Raz wanted to keep that spirit alive.

He popped open the hood and pulled out the slender rod that measured the oil. He rubbed it down with an oily piece of cloth, dipped it back into the well, and drew it out again. Down half a quart. That was a bad sign. He'd put a quart in only a week before.

But Raz whistled as he crossed the gravel drive to the garage and got a can from the case he kept on the floor. The garage was piled with spare parts and even had two tan Duster bumpers laid carefully across the rafters.

He didn't worry about things breaking. Making repairs was what he did for a living.

When he and Jane were first married, he'd been taking night courses in psychology. Then the idea was that he was only fixing things—cars, houses, furniture, machines—until he was ready to start his real career. But after a few years, he'd given up on school. Studying human behavior was fruitless, he told Jane. You couldn't fix the human condition, but you could fix things, and maybe that was, after all, the best contribution for him to make. He would keep the small machinery of life running, so people could go on making a mess of themselves. Besides the variety and solitude of his work suited him.

It embarrassed him now to think how well he'd succeeded in creating the illusion that this was his vocation, when all he was really doing was securing the freedom and privacy to drink. Not that he had seen it that way himself until recently.

Raz closed the hood and checked the tires. Then he went around behind the garage to tuck down the corners of the blue plastic tarp that covered his woodpile. If there was a storm, he wanted to keep the snow off his wood.

The yard behind their small old farmhouse stretched back to brushy woods. Most of it had been turned over to the vegetable garden, which covered a quarter acre. Raz walked to the edge and touched the soil with his boot. It was hard, full of frost.

Looking at the neatly turned beds gave him a measure of the distance he'd traveled that year. Last fall he had kept meaning to clean up the garden, but he never got around to it. The killing frosts had blackened the plants and vines, and then snow came, before he ever found the time. In those days it was hard to get anything done. There was just time to drink, and then find the next drink and drink that.

This past summer he and Jane had spent some of the best times they'd ever had out here. In the morning, they'd take their coffee out and work—planting, thinning, weeding, laying down thick fragrant layers of hay, pinching suckers. Not fixing things, just being in life. That's how Raz thought of it. He'd look up from what he was doing and see Jane's blue baseball cap bobbing along the rows of tomato plants as she worked, and it amazed him then that they were still together.

She'd threatened to leave him if he didn't stop drinking a hundred times. At least. But it hadn't made any difference. He had watched her get hysterical the way he would watch TV late at night with the sound turned off. Then all of a sudden she stopped. A silence filled the house that made it harder and harder for him to deny the sound of his own voice.

2

When the last pie was in the oven, Jane sat down at the pine kitchen table to rest before tackling the dishes in the sink. As she surveyed what she'd made—two pumpkin pies, one pecan, and an apple crisp—she could already imagine Tom saying "Do we really need to eat all this?" in a tone that implied both her hearing and her judgment were impaired. But it wouldn't seem like Thanksgiving if she didn't bake a lot, and, even though their family had shrunk this year, she guessed that everything would be gone by Saturday.

Jane yawned and poured herself some coffee. She would have liked a cigarette, but she had given up smoking when Raz stopped drinking six months ago to show her support. At least she was trying to give it up. She hadn't smoked that much—not enough to damage her health, she told herself—and taking a cigarette break had been an important way of relaxing for her.

She'd cheated a few times, bumming cigarettes from Bill Wisley, one of the other teachers at the elementary school, but she was uncomfortable about it. Sneaking smokes reminded her of high school, when she and her friends had started every day by smoking two cigarettes as fast as they could standing on the toilets in the girls' room.

The problem wasn't only that she had supposedly quit. Smoking was not allowed inside the school anymore, even in the teachers' room, so she had to go out in the cold. Once Bill had invited her to join him in his car, but there was something about the way he put this invitation that made her say no. Besides being outdoors kept the smoke from smelling up her clothes. She hoped.

She wondered what Raz would say if she told him she simply couldn't do it. Quit. It was too hard. Probably he would look at her the way he said she looked at him when he tried to explain why he couldn't control his drinking: with total contempt and disgust. Jane didn't believe she had ever looked at him that way. She didn't feel total contempt and disgust. Fear and despair were more like it. But Raz said that's what he saw.

Maybe, the counselor at the rehab center suggested, those were his own feelings he thought he saw on Jane's face. Maybe, Raz had said, shrugging his shoulders. He didn't look like he believed anything either Jane or the counselor said.

That was just part of the damage, they were told matter-of-factly. Their relationship would take a long time to heal. Sometimes Jane felt her life was like a neighborhood that had been strafed by bombs. The noise was over, but solid-looking buildings could suddenly collapse. Hidden fires burst out where least expected.

Still he wasn't drinking, and she knew that was sometimes hard for him. At night, when she couldn't sleep and began to crave a cigarette, she wondered if Raz ever lay awake craving a drink. If he ever cheated just a little bit too. Then with her heart pounding she would examine his sleeping face in the darkness and lean close to smell his breath.

So far, everything had been fine, and she was glad. Very glad. Their lives were beginning to turn around at last. So why did she find it irritating that Raz slept so innocently? She certainly didn't want him to get drunk again.

Getting up to wash the dishes, Jane resolved again to quit smoking completely. When the urge came, she'd drink a glass of water, chew gum, do jumping jacks. She imagined that she was making a bargain with the universe. If she didn't cheat—if she really quit—Raz would never ever drink again.

3

Raz came back into the house and found it silent. He crossed the living room with its faded green couch and chairs arranged in front of the cobblestone fireplace and looked in the kitchen. It was empty; the dishes were neatly stacked and counters wiped clean. Their bedroom upstairs was empty too. He checked the bathroom. Empty.

"Jane? What's going on?" Raz called. The anxiety he heard come into his voice annoyed him.

"I'm putting together a few last things," she called from the attic. "Come on up."

Raz climbed the steep narrow stairs to Jane's study. It was a tiny room in the attic that she'd fixed up for herself. "To correct papers," she'd told him, but he'd known it was really to have a place to be away from him. Once last spring he'd come up, wanting to know what she was doing, and they'd gotten into a fight that ended with his falling down the whole flight of stairs. Fortunately he was too drunk to get hurt.

He never went up again without an invitation, and the room still felt like part of some other house, not his home. If he were honest with himself, he had to admit he resented it: this separate world of Jane's.

Under the eaves she had put in low bookcases that were crammed with books, and there was a Jøtul stove hooked into the chimney. The large table where she worked stood in front of the window overlooking the backyard and woods. The slanting walls were covered with children's drawings, snapshots, and other memorabilia. On the flat wall she'd hung each of her class pictures in thin black frames, and Jane still knew every student by name. She said that had nothing to do with being a good teacher—but Raz couldn't remember having a teacher like Jane. His teachers were severe, angry women who called him Albert, emphasizing its two syllables, even though everyone else used the nickname his mother gave him, which was short for rascal.

Jane was a grown-up, hardworking and thoughtful, but she was also exactly the right size adult for seven-year-olds. It was easy for her to bend to hear what they had to say, she was quick to join them on the floor, her laugh was infectious, and her hands were almost as soft and warm as theirs.

"What are you doing?" he asked, standing awkwardly in the doorway.

Jane finished sweeping scraps of orange and brown construction paper into the trash and then held out a box filled with paper turkeys. The name of a family member was lettered on the feathers of each turkey's tail. "They're place cards," she explained. "Aren't they cute? We made them in school last week, and I thought it would be fun to make some for us."

"They are cute," said Raz. "I'm sure Tom will love them."

"I'm giving up trying to please Tom."

"That's good."

"Chrissy would have liked them," said Jane, neatly straightening the rows of turkeys with the tip of her finger.

"Yes, she would," said Raz, "but don't let's get into that now."

"Do you think they might call? Because of the holiday?"

"I don't think you call someone you haven't spoken to for three months to say 'Happy Thanksgiving'."

"I guess you're right." Jane turned off her desk lamp. "I just wish I knew where they were," she said. "It seems so mean. To just disappear. I'm sure Charlie never did anything to Maura to deserve that."

"You never know," said Raz. "What goes on in people's marriages can be pretty weird."

Jane looked up from the turkeys, and for a moment their eyes met. "I suppose," she said.

By the dim light coming up from below, they clambered down the stairs.

"So is that it?" Raz asked, looking at a pile of suitcases, jackets, and pastry boxes by the front door. It looked like they were going around the world, not on a weekend visit to Brettville.

Jane nodded. She held a bag of knitting, two novels, and the box of turkeys in front of her chest.

Armor, thought Raz.

"This is it," she said.

4

Raz loved to drive through the country with its rolling hills and canals—especially in November—the turning point between fall and winter. You could still see splashes of color—a clump of red leaves, a hedge of deep purple bushes—against the soft palette of silvered trees and fields dried to a pale yellow. Even though the landscape was littered with rusted cars and torn by new construction, underneath Raz thought it was very beautiful, gracefully shaped and unassuming.

They were almost to Syracuse when the snow began to fall. Thick clumps of flakes spiraled down from the darkening gray sky. They hit the windshield like bugs, sliding down the glass in wet trails. Raz turned on the windshield wipers and watched them cut their path through the snow, which piled up at either end of the arc. The heater was on, and they were listening to George Winston. The music was soothing like the heat and the lazily falling snow.

Jane sat slumped against her door, knitting. The plastic needles clicked softly. It was a complicated pattern of cables and Raz knew that if he spoke he would interrupt the counting that was going on in her head. She only had four more weeks to turn the shapeless mass into Charlie's Christmas present. A sweater.

"Mom says Charlie's started playing music again," she said suddenly, the needles pausing.

"Really? That's great." Charlie was the first of the Percys that Raz got to know. He and his older brother Ricky liked to play rock and roll in their garage, and Charlie kept showing up on his bicycle, an old Fender guitar slung across his back, until finally they let him play with them. The surprise was that even at thirteen he was really good. Before long they had formed The Dipstickers, and the Percys became part of Raz's life. "Has he joined a group?"

"I don't know. She didn't seem to know much more." Jane held the piece of knitting up to the air. It was a tweedy yarn of blues, greens, and purples that she said would set off Charlie's eyes. She and her brothers all had the same curly chestnut hair, but each with a different color eyes: Tom's brown, Jane's green, and Charlie's blue. They had the same compact bodies too—neither thin nor fat—but Jane was always watching her weight.

"I've always thought he bought that bookstore because of Maura," said Raz. "He wanted to show her he was going to be Mr. Responsible. A good father for Chris and all that."

"Don't you think he likes it though? Being his own boss? He's made it into a nice store."

"I think Charlie's really only cared about one thing, and that's music."

"But what about Chris? He loved Chris. And Maura too. At least in the beginning."

Raz gave Jane a sideways look, but didn't say anything. As far as he was concerned, Maura Reynolds had only been the latest in a long line of sharp-eyed women who had hooked the easygoing Charlie.

"He did too. I'm sure he did." She slouched down with her feet up against the dashboard. "Anyway I'm glad if he's started playing again. I've always loved his playing." After a moment the needles started clicking again. "I hope Mom bought a big enough turkey for leftovers," she said.

"If we had stayed home, we could be having any size turkey we wanted."

"Oh Raz. That wouldn't be the same."

"Exactly." The needles stopped. Raz glanced at Jane and saw her staring at him coldly. "Sorry," he said and turned back to the road.

5

By the time they reached Brettville, it was dark and the temperature had dropped. A finer, drier snow was falling fast, covering the ground. In the Percys' yard tufts of grass still showed, but the tall black walnut and maple trees were draped with white. The chalky white house with its Greek revival pillars looked even whiter against the snow. Lit windows glowed warm and yellow all over the house, welcoming them, but as Raz flicked on his blinker and pulled into the circular drive, he felt a flash of dread.

He wished he had insisted that they stay home and have their own Thanksgiving instead of making a joke of it. Jane didn't understand what it was like for him to be around people who were drinking. It was not so much the temptation as the mirror that he found it hard to bear. He no longer had any way to pretend that people who had been drinking were rational or to relate to them as if they were. Jane said she appreciated this, but she didn't. She wanted to believe that his getting sober meant some piece of her happy family fantasy was now going to come true.

Raz opened the car door, his foot sliding on the snow the instant it touched ground. He pulled it back and turned to watch Jane climbing out the other side. She reached into the back for the boxes of pies and other baked goods.

"Be careful," he said. She looked at him across the dimly lit car and smiled. She was excited. Her hair was lit from behind by the porch light, making a halo of red and gold highlights around her head.

Raz thought this was her favorite moment. The arrival at home. Getting out of the car, going up the steps to the front door with its oval frosted glass window. Standing there with him beside her. The sound of the bell echoing down the hall inside.

And then the rustle. The dark shape of someone moving toward them.

It was the best time of every visit. What she returned for. Because once the door opened and they stepped inside, nothing was ever as clear again.

Raz reached the porch with the suitcases just as his mother-in-law, Claire, swung the door wide and announced "You're here!" to the falling snow, then embraced each of them—boxes, suitcases, and all.

At sixty, Claire was still a beautiful woman, smelling of perfume, roasting beef, and bourbon, and dressed in a matching rust-colored sweater and skirt. Behind her, in the dimness of a hall cluttered with antiques and thick with faded oriental rugs, Jane's father Ben and brother Tom stood side by side holding cocktail glasses.

"Hi, honey," said Ben, folding Jane into a big hug.

"Hey, Raz," said Tom, reaching out to shake his hand.

"We're so glad you made it," said Claire.

"How was the drive?"

"When did you leave?"

"Charlie's just starting out," they said, all talking at once.

Raz excused himself to take the bags upstairs while Jane fielded the questions.

"I was so afraid he wouldn't come," he heard Claire saying as she shepherded Jane down the hall. For a moment Raz thought she was referring to him. His in-laws had never directly acknowledged that they knew he had been to rehab and stopped drinking, any more than they had acknowledged that his drinking had been a problem in the first place. Then he heard Jane repeat to her mother what he always told her:

"Oh, Mom, Charlie wouldn't miss Thanksgiving. He just likes to build up the suspense for his big entrance."

"Do you think so, honey?" Claire asked, and then she laughed, sounding relieved. "Well, maybe you're right. He was born late and has never caught up."

6

"Those pies look wonderful," Claire said, stacking Jane's boxes on top of the refrigerator. "I bought a mince pie at the store today, in case you didn't have time to make anything."

"I told you I would, Mom."

"But you're so busy with school. I don't know how you manage. I'm afraid Daddy and I don't eat as well as we used to, since I opened the shop. Of course, with you kids gone, what's the point? The two of us alone eating big meals. We'd only get fat."

Jane gave a little shrug and turned away from her mother, as if to deflect the reference—at least in her mind it was a reference—to the fact that, after ten years of marriage, she and Raz had no children.

"I don't cook that much every day," she said, trying not to sound sulky, "but I like to bake for the holidays."

"Well, it's terribly sweet of you, dear. Everyone appreciates it."

Jane took a handful of peanuts from a bowl on the island in the middle of the kitchen. Cocktail hour at her parents' meant gathering in the big old-fashioned kitchen to drink and talk and eat peanuts, while her mother prepared the dinner. It amazed her that, no matter how accomplished a cook she became, her mother seldom asked her to help. Instead she was given the tasks she'd been doing since she was a little girl: setting the table, snipping up parsley, finding the salad bowls.

"Want a drink, honey?" asked Ben, who presided at the bar.

"Just club soda, Dad," said Jane.

Ben wiped his hands on the towel he had tucked under the vest of his tweed suit. He looked disappointed. "Sure you don't want anything in it? A little whiskey? Lemon?"

Jane shook her head and smiled. "No thanks, Dad, really."

"How about Raz? Shall I make something for him?"

"No, he'll decide when he comes down."

"Where is Raz?" asked Claire.

"I think he's unpacking," said Jane, but her mother had already forgotten her question. She had her spectacles on and was peering at a greased-spattered cookbook.

"Jane, did you notice the wreath on the front door?" Claire asked, closing the book. She began whipping oil and vinegar together in a bowl. "A woman from Lowville makes them. How she found out about my shop I'll never know, but she showed up with a station wagon full of wreaths, and I bought a dozen! I hope you'll come in on Friday to see them."

"Those flowers in the dining room are from Jenna Jackson," Claire went on. "You remember her, don't you? She married Daddy's student Rich Jackson, who teaches at Cornell now. She recently published a novel, and they have two darling children, a boy and the cutest little girl. Anyway I'm sure you must have met them. Last weekend she hosted a retirement party for Marvin Specks—didn't you have him for Shakespeare?—and afterward she gave me some of the flowers. I think they look so pretty with the wallpaper."

Jane nodded. She started to get up to look at the flowers—and the wreath too while she was at it—when her father cut in, handing her a drink.

"You've read Emily's poetry, haven't you, Jane?"

"No," she admitted, but she knew to whom he referred; her father was a Brontë scholar and talked about the family as if they were close friends. Growing up Jane had felt as if the Brontës were the children she and her brothers should have been, but weren't. She'd narrowly missed being named Emily or Charlotte; Jane Anne was a compromise with her mother. "I've only read *Wuthering Heights.*"

Ben dismissed this with a wave as a given; he'd read the classics out loud to them himself when they were young. "You really should read the poetry," he insisted. "I'm reviewing Bill Dodd's new book about her non-Gondal poems. It's not bad as far as it goes, but some of his facts are completely wrong. I know because, when I was researching my book on Emily, I went to the original manuscripts, and what he did was base his research on later scholarship that was incorrect."

"Huh," said Jane, sipping her soda. "Isn't Dodd the one who thought Emily had a love affair with Robert Heaton?"

"Exactly," said Ben. He smiled as if she'd just gotten an A.

"Daddy, don't get into all that now," said Claire. "I want to get dinner on the table. What's happened to Raz?"

"He's unpacking," Jane said again, even though she guessed he was simply avoiding the family until dinner was ready. In the old days he would have been upstairs drinking out of one of the bottles he had hidden in their luggage. Now she couldn't picture what he would be doing.

"The problem with researchers today is that they are so anxious to get published they don't take the time to be thorough. And of course there's no editing to speak of any more."

"I hope you and Raz will approve of the way I'm doing the turkey," interrupted Claire. "I'm cooking it in a plastic bag. Have you ever tried that? You don't have to baste or anything. You can help me with it tomorrow. I do hope Charlie won't have trouble getting here."

"He won't," said Tom, who had come up from the basement with a big glass of Scotch. He snapped on the kitchen television and pulled a chair up close to the screen. The news was on, and he scowled as he ran through the channels.

Claire was bent over the oven, testing the roast with a meat thermometer, and Ben had disappeared up the back stairs to his study, so only Jane was aware of it when Tom began switching back and forth between stories about the new Vietnam Veterans Memorial in Washington and a local fire.

Footage of the massive black wall, where men, women and children were searching for names, alternated with scenes of flames shooting into the night sky. Fire and the wall. Fire and the wall.

"Hey Tom, I'd like to see that about the wall," she said.

He looked up at her and said: "Why?"

"I think it's beautiful. Important."

"Well, I think it's crap. The world's biggest fucking tombstone."

"Is that the weather forecast you're watching, kids?" asked Claire, as she lifted the roast onto a serving platter.

"No," said Tom. "But I can tell you the forecast. It's snowing."

"This storm will end soon," said Ben, coming back into the kitchen with a book in his hands. Yellow strips of paper flagged pages to the right and green strips flagged pages at the top.

"You see what I've done here, Jane," he said, as if their conversation had never stopped, "These yellow slips mark errors of fact." He turned to one page and pointed to a carefully underlined passage. "See where he says that Emily wrote this poem in 1840? Well that's incorrect—"

"Daddy," said Claire in an exasperated tone. "Dinner is ready, and I need Jane to set the table. Tom, would you please call Raz and tell him dinner is ready?"

"I'm watching something," said Tom stubbornly. The fire story had been replaced by a report on the collisions caused by the snow.

"I'll get Raz, Mom. Then I can look at the flowers too."

"But who will set the table? I want the blue plates."

"Now, Mommy," said Ben. "Don't worry. Everything will get done. Let me freshen up your drink."

Jane took the opportunity to put down the book and escape from the kitchen. She passed through the dining room, where a white linen cloth, already laid for tomorrow's dinner, glimmered in the dim light from the converted gaslight chandelier. Her mother had arranged Jenna Jackson's flowers in a silver bowl. There were orange and yellow lilies mixed with yellow roses and yellow and copper-colored mums. They did complement the pale gold wallpaper very nicely, Jane had to admit, although the Jenna Jacksons of her parents' world, with their professor husbands, published books, and cute children, made her feel suffocated.

On the mahogany sideboard stood an array of family pictures from her diminutive seventeen-year-old great-grandmother on her wedding day to Tom making his high school class valedictorian speech. Jane paused, as she always did, to look at these photos, as if she could divine something from studying them. She noticed Maura and Chrissy had been edited out of the collection, since the last time she visited. No doubt her mother had done this out of loyalty to Charlie, but how could she understand the family story if major characters disappeared without warning?

At the foot of the front hall staircase, she called "Raz! Dinner's ready!" and waited for a response.

"I'll be there in a minute," he called back, just as she was about to call again.

Jane stood, one hand on the newel post, wondering if going up to see what he was doing would show that she had not abandoned him or that she was hovering over him. She did not know the answer. She had only gotten as far as asking herself the question. To kill time, she opened the front door and looked at the wreath. Grapevine and dogwood. Brown ribbon edged with gold. Very nice.

She breathed in the icy air and lifted her face to the falling snow. Flakes lit on her cheeks and melted. At the house across the street, smoke curled from the chimney, and she could see a family seated around their table eating dinner. From this distance, they looked very tranquil.

She closed the door again with a sense of longing in the pit of her stomach. There was no sign of Raz. She almost called again, but instead she said "Okay!" up into the dark hallway above and went to set the table.

7

Whenever they came to the Percys' house, Raz and Jane slept in her old room. It was a large comfortably furnished room, with tall windows overlooking the back yard, and its own bathroom. There were twin poster beds covered with bright-colored quilts, a faded oriental rug, a vase full of flowers on the dresser, and everything was clean and neat.

Raz still remembered the first time he saw this room. Raz, Ricky, and Charlie had just started their band—they didn't even have a name yet—and they had driven Charlie home after practice. Raz came into the house to pick up a couple of records, and, as he was leaving, he saw that Jane's door was open. He had never really talked to Jane although they'd been in classes together for years. She was one of those good, smart girls who wore fair-isle sweaters and plaid kilts and knew all the answers in class. In those days Raz had preferred the company of bad girls in white lipstick and leather jackets who spent their afternoons in detention, but he was curious about Charlie's family, and, on an impulse, he looked in.

There had been only a few touches of Jane even then—a desk piled with her schoolwork, a bookcase crammed with children's books and classics, a teddy bear slumped in the corner of a rocker. It was much nicer than his room with its Sears rollaway and blue Bates bedspread, but he had had the sharp feeling that no one lived there. Not really. This made him wonder about Jane, and he began watching her and listening to what she said at school with more attention. Who was she? Where was she?

The first time he spent the night in this room, soon after they were married, he asked her whether she really liked it. They were sleeping together in one of the twin beds, their bodies pressed together.

"Of course," she said, sounding surprised. "I love this room. It's beautiful."

"Yes, but, Jane, where are you in it?"

She'd been silent for a moment and then turned to speak into his ear as if someone might overhear.

"I'm right here in this bed. Dreaming of you," she said. "Dreaming of our life together."

He had put his arm around her shoulder then and shivered with pleasure at the touch of her body all along the length of his own. It amazed him that their lives had finally so completely intersected.

Now he thought what a typical thing that was for Jane to say. It sounded like a truth, but it didn't answer the question at all.

8

The back kitchen, where they were to eat that night, was Jane's favorite room in her parents' house. She associated it with long lazy breakfasts, Scrabble games, watching movies, and talking by the fire until late into the night. There was an old pine table in front of the windows, chairs piled with pillows by the fireplace, and a wall of bookcases filled with a jumble of books and photo albums.

They had gotten the blue plates years ago during a sabbatical year spent in England, and it gave Jane great pleasure to set them around the table with the silver and glasses. They reminded her of when she was young and took for granted that her family would never change.

From the kitchen she could hear her father and Tom discussing the route Charlie should take to get to Brettville from Vermont. The tension that rose between them was as familiar as the plates, but that was all part of being home.

"Brettville is not home. Home is where we live," Raz would say when they had one of their arguments about the holidays.

And he was right. Of course wherever they lived was home, but then there was Home. The family home. She couldn't help it if she didn't feel that connection to their house. Maybe your own place only took on that dimension if you had children. Or maybe, as Raz contended angrily, if your life together was really important to you.

Jane couldn't believe he questioned how important he was to her. She had loved him ever since he turned up on the doorstep during the darkest winter of her life. Tom had come home from Vietnam wounded, and, with Charlie away at college, she had been the only one there to ease him back into life with hours of cards and Yahtzee and Johnny Carson. She had plodded through the days, trying to keep up with her own studies, but most of the time she'd been overwhelmed by sadness and anger at life.

She had practically forgotten all about Raz. It had been almost two years since he talked his way out of the draft and went off with a backpack to work for peace around the world. But there he was one afternoon—smiling and pink-cheeked, with icicles in his moustache.

"I'm home, Jane," he said, holding out snowy arms to hug her, and her body had moved toward him, knowing in advance of her brain that he was what she'd been waiting for.

She still believed in that moment.

Somehow it had held her to him, even as the clarity that sparkled in his eyes faded, and alcohol took over more and more of his life. Her life. She didn't really understand how or why that had happened, but living one day at a time was no news to her—only to Raz, for whom eventually there'd been no days or nights, months or seasons.

Now, she had been told, she was supposed to detach. Let go.

Fine, she thought as she lit the candles, and their reflected flames danced in the high gloss on her mother's plates. But there must be something you could hold on to as the years slipped by.

9

"So how was the drive, Raz?" asked Ben. Raz, Tom, and Ben were seated at the table waiting for Jane and her mother to finish running back and forth with last-minute necessities. Tom stared into his drink as Ben said, "You know this kind of weather is the worst for driving. When the snow changes to rain and then back again you get the thinnest layer of ice between the layers of snow, and it's treacherous."

"We didn't have any trouble," said Raz, sipping Coke. At each place except his own a glass full of red wine glowed in the candlelight. When he'd arrived at the table, there had been no glass at all at his place, but then Jane rushed in with the Coke. He didn't know why; he didn't like Coke, but she was gone again before he could ask her.

"That's good," said Ben, "because this is a bad time of year for accidents."

"Daddy, stop talking now," said Claire as she sat down at last.

"All right. This looks delicious," said Ben, looking down at his plate full of pot roast, oven-roasted potatoes and carrots, and salad.

It did look good, and Raz was about to pick up his fork to begin eating the food that had been sitting in front of him for at least five minutes, when Claire said: "Don't we want to say grace?"

She ignored any evidence that they did not and bowed her head. There was a dramatic pause while she waited for their attention. Raz saw Jane looking out the window at the snow illuminated by the back porch light. Tom had his arms crossed and was frowning at his plate. Raz took another sip of Coke.

"God," said Claire. "Thank you for this opportunity for us to share a meal together. Make us grateful for all that we have been given and for what we are about to receive. Amen." She waited, head still bowed, until they all muttered "Amen." Then she lifted her eyes and smiled.

Raz's father used to say: "I don't care what I eat for dinner as long as it's hot," and Raz agreed. Jane said growing up on TV dinners had given him a completely distorted view of what was involved in preparing a meal. How difficult the timing could be. No doubt, on this point, as on so many others, she was right.

Ben obviously liked his food tepid because he carefully cut everything on his plate into small pieces before he even took a bite. "This roast is gorgeous," he pronounced, when he finally began eating.

"Do you think so?" Claire asked. "I was worried it might be a bit overdone."

"No, it's perfect. Absolutely. Don't you agree, Tom?" he asked, but Tom didn't answer. He rattled the ice cubes in his empty glass, and then got up, leaving his dinner untouched.

Jane raised her eyebrows, but her parents ignored him.

"What do you hear from your father, Raz?" asked Claire.

"He's fine."

"He really likes it down there?" asked Ben.

"Yes. It's a great place for him."

"That's good," Ben said. "A lot of people think they're going to be happy at these retirement places, and they aren't. Mommy and I have decided we're going to stay right here. We love our house too much to move. It has a history."

Raz helped himself to some more potatoes. He could tell the professor was about to begin a lecture.

"You know we keep finding out new things about this place. For example, I recently discovered some old photos in an archive at the library that showed the way it looked back in the 1850s when it was a working farm. Did you know there were two barns and a silo at one time?"

Raz looked at Jane. She had an eager-to-please expression on her face that mirrored her mother's. They both appeared to be listening intently to every word, even though they heard this story the last time they were here.

Once he asked Jane if she really listened to her father's lectures, and she said indignantly, "My father is a brilliant man," so Raz let the subject drop.

Tom came back to the table with a big glass of Scotch, but he still didn't eat.

"We have dessert, you know," said Claire, when Ben had moved on to the subject of the tools used to make the decorative molding on the front staircase. Jane took the cue and stood up to collect the dishes. Ben went right on talking, but he focused his attention on Raz and segued to the history of furniture making in the area.

"That's enough now, Daddy," said Claire. "Raz was born in Brettville. He knows all about it. Jane, did you see what I did in the living room? Go and look. See if you can tell." Jane dutifully set down the dishes she was carrying and headed for the living room.

"Did you notice? Could you tell?" her mother asked when Jane came back.

"No," she said. "I couldn't see anything different."

Claire looked disappointed. "I had the couch recovered. Daddy, Jane didn't even notice the new upholstery."

"That's good," said Ben. "That's exactly right."

"I wanted something new and different, but Ben wanted the cover to look exactly the same as before. Do you have any idea how hard it was to find the same fabric as twenty years ago?"

Tom laughed. "I don't know why you bothered. What the hell difference does it make?"

Claire looked offended, but she didn't say anything. Instead she gathered up the cloth napkins and began folding them.

"Why don't you show me the turkey, Mom," said Jane.

10

Jane never thought of her parents as old until she looked into their refrigerator. For some reason her mother was no longer able to throw food away. The refrigerator was stacked with lumps of dried-up cheese, mayonnaise jars full of mucky soup, stiff pastries with red ribbons on them, and half-drunk bottles of wine. Although it didn't smell, it looked like it should, and Jane could barely restrain herself from holding her nose.

Sticking out on the bottom shelf, she could just see the pinkish-grey rump of a turkey encased in plastic.

"There it is," said Claire, as if sighting it were a discovery. "It's not as big as the ones I used to get, but I'm sure it will be plenty, aren't you?"

Jane looked doubtful. Whenever she and Raz had turkey they bought the biggest one they could fit in the oven and then went on an orgy of turkey eating. A turkey that could be eaten in one or two meals was hardly worth having in her view. "I guess so," she said.

"Well, we're only six this year."

"I know," said Jane, trying not to let her feelings show. Thanksgiving used to be a weekend-long house party, much more fun than Christmas because it didn't have the weight of expectation that came with exchanging gifts. Charlie would come with Maura and Chris; and Raz's father, brother Ricky and his wife and two children would be around every day. Now Raz's father was in Florida, Ricky and his family had moved to Montana, and no one knew where Maura and Chris were. "You're probably right. It will probably be enough," she said.

"Of course it will, and it's going to be a lovely weekend," said Claire. "It's better when there aren't too many people. That just makes everything so complicated.

"And the turkey isn't that important," she said, pulling out a limp head of celery, "We have so many other things to eat. All your wonderful pies. My goodness—shouldn't we be eating one of them now?"

"How about if Raz and I build a fire first," said Jane, putting her arm around her mother. "You make some coffee."

11

Going outside was like stepping into a cold shower, but for Raz it was a relief to get away from the house. He and Jane bumped together as they went down the back porch stairs. Under its layer of snow, the grass crunched under their feet, and the yard was dotted with black walnuts that had frozen hard to the ground. Raz cursed as he stepped on one that felt like a sharp stone, and Jane stiffened beside him as if she'd gotten snow up her nose.

The woodpile was at the back of the yard where, years ago, there had been a rabbit hutch. The Percys never had any rabbits, but in the summers Charlie had run extension cords all the way across the yard so that The Dipstickers could practice in the long low building thick with spider webs. Later, it was a place Raz and Jane went to neck, and Raz still remembered the smell of dust in Jane's hair. Since then the hutch had collapsed, so all that was left was the cement slab where Tom stacked the cordwood.

"They really ought to stack some of this wood on the porch," said Jane, picking up a log. The split wood gave off a sharp sweet smell.

"They should, but they won't, until Tom is too old to come out here. For some reason he likes doing it this way."

"Maybe we should get the wheelbarrow and bring up enough for tomorrow too."

"OK," said Raz.

He found the wheelbarrow in the garage and bumped back across the lawn toward the dark shape of Jane.

She threw an armload of logs into the barrow. They ca-thunked into the bottom, and she smiled at the sound.

"So what's the story on the turkey," said Raz.

"It's not bigger than a breadbox."

"Bummer," he said.

"I know. I'm sorry."

Raz set a log on the block and picked up the axe.

Splitting wood was one of those tasks that he could really enjoy again now that he was sober. He no longer had to approach it with that combination of rage, defiance, and dread that used to fuel him when he did things he knew he was too drunk to even consider doing.

He caught the log with the axe and hit it squarely against the block. He liked the noise it made and the feel of the axe sliding down between the fibers. When the blade reached the block and the two pieces fell away, his happiness seemed disproportionate to the event, but he tried not to question happiness any more. In fact he thought tomorrow he should come out here and make a mountain of kindling. That would give him something to do until it was time for dinner.

He picked up one of the half rounds and chopped it into sticks.

"Jane, I'm going to leave tomorrow after dinner," he said.

She had been gathering up the kindling, but now she stood up straight. "Because of the turkey?" she said.

"No, not because of the turkey," he replied, raising the axe over his head.

"Then what, Raz? What?"

He whacked a log in two before he spoke. He didn't know how to explain that ever since he left home, he'd been calculating how many hours it would be until he got back.

"This just isn't a good place for me to be right now," he said finally. He hoped she would let him leave it at that.

She gave him a long disbelieving look and then sat down on the edge of cement slab without speaking. Her head drooped, and she looked very tired.

With a series of rapid strokes Raz reduced the halves to a pile of fine dry sticks and tossed them into the wheelbarrow. He interpreted Jane's silence to mean that she was struggling to bring herself to say what she'd been trained to say rather than what she wanted to say. At the rehab, they had required family members to meet with a counselor too.

"I guess I can take a bus back on Saturday," she offered at last.

"OK," said Raz, sitting down next to her. He brushed the snow off her hair and shoulders. "I'll pick you up and we can go out to dinner."

"Raz," she said slowly, her mouth bent down toward her sleeve. "I do want what's best for you."

"I know, Jane," he said.

For a while they sat quietly, leaning against each other for warmth, then she said, "We'd better go back. Mom is waiting."

"I think we've got plenty."

"Ride me," said Jane hopping on top of the wood piled in the wheelbarrow. Raz grabbed hold of the handles, and the load shifted sharply to the right and left before he could get it balanced. As they lurched across the yard, the wheels made a narrow wobbly track through the thin snow.

Jane laughed and started to sing "Over the River and Through the Woods" then switched "A Turkey Ran Away Before Thanksgiving Day." Raz wondered if she were thinking of him.

She had gotten to the part about "they'll make a roast out of me if I should stay," when they reached the back porch. Raz flipped the wheelbarrow up, and Jane and the wood came tumbling out onto the ground.

"Ow," she said, breaking off the song. "You could've at least let me get off on my own."

"I thought you'd jump," he said.

Her face trembled, eyes glazing with tears before she turned, ran up the porch steps, and slammed the screen door. The angry swirl of her hair flashed in the porch light.

Raz sighed and pulled his jacket closer to his chin. His feet were soaked.

The windows of the Percys' house were lit up: warm gold like the windows of the Advent calendars Jane made each year. He turned away to gather up the wood. One armload at a time, he carried it onto the porch and stacked it against the inside wall. Each time he went out again he let the door slam until he began to be embarrassed by his own childishness.

When there was no more wood to stack, he sat down on the pile and stared out into the darkness. If he'd had a pint in his pocket, this would have been a good time for a drink. But he didn't have a pint, and he didn't want to drink. Not really.

A tapping on the kitchen window startled him out of his thoughts. He turned to see Claire smiling out at him. "Raz," she called from the doorway. "Don't you want any dessert? Jane has made the loveliest dessert for us."

It was a summons, and slowly he rose to meet it.

12

At eleven, Charlie arrived with three dogs. He came in stamping the snow off his feet and blustering about driving conditions that were so bad he'd considered stopping at a motel for the night. The family clustered around, hugging him, and giving him a hero's welcome as if he'd reached the North Pole by dogsled. Raz sat on the staircase and watched.

Charlie seemed pleased by their attention, but his eyes were red with fatigue. He looked thinner than Raz remembered and pale.

The dogs, a trio of mutts, were so happy to be out of the car that they raced up and down the hall between the people, whining and sniffing the furniture.

"I couldn't leave them," Charlie explained, setting two duffel bags and a guitar case down in a heap on the floor. "The guy who was supposed to take care of them decided to go to Florida this afternoon."

"Of course you couldn't," said Claire, hugging him again. "We're glad to have them," she added as two of the dogs ran across her feet.

"Which way did you come, Charlie?" Ben wanted to know.

"Come and have a drink," said Tom. "You look like you need one."

"That's Maura's dog, isn't it? Did Maura leave her dog?" asked Jane. She looked shocked. Charlie reached down to the little border collie mix who was dancing around him and picked up her front legs.

"Who's Maura, Minnie? Do we know anyone by that name?"

"I can't believe she did that," said Jane.

"Oh, Jane," said her mother.

"Way to go, Jane," said Tom.

Jane looked embarrassed and angry. "Well, I'm amazed, that's all."

"You mean you weren't surprised that she left me? Just the dog?" Charlie said.

Jane gave Charlie a punch on the arm. "You know I don't mean that, Charlie. I can't imagine anyone letting you go."

"Of course not. None of us can. Let me help you with your coat, dear," said Claire.

"But why are we all standing here in the hall when we have a nice fire in the living room?" asked Ben.

13

When the family began to move away from the door, back to the living room where drinks sat waiting, Charlie turned to Raz and gave him a hug.

"Hey man, how are you?" Charlie asked. "You look great. Healthy."

Raz laughed. "I didn't look healthy before?"

"No. The last time I saw you, you looked like shit. Death."

"Yeah. Well, I'm much better now," said Raz. "What about you?"

Charlie shrugged. "I'm surviving. I have Minnie as my best girl now, and we get along great." He rubbed the dog's head, and she gazed at him with dark, adoring eyes.

"I think we need some food," he announced, "What do you say?" All the dogs began to bark, as he took a bag of kibble out of one of the duffel bags.

"Charlie, aren't you and Raz going to join us?" called Claire from the living room.

"Sure, Mom, but I have to feed the dogs first."

Raz followed Charlie and the galloping dogs through the dining room to the kitchen. "This looks nice," said Charlie, pausing to admire the flowers. "God, it's good to be off the road. People were driving like maniacs and sliding all over the place."

"I'm glad you made it," said Raz. "Everyone's been obsessing about it all evening."

"Really? That's weird. So how's it going with you and Miss Jane?" Charlie asked, as he poured kibble into three plastic bowls.

Raz pushed his hair back from his eyes with both hands and watched the dogs plunge their snouts into the food. Minnie was the smallest and stood with her front legs protectively on either side of her bowl. The other two were Roger, Charlie's old black Lab mix, and a beagley-looking stray called Arthur who'd followed Roger out of the woods one day. Kibble rattled noisily as they ate.

"Overall, I'd say we're doing well."

"Hmm . . . Anything good in here?" asked Charlie peering into the fridge. He pulled out the leftover carrots and began eating them with his fingers. "That's a pretty lukewarm statement."

Raz shrugged. "Well, it's a big change. But sometimes, for Jane, it just isn't big enough."

Charlie laughed. "Nothing less than per-fec-tion," he said, waving a carrot at Raz. "God, these have a lot of butter on them." He put the bowl back. "Oh well, I'm not really that hungry. It's being in this kitchen. I feel like I ought to want to eat. Let's get out of here."

"Coming in for the drinks?" he asked as they returned to the hall, and Raz shook his head again. "Lucky you. Hey, check out my new guitar," he said, pointing to the heap of his belongings on the floor. "Will you be up for awhile?"

"I don't know," said Raz, "it's been a long day. I might go to bed."

"OK. Well, it's good to see you. I'm glad you're here, Razzie."

"Thanks. I'm glad to see you too."

"What would you like, dear?" Raz heard Claire say as Charlie went in through the door. "Tom will fix you whatever you want."

"Charlie," Jane's voice sang out, "come and sit by me."

"Oh, let him be closer to the fire. Don't you want to be closer? Take this chair, here, this will be better. There now, we're settled. Isn't this perfect, Daddy? Everyone's here."

"Everyone who's willing to be anyway," he heard Charlie say.

14

Raz took Charlie's guitar up to Jane's room and closed the door. He could tell from the case that it was an acoustic, which surprised him. Charlie had never played acoustic before as far as he knew. He was a Stratocaster man from way back.

This was something completely different though—an old Martin 12-string. Raz squatted over the case admiring the instrument—the voluptuous shape of the big body, the soft shine of inlaid mother of pearl and wood, the powerful-looking rows of doubled strings. He lifted it out carefully and ran his thumb across the strings. The sound was big and deep; it reverberated pleasantly in his chest. Of course it was nothing like the rush that came from whanging away on an electric guitar. Raz had always enjoyed that. But this instrument had a live sound that was very appealing. He sat down on the floor and began to fool around, picking out a few tunes with fingers that stumbled and struggled over the broad fingerboard.

After a few minutes, he gave up. He had never been a great guitarist, and anyway his instrument was the bass. Four strings. Simple lines. Charlie had been the one who played the flashy leads and riffs.

For Raz and Ricky, music had been more about noise, excitement, and attention than anything else, but Charlie inspired them to want to be a good band. He persuaded them to practice—not just fool around—and eventually they had gotten pretty good. They played almost every weekend at high school dances, frat parties, and weddings around the area.

In the summer of 1967 they reached their peak when Tom, with his long curls and angry eyes, joined them as lead singer. Then Raz had been amazed at how they all came together. He began to look forward to that perfect moment when the sound, light, and vibration would make the boundaries between them fade away. Really it was better than drugs. The energy between them was unlike anything he'd ever experienced, and the audiences felt it too. They had more job offers than they could handle, and a gang of high school girls followed them wherever they played. They had all had plenty of girlfriends then.

Everyone was shocked when Tom dropped out of college a year later and then let himself be drafted. The girl gang wept at his last performance.

The Dipstickers continued without him for a while, but the original group no longer satisfied any of them. Ricky decided he'd better spend more time studying. Raz had signed up for classes at the community college, but he was more interested in politics than school. He quit to focus on the anti-war movement and his own plan for staying out of the service. Neither one of them wanted to end up where Tom went—into the thick of the war.

Had Charlie felt abandoned? Jane said he did, but Raz didn't believe it. He formed a new band with guys from the high school within weeks of The Dipstickers' demise.

Raz missed the excitement of performing, but he had never imagined he'd be a musician. Charlie was the one who had the true passion—the one they all thought would make it. He stayed on in L.A. when he graduated from college, but, after three years of unsatisfying studio gigs and unsuccessful efforts to get a good band together, he quit.

"Music has changed," he once told Raz, "and I can't get behind what these people want to play."

He said he was "done" with music, but Raz thought a sheen of disappointment settled on him when he moved to Vermont. He began working in the bookstore that he eventually bought, married Maura, and devoted himself to being a family man. Now that was over too.

Raz strummed his fingers across the guitar strings again, feeling the reverb in his chest. When one door closes, another one opens. Or so his AA sponsor continually told him.

15

Jane studied Charlie for signs of grief as she sipped her drink. He was seated in an armchair with Minnie on his lap. Roger and Arthur were sprawled next to him in front of the fire, snoring softly. He held a glass of bourbon and was stroking Minnie with his free hand. He did not appear to be listening to the conversation—an analysis of his trip with Ben and Tom still taking opposing sides.

He looked tired. There were circles under his eyes, and his hair looked shaggy and neglected, curling over the collar of his shirt. Still he didn't look the way she'd imagined he'd look: Devastated. Transformed. Overall, in fact, she had to admit he looked pretty normal and that surprised her. She thought the amputation of your family ought to mark you in some permanent, visible way.

During the holidays a year ago, she had been envious of Charlie. He had everything she wanted—work he loved, a home, a partner, a child. And dogs too. She'd even been jealous of the dogs. Not that she didn't like teaching, she did; but at that time Raz had begun spinning completely out of control and every minute of her waking life was devoted to maintaining some semblance of sanity.

At the same time she had become obsessed with the idea of disappearing. Her plans were extremely detailed—she had bus schedules, lists of clothes she would take, and an anonymous-looking motel in another town picked out—but in the end she could never really see herself leaving Raz.

What would happen to him if she did? What would happen to her? She believed marriage was a lifelong commitment. The whole point was that you committed yourself. The point wasn't that it would always be fun.

Charlie believed that too, she knew. They had had long talks about it when they were younger and, he, even more than she, was very passionate about whatever he believed in.

He said he'd had no warning that Maura was thinking of leaving. He'd gone to work one morning and, when he came home, she and Chrissy were gone. Minnie was scratching at the front door whining and pacing, and she wouldn't stop. He said that's what forced him to admit that they hadn't just gone on a spur-of-the-moment jaunt. A mother–daughter adventure. They were really gone. The very idea made Jane shiver.

Still she was sure there had been warnings, and Charlie simply didn't notice them. Other people had to come on strong to break into Charlie's world. He would probably never have gotten married at all if Maura hadn't come to work for him at the bookstore. If she hadn't decided that she wanted him. Charlie went with the flow. Not that he didn't love Maura, she was sure he did, and he completely adored Chris. But Charlie's philosophy about women was to be a net and see what floated in. Maura had swum straight in—and five years later she had swum straight out again.

Charlie was very stoned when he called to tell Jane. If it weren't for his dogs, he said, he didn't know what he'd do. His voice sounded like it was coming down a long tunnel.

"I don't even know where they are," he said. "No one will tell me anything. Not even her sister Martha, and we were always good friends. That's the thing that kills me. I mean do they think I'll come after her or something? Stalk her? I mean what kind of a guy do they think I am?" And then he cried.

Jane had felt a terrible sharp pain in her chest listening to him. She didn't understand why Maura had to leave Charlie—Charlie was one of the nicest men she'd ever known—but she thought she did know why she'd left without a trace: the negotiation period was over. It was too bad that Charlie had missed it, that he had not understood what was going on. But she was sure, for Maura, there had been such a period, and when it was over, it was over. She was not willing to go through it again.

The amazing thing to her was that, in her own life, things had changed for the better even though she hadn't left. She had come to another kind of absolute end where there could be no more negotiating. It had happened the day she screamed at Raz to get out of her room, to go away, she couldn't stand to see him drunk anymore, and he'd fallen down the attic stairs on his way out. The stairs were very steep and she heard him slip, then tumble all the way down. It was a horrible scraping thudding sound, but the silence that followed had been worse.

She had sat at her desk listening for a minute and then turned back to her work. She didn't know if he was dead or not. The whole house was completely quiet. She could hear her own breathing, and she remembered staring for a long time at the page she'd been reading before he came in. The type seemed to lift off the paper—it was so black, the page so white. She read the words slowly and deliberately. She felt nothing. Not then and not some minutes later when she heard Raz get up.

Two days later he told her he had arranged to go to rehab. He wanted to know if she would mind driving him there. She had looked at his drawn, exhausted face and shaking hands and she'd felt a pang of something. Hope, maybe. Love, possibly, but more likely it was nostalgia for the boy who'd gone around the world and come back to declare, "Jane is my favorite country on earth." Without that pang, their relationship would have ended right then, she was sure. But instead she'd said, no, she wouldn't mind.

"Does it really matter how I got here?" Charlie finally said, interrupting Ben and Tom.

"Of course not, honey," said Claire. "Being here is what counts. Now Daddy, tomorrow is a busy day. We should go to bed."

Ben scowled and rattled his ice cubes. "I'm not finished with my drink," he said. "I want to sit here and enjoy my children."

"Well, I'm going to bed. The shop was very busy today, and I'm exhausted," said Claire. She came around and kissed each one of them, including Tom, who stared gloomily into the fire and didn't respond. A shadow crossed Claire's face. Jane saw it and stood up to give her mother a hug.

"Are you going to bed already?" asked Charlie her.

"No, I'm going to see if Raz is still up. If he'd like to take a walk. We could take the dogs, if you want."

16

The snow had stopped. A few pale puffy clouds remained, but most of the sky was clear and glittering with stars. Jane and Raz went down the Percys' drive to the road, where Jane automatically turned left toward the village, but he put his hand on her arm and said: "Let's just go to the pond. It's late."

Turning right took them down through a neighborhood of big old houses like the Percys'—set back well from the road and surrounded by large trees and shrubs. They walked in the middle of the street, which had been plowed once and partially refilled with snow. There was no danger; hardly any traffic passed at this time of night. Most of the houses were already dark, and Raz and Jane passed in and out of the pools of streetlight, walking at a fairly good clip to keep warm. The snow squeaked under their feet.

"Why do you think Maura left Minnie behind?" Jane asked, as they followed the three dogs down the silent street. The dogs ran ahead of them, going from tree to tree, sniffing the trunks and kicking up little fountains of snow. Every now and then one of them circled back for reassurance and then bounded off again.

Raz took so long to answer that Jane thought he was going to ignore her question, but finally he shrugged, pulled his scarf higher around his neck, and said: "I have no idea."

"I thought it might be a sign that she plans to come back."

"Jane, she's been gone three months without being in touch once."

"So?"

"So, she isn't coming back."

"You don't know that."

"No, you're right. I don't. But let's not waste our walk arguing about Charlie's marriage."

"OK," said Jane. She walked silently for a few minutes, watching her breath puff out in front of her, and then said: "I just can't imagine what could have happened to make her act like that."

"Well, there must have been something, but we'll probably never know what. Frankly I think Charlie's better off without her."

"Oh, come on. I don't see how you can say that. Maura and Chris were his family. He loved them. Don't you remember how cute they looked last year in those Christmas hats?"

"Jane, you made those hats for them. That's what I remember. All they did was put them on so you could take a picture. That wasn't them. Chrissy was great, but Maura could be a real pain in the ass. She was always trying to control Charlie, and then claiming her own feminist right to total freedom."

Jane laughed. "She wasn't nearly as bad as Martha. Once when we were visiting, she came over when you and Charlie were off somewhere, and she wanted to show Maura and me how to look at our cervixes. She had this special mirror and stuff in her bag."

Raz laughed too. "Did you do it?"

"Are you kidding? No. But Maura did. She thought the world of Martha, and they both lectured me about the danger of being closed off to knowledge of my true self."

"Well, they were right about that. Your cervix is one of my favorite parts of you. You should get to know it better."

Jane gave Raz a poke, and they both laughed again. In the dim light, he looked, for just a moment, like a boy you'd call Rascal, and she felt lucky and happy that they had survived. Charlie and Maura had broken up, but they were still married. Still friends.

At the end of the long block, they came to an expanse of brushy woods that edged a shallow pond. The dogs dipped in and out of the woods, and Jane would have liked to go down to see if the pond was frozen enough for skating, but Raz said it was too late. He clapped his hands for the dogs, and they all turned back.

"Raz," said Jane, walking close beside him as they retraced their steps.

"What."

"I used to think about leaving you like that. Just disappearing."

"I know," he said.

"Really?" she asked, glancing quickly at him and then away.

"Yes. I've seen it on your face lots of times."

"Not recently though."

"Yes, recently too."

Jane blushed. "Well, maybe. I never meant it though. Not really."

She looked up at him again, but he was concentrating on the slippery ground beneath his feet. Jane wanted him to say that he was glad she didn't leave. That he was grateful. But he didn't. He just kept walking, and the warm lucky feeling faded into a dull familiar anger.

As they turned the corner and arrived back at the Percys' drive, Raz said, "I've had enough. How about you?"

17

When Jane and Raz arrived back at the house, only a few lights still burned. Ben and Claire had gone to bed, but from downstairs Jane could hear the thump-thump-thump of a bass line. She headed for the basement door without even taking her coat off.

"C'mon," she said to Raz. "Just for a little while."

He frowned, and Jane's anger flared, but he said nothing, and, in a welter of panting dogs, he followed her down the stairs.

The Percys' basement had served as the winter quarters of The Dipstickers since the Carters' garage was unheated. In those days, it had been a bare room with posters on the walls and a couple of sagging couches. Jane had spent many a Saturday afternoon listening to the band practice and reading, to the point where she thought all literature ought to have a four-four backbeat.

After Tom came back from the Army, he said he would never sleep in his old room again—although Claire preserved it as if the person who once lived there might yet return. Instead he had taken over the basement, painting the walls white, upgrading the couches, and installing his stereo equipment, a TV, icebox, and bar. Even though he eventually bought his own house in Eastville, he periodically came back to the basement, sometimes for weeks at a time. Jane thought this was weird, but her parents never questioned his changes of venue. Claire simply asked him if he'd be joining them for dinner. Usually he said no.

Apparently he'd been in residence for quite awhile this time. A pile of laundry lay on the floor next to two shopping bags full of empty bottles. The typewriter on his desk was surrounded by the crumpled remains of works in progress, and a jacket and tie hung on a hanger over the door to the furnace room.

Charlie sat cross-legged on one of the couches, eating mince pie piled with ice cream. The 12-string sat on the couch beside him as big as a person, and the air smelled strongly of marijuana.

"Hey, come on in," he said, waving them down the stairs.

The dogs rushed over to him and thrust their icy noses at his crotch. "Whoa!" He lifted his plate out of their reach and ordered them to lie down, which after the necessary amount of circling, they did.

"This pie is great, Janer," he said.

"Thanks, C," said Jane. "What're we hearing?" She flopped down onto the other couch.

"I'm trying to convince Tom that music is finally coming back from the dead."

"So far he's failed." Tom sat on a wooden stool, his arms crossed, like an interrogation subject. He held a large Scotch in one hand.

Charlie laughed. "I made him listen to some of Springsteen's new album."

"The one he recorded in his bedroom?" asked Jane.

"I like that," said Raz. "It's uncommercial."

"Ugh," said Tom. "If I wanted to listen to dreary folk music I'd move to Vermont."

"He doesn't like reggae either," said Charlie. "Too political."

"Too religious," added Tom.

"Too bad," said Raz. "I like Bob Marley."

Jane sat with her back against the arm of the couch, but she pulled up her feet to make room for Raz as he sat down. She felt her body begin to relax as if she had just completed a long, arduous task. "So what's next?" she asked. "Are you going to play something, Charlie?"

Charlie picked up his guitar and bent his head down over it. His fingers danced over the strings, but without touching them, and no sound came out. Tom swirled the ice cubes in his glass round and round, and Raz took off his boots. Then he scrunched down on the couch, with one foot propped against a battered Vuitton trunk that Tom used as a table, and the other absently rubbing

Roger's belly.

They all waited in silence, but Charlie seemed to have forgotten them. When he looked up and saw them watching him, he said, "Oh, sorry," and set the guitar back down. "No, I'm too tired to play tonight."

"OK, we can wait," said Tom. "But we have to end the evening with something better than that chunka-chunka stuff." He got up and began fingering his way along the shelf of records until found what he was looking for.

"Now why do I think I can guess what this is going to be?" said Charlie.

"Oh, be quiet," said Tom as he put on the record, returned to his stool, and closed his eyes.

Of course it had to be The Beach Boys' *Pet Sounds*, Tom's all-time favorite record. A couple of years ago Jane, Raz, Charlie, and Maura had each given him a copy for Christmas as a joke, but he'd been delighted.

"This is what I call security," he'd said.

As the song began, Jane felt a shiver go up her spine, and she saw each of the others withdraw into listening. Remembering. "God Only Knows" was the song The Dipstickers had used to close every show. They had sung it *a cappella* with a sincerity and sweetness that Jane would never forget.

She wished they would sing along, as they sometimes did, and then she could sing too. When they were all singing, they recovered something from that time. When they were what? Happier? No, not really. Younger? For sure, but that wasn't it either.

Maybe it was just that they were together then like a litter of puppies. They were each so much more alone now, and her own separateness felt like a wound bleeding slowly, deep inside. Surely that wasn't right. Wasn't what she ought to feel.

When the song ended, no one moved. The furnace hummed in the silence. Then with a precision borne of long practice, Tom swiftly lifted the needle before the next song could begin and shut off the record player.

"Well, that's it for me," said Charlie, standing up. Minnie jumped to her feet, as if she were afraid to let him out of her sight. The other dogs yawned and stretched, then got up too.

Jane didn't want to move, but Raz put his hand on her head and stroked her hair.

"C'mon Jane," he said. "It's time for bed."

18

"What are you thinking about?" Jane asked, as they lay in their separate beds in the darkness.

"The day we met again. When I came back from my trip."

He heard her rustle her blankets contentedly. "Why are you thinking about that?"

"I always think of that when I'm in this house. When there's snow."

"I was surprised to see you. You'd never come over to see me before."

"I know."

She was silent for a moment. The room was dimly illuminated by the back porch light, but Raz couldn't see Jane across the room. He listened to the sound of a car swishing by on the street.

"Raz," she said. "Without you, I really don't know where I'd be."

"I think that's just a song lyric, Jane," Raz said, but she hadn't wanted a joke. He could feel her waiting in the dark for something more, so he added: "We've had good times."

Jane shifted in her bed, punching up the pillows.

Probably his face, he thought, but he couldn't help it. He wanted to be honest, and he couldn't think of another thing to say that would be completely true. A coolness settled on the room. Then, down below, someone switched off the porch light and the room was plunged into blackness.

II. Thursday

1

In the morning Raz woke up in bed with Jane. They were curled together, naked. He could feel her breath on his arm, warming that one spot.

She was sleeping soundly, her expression peaceful and content, but he was uncomfortable. The arm that was under her had become stiff and tingly. He tried to move it without disturbing her, but she nestled closer to him, so he stopped. He didn't want to waken her.

Instead, he lay there thinking about the promise and the lie of sex. He didn't know why he had left his bed and climbed in with Jane last night. He'd hurt her feelings, and it was a way of apologizing, he guessed.

He hadn't lied: They had had good times, especially early in their relationship before his drinking really took off. But when he got sober, he'd had to face the fact that some of Jane's most intimate memories were about events that had taken place while he was in a blackout. The shared reality that she experienced had been one-sided.

When he tried to explain this to her one night at dinner—that there were total gaps in his memory—she refused to believe him.

"But we talked," she argued. "Did things. Went places. How can you sit there and tell me that you weren't really there?"

In his stomach Raz had the feeling that came with trying to tell the truth when lying still seemed so much easier: like he was about to jump a chasm with no safety rope.

"Because it's a fact, Jane," he said. "A simple fact. It wasn't anything I was doing to you. To us."

"Oh, right. And I suppose this is where you're going to remind me that alcoholism is a disease. You're not responsible for it. Well, fuck you, Raz Carter," she said, slamming her fork down on her plate. "Whatever happened to you in the past twelve years—whether you remember it or not—happened to me too. So don't try to pretend otherwise." Then she got up from the table and banged out the kitchen door.

Raz had waited at home all evening, unsure what to hope for—that she was really gone or that she'd come back. It seemed impossible that they could ever recoup their losses. Perhaps, he'd thought, it might be better to give up than to go on.

But she had come back, finally, and said she was sorry. She knew he hadn't willed himself to become an alcoholic any more than she had willed herself to be right-handed, but sometimes it was still hard to accept.

They'd made love that night too, and afterwards, talking in the dark, she said, "You know, when we started going together I thought you were the one person I knew who was really choosing his life. Tom and Charlie and I seemed to be, I don't know, floundering. We tried to do what was expected of us, and it wasn't working. But you went out and acted on your beliefs. Did what you wanted. I thought that meant that if you wanted me, it couldn't be wrong."

"I did want you, Jane. I still want you," he said. "But you have to think about what you want. Is this the life you choose?"

"I don't know. Sometimes I feel like I don't really know anything about you, so how can I know about us?"

"You know me, Jane. You probably know me better than I know myself."

She had been pleased when he said that, but he regretted it. It was as if he had given himself to her. Not only their shared past, but also the blank spaces and the future. That was wrong. His life was his, and hers was hers. That's what he should have said to her: It's yourself you need to know.

Now he touched Jane's tousled hair lightly with his fingers. As he moved closer to her, pressing his angular body to match her soft curves, he shut his eyes, but it was no good. The stillness of the house rang in his ears. He could not go back to sleep.

Finally he slipped his arm out from under her and got out of the bed. He pulled on his clothes quickly and went out into the shadowy, silent hall with his shoes in hand. At the bottom step, he sat down and put them on. The keys to the front door were in a small silver dish on the hall table.

He opened the locks as quietly as he could and then he was out: released from the house. His spirits lifted instantly in the bright cold morning. The snow was pink and blue in the light from the newly risen sun. Raz took a few deep breaths of the icy air then set to work clearing the snow off the Duster. When it was clean, he sat down on the cold seat, said a quick prayer, and turned the key.

2

In the village, the streets were plowed, but no one was out—not even children or dogs. Here and there a plume of smoke rose from a chimney, thin and pale against the bright sky, but for the most part Raz felt like he had the place to himself.

He drove slowly, with no particular idea in mind except to be away from the Percys for a while. In Brettville that wasn't easy to accomplish. He passed the brick elementary school where he'd first seen Jane; the three churches where The Dipstickers had played for so many dances; and the library, where Jane had worked in high school, watching him silently as he came in and out with other girls who had no intention of spending their time in its dark corners reading.

The center of the village was built around a small green with a single snow-covered bench and a stone commemorating the local veterans. New shops selling clothes and antiques had crowded out the drugstore, grocery, and hardware store that Raz remembered, but there was one familiar spot left: Hope's, the restaurant/bar where his father had gone for one beer every Friday night for years.

Of course he went by his own house. A grey shingled ranch in the first layer of post-war building that had surrounded the village, where each house had a one-acre plot and the trees and shrubs had, after nearly forty years, grown to impressive heights.

He circled that block twice although there wasn't much to see. A large snow-capped pumpkin on the stoop was the main thing that distinguished his house from the neighboring houses. He guessed a family must live there now, since two blue plastic sleds leaned against the wall by the back door. Snow, melting in the morning sun, dripped from all the eaves.

The backyard, which had been known as his mother's garden long after her death, and where, in the summers, Raz had played in a jungle of tall grass and vines, was now, under its coating of snow, tamed and neat.

Overall it looked like a normal family house. This always surprised him. He expected it to retain an aura of its past as that anomaly of the fifties—an all-male household.

Raz had been only five when his mother became sick, and he was eight when she died. He had very few memories of living with her; life seemed to begin when his father stumbled out of his grief and laid down the ground rules for their new family. No riding your bike in the house. No uncaged pets without everyone's consent. Be home by dinnertime. Leave a note that says where you are. Ricky, who was older and more conscious that this was not the way his friends lived, found it harder to adjust. Raz was just glad to feel like he finally knew what was happening.

"I thought you looked like Peter Pan when you were little," Jane told him once. "You and Ricky reminded me of the Lost Boys."

"We weren't lost," Raz said, feeling a familiar need to defend his family. "We were fine. We just didn't comb our hair. That wasn't important to us."

'All people are created different and everyone is as good as everyone else' was his father's version of the Declaration of Independence. Why try to be like anybody else? he counseled his sons. You were born different, try to find out about it and enjoy it.

Raz didn't say it to Jane, but he thought his father's upbringing had had better results than Jane's parents'. You're special was definitely not the same message as you're different, and obviously a lot harder to believe. Not that he hadn't himself been impressed by the specialness the Percys were capable of conveying. He'd been attracted—even seduced—by it. At one time he'd even thought that he might acquire some of it himself by his association with them. All that showed was how far he'd strayed off his own path, he thought now.

And what was his path?

Something other than drinking himself to death, he hoped.

As he circled back into the village and parked in front of Sweet Sue's Hair and Nails, he was filled with nostalgia for the sight of his father heading home from the grocery with a bag full of TV dinners under one arm and a folded newspaper in his hand held up where he could read it while he walked.

Even though he hadn't admitted it to Jane, Raz missed having his family around at the holidays too. They all acted differently when the two families came together. They made a reasonably polite effort to seek a common ground, and it gave Raz a fresh perspective on how he and Jane fitted together, each contributing half of the hopes and fears that made up their relationship.

When he was alone with the Percys he was not himself but the un-Percy, a phenomenon he and Maura had discussed the last time he'd seen her. It was a year ago, late Christmas night, and they were alone in the living room, after a long day of drinking and celebrating.

"No, no, we're not un-Percys," she'd declared, waving her champagne glass as if to make a proclamation, "We're the Im-Percys, Raz. The Im-Percys. That's why we have to stick together." And then she'd slapped his knee in a way that made him suddenly alert and uncomfortable.

Raz shivered as he climbed out of the warm car into the cold morning air. He remembered thinking then that Maura, in her red holiday dress with her long dark hair hanging to her waist, was a very beautiful woman. And he was glad that, even drunk, he'd had the sense to ignore what seemed like an invitation to connect.

At least he was pretty sure he had, but that was one of the problems with blackouts. Not only were you not really there when people thought you were, you also went places and did things that you could never recall.

3

Raz looked up and down the street and considered the possibilities for coffee. One of the lesser-known fast food chains had edged its way into the village with a bright red-roofed restaurant and windows full of colorful photos of hamburgers and ice cream. He would not have gone there even if it were open this early, which it wasn't.

Hope's was open, of course. The small neon sign that said "There's always Hope's" glowed over the oak door. Billy Hope kept his place open until three a.m. for the village drunks who came early and stayed late, as well as the kids who would finish up an evening spent at fancier nightspots with Billy's 15-cent drafts and an order of his special French fries with gravy. Like his father before him, Billy was open again at seven, brewing coffee, cooking eggs, and serving "hair of the dog" specials. Even though the place was scrubbed clean, the rank smell of beer and cigarettes still competed with the more wholesome fragrances of coffee and grease.

Raz paused in the doorway, letting his eyes adjust to the dimmer light and noted that his pulse quickened as he approached the bar. He had spent a lot of time and money in this place over the years.

Now all he wanted was coffee, he told himself, and the chance to see a familiar face. Billy Hope had been a year ahead of Ricky in school, three years ahead of Raz. His family, like their business, was a fixture of the Brettville scene.

"Yo, Raz," said Billy hardly looking up from the paper he had spread on the bar. A cigarette burned in the ashtray beside him, its smoke hanging in the sun. A man and woman Raz didn't recognize were seated at one of the old red leatherette booths eating breakfast. No one had turned on the jukebox yet.

"Hey, Billy," said Raz, sitting down on a stool. It felt strange, very strange, to sit on a bar stool, his wrists resting on the smooth round lip of the bar.

"The usual?" asked Billy, reaching behind him for the Jack Daniels. The bottles full of colored liquid glowed invitingly in the sun that came in through the front window. Raz felt a chill go up his spine in the pause before he said:

"No, thanks. Just coffee and two eggs over easy."

"OK," said Billy, folding the paper shut. He gave Raz a curious look as he poured the coffee and placed it in front of him. Since the day he turned 18, Raz had never come in here without ordering a drink, but Billy, he knew, was too experienced a bartender to ask questions.

"How's the family?" Raz asked when Billy came back with the plate of eggs, toast, and home fries. Billy rubbed his hands on a dishtowel stuck into his belt. His round stomach, ridged with scars from the war, pressed against the fabric of a faded Brettville Bees t-shirt.

"Good," said Billy. "Real good. My oldest kid is at the high school already. He played jay-vee football this year. Can you believe it?"

"Jesus. That is incredible."

"How's your old man?" Billy wanted to know.

"He's fine," said Raz. "He really likes Florida. For some reason."

"Old babes in bikinis," said Billy. "That's what I've heard."

Raz laughed. "Maybe that is it. No snow anyway."

"My folks are talking about Arizona. Don't ask me why. I think it's all lizards and sand out there."

"Whatever turns 'em on, I guess. How're things here?"

"Shitty. A lot of guys have been laid off. What about you?"

"I'm keeping busy."

"That's good. You up at the professor's house for the holiday?"

"Yup," said Raz, spreading jam on his toast.

"How are all them?" asked Billy.

"Fine," said Raz.

"Lieutenant doing OK?"

"He's back in his old place at the moment."

"Uh-huh," said Billy sympathetically. "Well, that's the way it goes."

Nothing as overt as a look had passed between them, but Raz felt like a burden had been lifted, and he was suddenly very hungry.

Billy went out to collect the money and pick up the dishes from the couple that had finished eating. They left, letting a gust of cold air rush through the door.

Raz ate and studied the pictures of the Brettville High football teams that surrounded the mirror on the wall behind the bar. They went back about 20 years and all looked the same. One of those little round heads with shoulder pads and breeches was Ricky, but Raz couldn't remember which year it had been that Ricky decided to become an all-American. Raz never entertained any such fantasy and his long hair put him permanently on the bad side of all coaches. In the center of the display was a black-and-white portrait of Billy in his football uniform, and next to it, his Bronze Star and Purple Heart in a frame.

By the time Billy came back to the bar, Raz was finished. He stood up and laid down a five-dollar bill.

"Tell your missus I sent my love," Billy said, ringing up the bill. This was a line he used on guys who spent their paychecks at the bar. Raz frowned. "Hey, just kidding. You look great, man. Whatever you're doing, keep it up."

"Thanks, Billy. You too."

As he stepped outside, Raz was embarrassed to realize he couldn't resist glancing around to be sure no one he knew had seen him come out of the bar. Why, he didn't know. No one here knew he'd gotten sober in the first place. He zipped up his jacket although he felt a trickle of sweat run down the center of his back. When he got in the car, he locked the doors. Now what, he wondered.

He pictured his empty house and the time it would take to get there. He asked himself if that was where he wanted to be and was surprised when the answer floated up: No.

He sat in the car with his hand on the icy gearshift and did not know where he wanted to go.

4

When Jane woke up, Raz was gone and the space he had occupied in her bed had grown cold. The room was cold too, but she didn't mind. She liked that contrast: cold room, warm bed. She pulled her nightgown back on, then stretched out and spread her body over the whole bed, pressing herself into it, as if Raz were still there beneath her. Only his scent remained, but she was happy. It had been a nice night, sleeping with him in the high narrow bed. At home too often they slept at opposite sides of their bed, facing the darkness.

She dozed and woke up and dozed again, in no hurry to start the day. When she looked at the clock, it was nearly nine. Normally she'd be about to start teaching, but this was not a normal day. This was Thanksgiving.

She was glad she had slept late, even though the mingled smells of coffee, toast, and onions coming from downstairs told her that her mother had already started cooking the dinner. She would hear about that, no doubt, but she told herself she didn't care. It was a holiday and she meant to enjoy it.

She was dozing again, snuggled deep into her rumpled covers, when she heard a tap on her door.

"Jane?" Claire called softly. "Are you awake?"

"Yes," she answered, pushing herself up against the pillows.

"I brought you some coffee," her mother said. "I thought we could talk about the plan for the day."

"All right. Thanks," said Jane, wrapping her hands around the mug she held out.

Claire was already dressed in a brown tweed skirt and heather sweater that set off her green eyes. Her hair was freshly combed and her face made up, ready to go out. Jane ran her fingers through her own tangled hair self-consciously. She wondered if her mother would notice that she smelled of sex and pulled the covers up to her chest.

"The creamed onions and Brussels sprouts are done," said Claire, "and the dressing is ready to go in, but I still need to make the mashed potatoes, sweet potatoes, and cranberry sauce. The turkey should go in at noon, so we can eat around four. I'm going out now to do some last-minute errands. Would you like to come?"

"Not especially. You're all ready, and I don't feel like rushing," said Jane. "Why don't I help with the cooking?"

Claire looked disappointed and began picking at some lint on the quilt covering the bed. "I suppose. Charlie and Raz have already left with their list."

"Well, what could I do here?" she repeated.

"I guess you could make the cranberry sauce, but be sure to make it sweet enough. You know Tom doesn't like it too sour." She looked at Jane in her childhood bed and said: "Maybe you should just peel the potatoes."

"I'll do both. I'm going to make rolls too."

"Really? Is there time? I bought some, but if you want to make them," her mother said doubtfully.

"I do."

"You'll help me with the table later, won't you?"

"Sure. I brought a surprise for the table."

"Did you? That's nice." Claire crossed the room and began fiddling with the flower arrangement on the bureau. "Daddy and I had a good talk with Charlie this morning," she said.

"About —"

"About divorcing Maura, of course. Daddy thinks he should do it as soon as possible."

"Why? They might still work it out."

"Oh Jane, there's nothing to work out. He never should have married that girl in the first place."

"Why not? He loved her."

"I suppose he did, but you know how that goes. She wasn't the marrying type really. I knew that the minute I heard that she refused to change her name."

"Mom, everybody does that now. It doesn't mean anything."

"But if she wanted to be so independent, why did she get married? She should have been grateful a man like Charlie would marry her and give his name to her and that poor child. But no. She was sticking with Reynolds and her child had to have a name of her own, she told me. Chrissy Rainbow. I don't know why she didn't just call her Chrissy Cabbage Leaf."

Jane laughed, but she was surprised at her tone. "I thought you loved Chrissy."

"I did," said Claire with a shrug. "She was a sweet little girl, but I couldn't help wondering who she was. How did she end up in our family?"

"You're talking about her in the past tense, Mom. She's not dead."

"To me she is. I mean it. That whole arrangement was ludicrous from the start."

"I hope you didn't say that to Charlie."

"No. I know he's terribly hurt, but we encouraged him to get on with his life. Find some nice girl and have his own children."

"What did he say?"

"Oh, he knew we were right. He's a sensible boy at heart. So—don't you want to hurry up and go with me?"

"No," Jane said again. "I'll do something with you later, if we need to."

"All right. But I hope tomorrow you'll come into the shop for a while. I want to give you one of those wreaths for your front door."

"Thank you," said Jane, despite the fact that she'd already made a wreath for her door.

"Breakfast is ready," Claire said, taking Jane's empty coffee mug from her hand. "You can help yourself. The boys and Daddy and I already ate. Raz didn't want anything. Not even coffee. He said he ate breakfast at Hope's."

"Really?" Jane's heart jumped, but she was careful to control her expression.

"That's what he said. I didn't even know they served food there."

Jane laughed. Her mother was shocked not because Hope's was a bar—she knew nothing about people who drank in bars first thing in the morning. It was the idea that someone would even consider going out for breakfast when they could eat at home. That's what shocked her.

"Well, you know Raz," Jane said. "He likes to be independent too."

5

"No," Tom was saying. "No. If that's what you want to do, fine. Do it. I don't want to talk about it anymore." His voice was sharp.

Jane paused in the dining room, half-listening, not wanting to interrupt.

"Don't call again until you've made up your mind," he said angrily. Then Jane heard him hang up the phone.

"Christ," he said, as she entered the kitchen. He was slouched on the bench that ran underneath the windows, head bent, hands between his knees. In his starched white shirt, gray flannels, and navy cashmere V-neck sweater, he looked like a pink-cheeked executive—immaculate and perfect, except for the slight sag of his left, damaged shoulder.

"What's up? How come you're all dressed up?" she asked, pouring herself some coffee.

"I thought it was Thanksgiving," he said, looking at Jane critically. She had brushed her hair before coming down, but she was still wearing her faded flannel nightgown and a pair of Raz's socks.

"Ha, ha," said Jane.

Sun was pouring through the window and the sound of melting snow dripping from the eaves mingled with the steady tap-tap-tap-tap of Ben's typewriter coming from his office overhead.

Jane noticed that the snow outside the back door was already punched with several lines of footprints and felt a twinge of guilt at being the last one up. She sat down on a stool at the island. A pan full of congealed scrambled eggs and a bowl of cold buttered toast awaited her. She took a piece of toast and dunked it in her coffee. "Is anything wrong?" she asked, unsure if she really wanted to know.

"No," Tom said at last. "Everything's great."

"So what are you working on these days?"

His face contracted from a blank expression to an angry glare. "Some shit for a bunch of assholes."

Jane laughed. "That's descriptive," she said. "It must be advertising."

"Of course, it's advertising. Sandy's Candy. Bob's Bar-be-que. Hot stuff. The economy up here is in the toilet. Not that it was ever anything else."

Jane took another piece of toast and began spreading strawberry jam on it. "So do you ever think of moving? Going to New York? I'm sure you could get a job there."

"Christ, no." He got up then and went to the refrigerator, rummaged around, and pulled out a beer. "I don't know how Mom can stand this refrigerator. It must be a hundred years old."

"Actually it's only the food in it that's a hundred years old," said Jane. Tom looked at her as if he didn't know what she meant, popped open the beer, and took a long drink.

Jane watched the movement of his throat as he swallowed. "So who was that on the phone?" she asked.

"Sheila."

"Oh," said Jane. "You're still seeing her?" Sheila Reagan, the homecoming queen of Jane and Raz's high school class, had been Tom's girlfriend in high school, but she married someone else while he was in the Army. Now they'd been having an affair for four years.

"Who knows. A week ago we broke up. Again. Now she says she wants to come over today."

"Good, I hope she does. I mean, Thanksgiving always seems more festive if it's not just the family," she said.

"Festive. Is that what you call it? You mean like when you and Chrissy used to sing those awful turkey songs while Maura tried to play footsie with Raz who was too drunk to notice?"

"Chrissy and Maura were part of the family, not guests, and that never happened."

"If you say so. Anyway I wouldn't count on seeing her. A month ago she was going to move in with me, and then suddenly it was all off."

"What happened?"

"Joey bought her a new car. I suppose that's as good as having sex. You wouldn't know though, would you?"

Jane blushed at Tom's knowing look and busied herself gathering up her dishes. Her mother had stacked the rest of the family's breakfast dishes in the sink—a cue she recognized. She poured herself some more coffee and squirted soap into the dishpan, glad to have something to do.

"So is that why you moved back here?"

"I suppose. That and a six-pack will get you a degree in psychology," he said. Tom crumpled his beer can and tried to toss it left-handed into the trashcan. It missed and clattered across the linoleum floor.

Jane did not move to pick it up. "Very funny," she said. "So where'd Charlie and Raz go?"

"Mom had a list of things that need fixing. She's been saving them up for Raz, but I don't see how she thinks they're going to get anything done today though. Nothing's open."

"Maybe they just went for a ride."

"Maybe," said Tom, going to the fridge for another beer. "They didn't consult me about their plans."

"Mom told me she and Dad were already on Charlie's case about getting a divorce."

"That's a laugh. I doubt Maura will wait for Charlie to decide anything. She's probably already divorced him and found someone else. He just forgot to open his mail and get the news."

"God, you all talk about Maura like she was some kind of monster."

"No, but I think when that Chicago cop cracked her on the head, he knocked a few things loose."

"Don't be ridiculous. That was fourteen years ago."

Tom shrugged. "Whatever. And how are things with you, Miss Jane?" he asked.

Under his scrutiny, Jane felt exposed. She wished she were not standing there in her nightgown, her faced flushed and damp from the hot water.

"OK," she said, scouring a juice glass. "I mean good. Really good. We need a new car. That's all." She didn't know why she said that. Dragged on his bad joke. She ran fresh water into the tub for the silverware and began washing each piece separately.

"So Raz is really off the sauce?"

"Of course, he is. He's been sober for nearly six months."

Tom looked skeptical. "I heard he went to Hope's for breakfast. That sounds like the old Razzie to me."

Jane felt her ears turn hot, but all she said was: "Well, he says he hasn't, and I believe him."

Tom laughed. The same horrible infuriating laugh he had used to belittle her his whole life.

"That's because you are such a loyal little wife," he said.

"It is not because I'm his wife. It's because it's true," said Jane, crashing a handful of silverware into the drainer. "You think I don't know the difference between drunk and sober?"

"Hey, I'm only teasing. If it's true, more power to him. I'm very happy for him. For both of you. Really." He came over to her then and put his hands on her shoulders.

"It's not an if. It's a fact," said Jane in a sulky voice, but she didn't resist when Tom pulled her into a hug. Even though she was acutely aware of her naked body under her nightgown, she hugged him back hard.

He kissed her with lips that were soft and smelled of beer. She turned away from the smell, and put her face against his shoulder. "I wish you could be happy for you, Tom," she said.

"Thanks, sweetie, but that is not my strong suit," he said, letting her go.

6

When Claire came home, Jane was looking at old photographs she'd found in the bottom drawer of the dining room chest. This, she'd discovered, was where all the family outtakes had ended up: the pictures of Maura and Charlie's wedding, Charlie holding Chrissy as a toddler, Chrissy dressed as a bat for Halloween, Tom playing the trumpet in the high school band, Raz and Jane with long, long hair in patched jeans and embroidered shirts.

"What in heaven's name are you doing, Jane?" asked Claire. She had a grocery bag in each arm and looked down at Jane, seated on the floor surrounded by pictures, as if she were a puppy who'd peed on the rug.

"Looking at stuff," said Jane. She had just pulled out the framed photo of Tom in his dress blues, taken when he graduated from Officers Candidate School. It had been at the very bottom of the drawer. "Why isn't this on your bureau anymore?" she asked.

"Because Tom threw it in the trash. Really, Jane," Claire said impatiently, "It's after eleven o'clock. Are you planning to spend all day mooning around in your pajamas? Because if you are, I think I'll go back to bed myself and forget this whole Thanksgiving."

Jane gathered up the photos and shoved them back into the drawer, then took one of the grocery bags from her mother.

"The potatoes are cooking. Did he say why he wanted to get rid of it?"

"Who?"

"Tom. Does he know you kept it?"

"What?"

"The photograph!"

"I don't know. We didn't discuss it. I just took it out, cleaned it up, and put it away."

"I don't see why. Frankly I think it's a good sign. Maybe it means . . . I don't know what it means. But I've always thought that photo made him look like the Army had sucked all the life out of him."

Claire's eyes flashed. "That's nonsense. He looks like a brave young man ready to do his duty to his country."

"Mom, we were all trying to do our duty to our country back then."

"Well, you did it your way, and Tom did it his—something I wish you other kids respected a little more. It certainly cost him enough pain and suffering."

Jane stared at her mother. Her face grew warm. The rush of responses that came to mind piled up so fast that she said nothing. Instead she carried her bag into the kitchen and set it down, amazed that she could do these things when inside she felt like she'd just narrowly missed a high-speed collision.

Claire busied herself unpacking groceries with a concentrated, self-righteous air. Her lips were tight as if she were doing addition in her head. She didn't speak until everything had been put away. Then she asked: "Where are Charlie and Raz?"

"They aren't back yet."

"Well, I hope they haven't gone gallivanting off somewhere. All I asked them to do was a couple of errands. They should be back by now."

"I'm sure they'll be home soon."

Claire looked at her as if her judgment were not the most reliable indicator of anything.

"I'll go take my shower," said Jane. "Then we can stuff the turkey."

7

Jane knew from the barking that the boys were back before she even got downstairs. They were all in the kitchen: Tom, stiff and overdressed; Raz and Charlie, red-cheeked from the cold; and the dogs dancing around excitedly at the smell of the turkey.

The turkey sat on the island like a naked baby. Charlie was telling the story about the year one of their golden retrievers, Rufus, jumped up on the counter and gobbled up one whole side of the turkey while they were having their soup course. Even though they all knew the story, everyone laughed.

Jane was struck by the fact that Raz looked more happy and relaxed than he had in months, and she wondered where he and Charlie had been. What they had been doing and saying to each other.

"Rufus was a crazy dog," said Tom.

"Fortunately these dogs are not crazy dogs. These are very, very good dogs. So nothing bad is going to happen to the turkey today, is it?" Charlie concluded, admonishing the dogs who barked as if he'd just told them he would give them the turkey.

"There you are, Jane," said Claire. "I told the boys we were letting you have a real holiday."

They all turned to look at Jane, still damp but neatly dressed in navy slacks and a cranberry-colored turtleneck sweater. She smiled self-consciously. Making an entrance.

"Any day I don't have to spend with twenty-five kids is a holiday," said Jane. "No matter how much other work I do."

"Poor Janer, slave to childhood," said Charlie, putting his arm around her shoulders.

"Jane's kidding. She loves teaching. In her heart of hearts she'd like to have us all sit in neat rows and obey her orders," said Raz.

"Ra-az," said Jane, turning to him, "that's not true." She started to punch him on the arm, but he grabbed her first and pulled her backward into his arms, hugging her tight.

She didn't resist. She was happy to be publicly claimed by Raz, to lean back and feel his warm body behind hers.

"Now kids," said Claire. "Stop teasing. Jane, we have to get this turkey in or we'll never eat."

"All right, Mom," said Jane, moving away from Raz.

"We're going to watch football downstairs," said Tom.

"That's fine. You boys have been a big help already. You go and have fun. Jane, if you'll mash the potatoes, I can get started on stuffing the turkey."

"OK," said Jane, taking up one of her mother's aprons.

Once the boys had gone downstairs, Jane and her mother fell silent. It was not an easy silence, but someone peering through their windows would have seen a busy contented family—from her father in his study to the boys in the basement. Jane sighed. A faint sweetness rose from the potatoes as she mashed butter and milk into them. So like the day, she thought.

Behind her, Claire was busy packing cornbread stuffing mixed with oysters, onions, celery, apples, and chestnuts into the cavities of the turkey. It was a family specialty, a recipe evolved to accommodate everyone's favorite element of the stuffing.

"The price of oysters was high this year," her mother said, breaking the silence. "I almost didn't buy them. But then I thought Charlie would be disappointed, so I got them after all." She had woven together the last flap of skin with a big metal pin and now gave the turkey a pat. "Jane, will you check to see that I set the oven at three-fifty?"

A large plastic bag lay on the counter next to the roasting pan.

"Mom, you're not really going to cook that turkey in plastic, are you?"

"Why, don't you think I should?"

"I don't know. It sounds so unhealthy."

"It keeps the oven clean. And you don't have to baste."

"But it's like steaming it."

"It's supposed to come out very moist."

Jane wrinkled up her nose. "How does it get brown? How does it smell? Like roasting plastic?"

"Oh Jane, don't be silly. You brown it at the end. You're just like Daddy. You always resist anything new."

Jane pulled herself up sharply. "I do not."

"Yes, you do. Trust me. Everything's going to be fine."

Jane turned her head away as Claire set the turkey, wrapped in its plastic shroud, into the oven.

"There," Claire announced with satisfaction. "It's in."

8

"I need to lie down for a little while," Claire announced once the turkey was in the oven.

"That's a good idea," said Jane. She turned on the water and began to fill the dish tub so she could clear away the latest round of dishes. "I'll keep things moving here."

"When I get up we'll do the table," said Claire, untying her apron.

"Sure," said Jane.

"I mean it. I don't want to wait until the last minute."

"Fine. I'll do it now, if you want."

Claire frowned. "You can't do it alone."

"Whatever you say."

"I mean it's nicer to do it together, don't you think?"

"Of course." Jane looked at her mother. Her expression had turned hurt and dissatisfied. "Mom—I didn't mean to be critical about the turkey. I'm sure it will be wonderful."

Claire had hung up her apron, which matched the colors of the kitchen curtains, and was carefully smoothing out any wrinkles with her hands.

"Oh well. You all seem to think I'm not capable of having a good idea, but I'm not some moron, you know. My shop has turned into a very successful business, and I do everything myself."

"I know you do, Mom, and we're all very proud of you," said Jane.

Jane dried her hands and, coming up behind Claire, put her arms around her waist.

"Take your nap. You must be tired. Working all day yesterday. Up this morning early.

Claire did not return the hug, but she managed a smile.

"You always clean things up so nicely, Jane," she said and then she left.

Jane expected to feel relieved with Claire out of the way. She had a lot to do, and, now that she had the kitchen to herself, she should get to it. But once she'd finished the dishes, she went into the back kitchen and lay down on the upholstered bench instead. When she was sick as a little girl, this had been her favorite place to spend the day. Bundled up with blankets, she could doze and listen to the comforting sounds of her mother puttering in the kitchen, her father typing away upstairs.

Now a patch of sun came through the window, and she curled herself as small as she could to fit into it. She wasn't going to sleep. She simply needed to relax for a few minutes. The day felt like an over-wound top already.

If Maura were there, they could joke about the family's quirks and none of them would matter so much. Laughter would dispel their importance. But Maura was gone, and Raz was probably right. She would not be back. Jane would never see Maura or Chrissy again. Although she was innocent of any wrongdoing—had done her best always to be a loving, affectionate sister and aunt—she had lost them.

She was surprised that behind this feeling was anger at Charlie. She didn't want that. She had no idea what had happened, and, even if she did, what would she gain by being angry with him?

She sighed and went back to work. Moving quickly and efficiently as if she were in a time and motion study, she made the cranberry sauce and mixed up the bread dough. She liked thinking about how to sequence her moves. It made cooking into a kind of dance, and it took her mind off other things.

She was kneading the dough for the rolls, when Charlie came up the stairs looking for something to eat. He wore a hand-painted t-shirt that said Peace and Freedom Festival 1970.

"God, that's a relic," said Jane, turning the dough over.

"This?" Charlie looked down at the shirt as if he hadn't noticed what he was wearing. "Oh, I know. I had it on under my sweater. Tom's got that place as hot as a furnace."

He peered into the stuffed refrigerator.

"Where's that pie?" he asked.

"You can't eat pie now—we're having dinner in a couple of hours."

"Exactly," said Charlie. "I'm hungry now."

"What's going on downstairs?"

"Tom is beating the pants off us at Yahtzee."

Jane laughed. She knew from experience, no one ever beat Tom at Yahtzee.

"Is Raz all right?"

"I don't know. What's all right mean? He and the dogs have eaten so many potato chips they're probably going to throw up."

Tom appeared at the top of the stairs. "Charlie, the game's starting again," he said. "Is there any more cold beer up here? Jane, why are you baking bread?"

"It's not bread, it's rolls. They'll go in as soon as the turkey comes out."

"Jesus. I don't know why you have to make more work for yourself. Isn't this day complicated enough already?"

"She just doesn't want to play with us," said Charlie. He had rummaged through the refrigerator and cupboards until he found a hunk of cheese, a box of Triscuits, and a six-pack. "You'll come down later, won't you, Jane?"

He smiled as if her coming really mattered, and Jane said, "Sure," pleased to be wanted. "I'll come after the massacre."

Alone again, she concentrated on pinching the bread dough into small rounds and setting them in a pan to rise. Last year, she and Chrissy had made bread dough turkeys. They colored the tail feathers with paprika and saffron and gave them poppy-seed eyes. Claire said they were too pretty to eat, but

Charlie had delighted Chrissy by pretending to carve his with his knife and fork. How could you not love someone who did that?

Once she'd cleaned up again, Jane made herself a cup of tea and went back to her spot on the bench. The sun had moved though, and now it was chilly there. She pulled a lap blanket up around her and sipped her tea. The quiet wouldn't last much longer. Her mother would be up soon, refreshed and full of new demands.

She wished Raz would come instead. She hadn't seen him alone all day. Even though he was only downstairs, he felt far away. She wanted him close, like he was last night. Not only physically close, but with her.

After he got sober he'd apologized—made amends, he called it—for all the times he'd been in a black out. He said he hadn't even known where he was, what he was doing or saying. She'd thanked him and she was glad, every day, that they'd survived his drinking. But he had new ways of being absent that she wished she could cure him of. The abstracted look. The long hours off "at AA." The vagueness about everything future.

Not that she had that many opinions about the future herself. She enjoyed her job, but she couldn't imagine doing the same thing over and over for her whole life. The first students she'd taught would be graduating from high school this year. That made her simultaneously feel very old and left behind—stuck forever in the second grade.

Sometimes she thought about opening a bakery. She liked the idea of spending the day baking instead of managing a classroom full of seven year olds. It would be a peaceful life by comparison. But then, bread didn't give much back, and she needed kids in her life. Somewhere.

Claire thought there must be something wrong with her and Raz. When they were alone, she asked Jane questions like "Don't you want a baby? Aren't you trying?"

Jane refused to respond to these questions. She couldn't explain to her mother how complicated it was to make a decision about having children these days. What she wished was that it would happen and then there would be no decision to make. But so far, nothing had happened.

Whenever she and Raz made love, afterward Jane would lie in bed and wonder: Is this the time? Is it happening now? This morning she had counted back the days to her last period and decided there was a chance she could have become pregnant.

She rested her hands on her stomach and thought if she were pregnant, right now, this minute, then next Thanksgiving they'd have a baby in the house, and everything would be different. That would make this the last Thanksgiving of her childhood. Or her adolescence. Or whatever this was.

9

After the Yahtzee game, Raz went out to split some more wood. Two hours in a basement with Tom and Charlie drinking were more than enough for him. He didn't care about the football game, and he didn't care about Yahtzee either. In the past he'd enjoyed these Thanksgiving rituals because they offered an opportunity to drink all afternoon without having to hide it. Sober, it was harder to remember why he was there.

"You'll come back though, won't you?" asked Charlie, when Raz said he was going out. "We want to jam after the game."

"Sure," said Raz, but he didn't mean it. He was thinking about how soon after dinner he could leave. Definitely not before dessert. Jane had made the desserts.

The afternoon sky was bright as he crunched his way across the snowy backyard. The warmth of the sun had made most of the snow fall off the trees. They were etched black against a blue and white landscape. The yard was quiet except for the twittering of a few winter birds. Everyone must be at home eating dinner; almost no cars went by on the road.

The woodpile was covered in snow. Raz had to knock the snow off each log before he split it, sending up a little shower of snow crystals that glittered in the sun and blew against him. They prickled and melted on his face.

Splitting logs, Raz watched his breath explode from his body. He worked fast, wishing his mind would go blank. As he warmed up, he felt a tension in his chest begin to relax. He swung the axe with more pleasure, less vengeance. Wood piled up around his feet, and he stopped to stack it.

When he had repeated this process three times, he sat down with aching arms, and unzipped his jacket. He tipped his head back so the sun was full on it, and slowly the thoughts he'd been holding off seeped back in.

He didn't know what had triggered it—another memory from that night last Christmas—but it had been with him all afternoon. It was his own voice, thick and blurry, protesting that he loved Jane and the sound of Maura laughing. She seemed to be leaning over him with her long dark hair falling into his face.

"You're wasting your time," she'd said. "The only people those Percys really care about is each other." In the background, Christmas lights blinked on and off.

Then what.

Nothing. He was sure nothing had happened. It seemed like she was coming on to him, but she probably wasn't. Maura had a confidential way of talking that pulled you in as if you were in the inner circle of people who understood a secret. It was flattering, but that was all. It didn't mean she wanted to seduce you. He'd seen her do it with Jane a hundred times. And anyway, even if she'd wanted to, he couldn't have had sex with Maura. She was Charlie's wife, and he liked Charlie a lot more than he liked her.

But he did identify with her, and, in a way, he admired what she'd done. By vanishing, she'd made an impression on the Percys that they would never forget. She'd have a permanent place in their history.

Charlie said he'd tried to find her, but he wouldn't have tried that hard. He would be too proud to go to the necessary lengths. The Percys lived by a list of unthinkable things. Leaving was one of them.

He knew Jane had wanted to leave him and sometimes he'd despised her for not doing it. He'd left himself as often as he could, spiraling farther and farther away from whatever notion he'd had about who he might be, what his life might be about.

He didn't agree with Maura that the Percys didn't love anyone else. The dead weight of Jane's love and trust had sometimes been almost more than he could bear. Maybe for Maura it had been the same. She had had to get out from under to breathe.

He picked up a log and set it on the block.

At rehab he'd been told to list what he liked and what he didn't.

"You have to rediscover who you are," the counselor had said.

Raz remembered sitting for a long time on his narrow bed holding a yellow pad with two neat but empty columns drawn on the page in front of him. It was the one time he'd broke down and later when he tried to explain how it made him feel—that he had been completely erased by alcohol—the counselor had smiled sympathetically and said: "Try to think of it as a clean slate instead."

After six months, he still didn't have two lists, but he was beginning to have questions: Was that guy who could stand up for his convictions really gone forever? Did he want to spend his life fixing things? Was he always going to be the disappointing guy who married good old Jane?

"No," he said, bringing the axe swiftly down to the log.

No and no and no.

10

In the dining room, Jane watched as Claire brought out seven crystal water glasses and seven wine goblets to set on the table.

"Why are you setting seven places?" she asked.

"Tom's Sheila is coming," Claire said, rubbing away a water spot with the edge of her apron.

"Really? I guess she plans to slip her husband a mickey in his after-dinner coffee then."

"Jane!"

"Well, how else is she going to get away? What's she going to say? Bye, honey, I'm going to Tom's now?"

Claire sighed and sat down in one of the lyre-backed chairs. In front of her were the rolled gray flannel cases of silver flatware handed down to Claire from her grandmother. "I don't know. I thought he was finished with that whole situation, but I never ask him questions about what he's doing and maybe that's wrong. Maybe he needs more guidance. As it is, he comes and goes like an angry ghost, and all I do is try to welcome him. I'm just so afraid we'll lose him altogether."

Jane was shocked. "What do you mean lose him altogether?" she asked, but Claire didn't answer. She picked up one of the flannel cases and fiddled with the faded ribbon knotted around it. "I think we need to confront him about his drinking. Have one of those interventions." She didn't know why she said this. Her own experience showed other people's opinions didn't carry much, if any, weight where drinking was concerned.

"I can't do that, Jane. After all he's been through. I know he drinks too much sometimes now, but you don't remember what it was like when he first came home. You ran off with Raz."

"I certainly do remember. I was living here then too. And I didn't run off with Raz. We fell in love, and we wanted to be together."

"Yes, in a teepee, as I recall."

"We only lived in that teepee for one summer, and it was really nice. An adventure."

"I suppose. I just imagined you would. . . but then, I've never been outdoorsy," Claire said with a sigh. She unrolled the first flannel case to reveal twelve carefully polished silver dinner forks. Each was engraved with an "E" for "Eaton," Jane's great-grandmother's married name. As she pulled each one out, she handed it to Jane, who walked around the table setting it in place.

144

"I don't know why I bother keeping all this up. None of you kids will ever live this way," she said, as she passed Jane the salad forks and dessert spoons.

"What way? We do live in a house now, you know. Our own house, I might add."

"But you and Raz don't entertain, do you? And keeping up with silver takes a lot of time. A good set of stainless is much more appropriate. Besides, who will you hand all this on to?"

"Mom, I'm only thirty two. I'm not worried about who I'll hand things on to yet."

"By thirty two a person's life pattern is pretty well set. You and Raz have been married for ten years."

"I don't need you to tell me that."

"No. Of course, you don't."

Claire handed her the dinner knives, butter knives, and teaspoons. Jane went round and round laying each place with care and turning the blades of the knives in, an act of ritual importance.

"I don't think you understand how things have changed this year. I feel like I have a whole new life ahead of me now that Raz is sober," she said. She hoped she sounded more confident to her mother than she did to herself.

"You're right, I don't really know about things like that," said Claire, gathering up the flannel wrappings. "It always seemed to me that he would be fine if he would just finish college and find a real job. Tom too. He was such a bright boy I never imagined he would end up with no education. I must say a degree doesn't seem to have helped Charlie though."

"Charlie wanted to be a musician."

"Oh, I know, but he could have been a scholar. He has a wonderful mind like Daddy. But all you kids grew up with big ideas about changing the world and no sense at all about your own lives."

"Thanks, Mom."

"I'm sorry, but that's what I think," said Claire primly. She walked around the table making minute adjustments in the arrangement of the silver. "The sixties ruined all of you. Not just Tom. Daddy says it happens like that sometimes."

"You mean we're a bad crop."

She frowned as if she were seriously considering this possibility. "I don't know, but you were such promising children, and each one of you went off the rails. I have no idea what will become of any of you."

"I am not off the rails," said Jane.

Claire stepped back from the table to study it then began tweaking the flower arrangement, which looked already perfect to Jane.

"You're a good steady girl, Jane. You always have been, ever since you were a baby. But I worry about you anyway. The life you've chosen."

"The life I've chosen is fine," Jane said stubbornly.

"Maybe you're right," said Claire, pulling a flower that had begun to droop out of the centerpiece. "Things will get better. Didn't you say you brought something for the table? Why don't you get it?"

11

Jane told herself there was no point in getting mad. Claire always said whatever she thought, and it never even seemed to dawn on her that she could be hurtful. Or maybe it did, but she didn't care. Jane had never been able to figure that out. It didn't really matter though. This was Thanksgiving. She didn't want to spend the day being mad.

She went to her room to get the box of paper turkeys. She had to finish the table so she could get back to her rolls, which were probably, at that very moment, rising into small bags of air, but then Tom's voice in her head said: "What do we need rolls for anyway?" and she felt her energy sag like punched-down dough.

She sat down on her bed instead. The paper turkeys, with their magic marker faces, looked up at her. "What's happening? Are we going?" they seemed to ask.

Their expressions were silly and hopeful, the way Jane had felt when she made them, surrounded by piles of construction paper and glue, safe in her own room, in her own home. Now she had the urge to throw them away. The moment of pleasure that she had imagined, when the family would walk around the table looking for their names, was simply another one of her fantasies.

As she lay back against the pillows, the turkeys slid and tumbled against each other in the box. "Yikes!" they said, but she didn't care anymore. She looked up at the ceiling. That smooth white answerless surface had never changed in all the years she'd spent searching it.

Even when she heard footsteps coming up the stairs, she didn't move. It didn't matter who it was.

The door opened and she could hear the small breath, drawn in surprise at her presence, as someone came into the room.

"What are you doing?" Raz asked.

"Hiding," said Jane.

He raised his eyebrows. "From?"

"My loving family. What are you doing?"

"I just split a bunch of wood. I had to get out of the basement. Your brothers are getting very drunk. No doubt for their own very good reasons." He sat down on the other bed, kicked off his shoes, and lay down. "Your mother thinks you decided to change your clothes."

Jane laughed bitterly. "I guess she doesn't like my outfit."

"We could be at home right now, you know. Getting ready to eat," said Raz, folding his arms under his head. "Big turkey in the oven. A fire in the fireplace. Some soft music on. A couple of friends about to arrive. . ."

"Oh, I know. I'm sure you're right, that would have been very nice," said Jane, getting up. She went over to his bed and bent down to hug him, her head on his shoulder. His chest was hard and warm, and his hair smelled like fresh cut wood. He edged over and she lay down next to him. Close. For a moment, with his breath on her face, the feeling of loneliness lifted. "Are you still leaving tonight?" she asked.

"Yes. You can come with me if you want."

Jane did pause and try to picture herself doing this, but it was impossible. She could not disappoint her family in that way. "No I can't," she finally said.

"Suit yourself. Did you ever think what that means, Jane?"

"No," she said, kissing his neck. "I was born to please others, and I wish, just this once, you would stay to please me. You could go back in the morning. Charlie's leaving early. Why not go then?"

"No," said Raz, abruptly pulling himself up against the pillows. "I'm going tonight."

Jane stood up and straightened her sweater. "What's the difference? Either way you're asleep most of them time."

"The difference is this holiday will be over. I'll sleep in my own bed. Wake up in my own house."

"Oh, c'mon, Raz. It's only one night. Please stay with me. I'll be so lonely without you. I don't have anything in common with my family anymore."

He looked at her coldly. "I'm not staying here to hold your hand. You can either come with me or not."

"I can't."

"You mean you won't. But tell me one thing. Tell me you do know this is your choice."

Jane went to the door and stood with her shoulders back, a pose she recognized suddenly as her mother's. She could see in Raz's face that he recognized it too. A moment hung between them like a spider's web then Jane said: "I'm going down."

12

At four o'clock, when Raz came downstairs, the kitchen was at the peak of chaos with Claire at the hub. She was tasting and seasoning and sending Jane back and forth to the dining room with serving spoons and pitchers of water and dishes of condiments. Charlie had fallen asleep on the bench with Minnie on his stomach. Ben had still not appeared—the sound of his typewriter continued unabated—and Tom was on the phone.

"All right. No, you're right," he was saying. "Yes. OK. OK. I promise. Me too."

"Was that Sheila, dear?" Claire asked. "I hope she's still coming. We're all looking forward to seeing her."

"Really?" said Tom. "I don't know why."

"Daddy!" Claire shouted up the back stairs. "It's time to come down! Right now!"

Raz went out onto the porch and brought in an armload of firewood.

"Oh, Raz, thank you!" said Claire. "That's just what we were missing. A beautiful fire."

"It looks like it's going to snow again," he said.

"Really?" said Jane, hopeful. As if a blizzard would keep him from leaving.

"Really," said Raz, and she turned back to chopping the giblets.

By five, the turkey had been removed from its bag and was out of the oven, looking remarkably golden brown and handsome, enshrined on a large platter garnished with parsley. Everyone gathered in the kitchen to have a drink and eat peanuts and olives, while Claire stirred frantically to keep the gravy from separating.

"This looks like the best turkey we've ever had," said Ben, who had come down at last. He wore a faded green felt vest with brown felt turkeys pasted on it that Jane had made him when she was a little girl.

"Oh, I don't know," said Claire. "Next year I think we should go out. Thank God," she said as she poured the gravy into a gravy boat. "That's the real thanksgiving of this day."

Everyone laughed with relief, and then Tom said, "I'll pour the wine."

That was the cue that it was time to go to the table and, when Raz found the paper turkey marking his place, he also found his glass had been filled with red wine. At first he thought this must be a mistake, but Tom said: "You can hold it for the toast. Can't you? I mean that won't corrupt you, will it?"

Jane looked nervously at him, and her reaction angered him as much as Tom's remark. Without a word, he pushed back his chair, picked up the glass, and took it out to the kitchen.

"Oh Raz, is that really necessary? You know someone will drink that," said Claire.

"Anyone who wants it is welcome to it," he said more sharply than he intended. Claire looked rebuffed and busied herself by handing the potatoes and creamed onions around the table away from him.

"What'll you have, Raz? Dark meat? Light meat?" Ben jumped in, pointing at the turkey with his carving knife. "How about you, Jane—a leg?"

"Just some dark, Dad," said Jane. "Mom, everything looks great."

"It does," said Charlie. "I think the plastic bag lent a special aroma to the turkey."

"Charlie!" said Jane, but Claire laughed and looked pleased.

Once the plates were all filled and passed around, Ben asked, "Aren't we going to sing before we eat?"

"Of course, we are," said Claire. "It's Thanksgiving!"

Singing grace was a custom the family picked up during one of Ben's sabbaticals in England. Tonight Claire suggested a medieval round that was Raz's favorite, but Charlie said, "Let's do 'Dona Nobis Pacem' instead."

"All right, dear. That's a lovely idea. Peace. I think we can all agree we need more of that in this world."

They settled themselves and glanced around the table expectantly. In the momentary shift of their attention to each other and the anticipation of making music together, Raz thought their faces changed, grew more open and relaxed. Even Tom's eyes lost some of their guarded look.

Jane and Claire began the round, their pure clear voices rising and falling as one. In the candlelight, Jane looked young and enchanted, the way she had when he first fell in love with her, and maybe it was worth it to be here to see that expression on her face again.

Charlie and Ben came in second. Ben sang with gusto, and Charlie softened his own voice to blend in.

Raz was supposed to sing the third part with Tom, but he usually didn't. He thought it was so much nicer to listen. Before he met the Percys he had never even imagined that there were families who sat around the dinner table singing in Latin like monks.

Do-na. No-bis. Pa-cem. Grant us peace.

The layered harmonies filled the room like the flickering lights cast by a twirling prism. As if by unspoken agreement, they continued to repeat the verses over and over.

Do-na. No-bis. Pa-cem.

Raz felt suspended in music. Cleansed. Full. Grateful even. And it occurred to him then that this was Jane's beanbag chair. The comfort she could not find anywhere else.

They dropped out in the same order as they began—Jane and Claire, Ben and Charlie—until only Tom was left singing in his rich warm baritone: "Dona. Nobis. Pacem." The silence that followed held them together like a bubble, then, from under the table, Roger groaned in his sleep, and they all laughed.

13

"Hey, I think we sounded pretty good tonight," said Claire, smiling at everyone around the table.

"We always sound good, don't we?" said Ben.

"No, we don't," said Tom.

Charlie laughed. "I have never been able to figure out how you ended up in advertising, Tom. You certainly don't have a gift for the comfortable lie."

"My rolls!" said Jane, jumping up from the table.

By the time she returned with a basket of hot brown rolls, Raz had begun to work his way through more food than he would normally eat in three dinners. Later he would have a stomach ache, but now he didn't care. It was Thanksgiving, he was hungry, and his ears were ringing with pacems.

They had only been eating for a couple of minutes, when Tom rapped on his glass.

"I want to make a toast," he said.

A little reluctantly everyone put down their forks and lifted their glasses. When Raz picked up his water glass, Tom looked at him disapprovingly.

"To our family—all present," said Tom.

"That's sweet, dear," said Claire, her eyes misting up.

"If we're all present, why do we have an empty chair?" asked Charlie.

"Is that for the ghost of Thanksgiving past?"

"No, honey, that's for Sheila. She's coming for dessert."

"Oh," said Charlie. "I get it."

"To our family," they said and clinked glasses all around.

Charlie knocked back his glass of wine and refilled it. "I want to make a toast to my family," he said, and everyone looked anxious until he added, "Roger, Minnie, and Arthur." The dogs had positioned themselves at strategic points around the table where they'd be ready to catch any morsel that fell, and their ears pricked up when they heard their names.

"To the dogs. All our dogs, past, present, and future," said Jane. She lifted her glass to Arthur, who was closest to her, and he half rose on his haunches to meet her hand, then sat back down when he realized there was no food involved.

"Oh, please. Daddy and I don't want any more dogs," said Claire. "Not that we don't love having yours here, Charlie. But at a certain point you get too old for babies and dogs."

"I'd like a dog," said Jane, much to Raz's surprise. She patted Arthur's head and slipped him a piece of turkey, which incited Minnie and Roger to rush to her side of the table.

"You can never have too many dogs or babies in my book," said Ben chuckling.

"Oh Daddy. You know what I mean."

"Stop feeding the dogs, Jane, and let's toast, for Christ' sake," said Tom.

"Yeah, c'mon, they don't care if the food is cold, but I do," said Charlie.

"It's their toast. They should get something," said Jane, but she turned away from their eager faces and picked up her glass. "To dogs—ever loyal and uncritical," said Jane, holding a smile.

"Dogs," said Raz, as he clinked his glass with Ben, and Arthur barked a high-pitched beagley bark.

"Babies," said Ben, as he clinked with Jane, who blushed.

Then at last they began to eat again, and there was silence until Claire said:

"Daddy, we forgot to put on some music!"

"Let's not have music," said Tom. "We'll spend ten minutes arguing over what it should be and then another ten minutes over how loud it is. Why don't we just talk for a change?"

Charlie laughed. He'd already refilled his wine glass a third—or was it a fourth—time.

"OK, Tom. You start. Why don't you tell us what's new in your life?"

Claire headed off this topic, but not before Tom glared at Charlie and left the table to refill his Scotch glass. "I thought we always had music," she said. "It doesn't seem too much to ask to have someone put on some music. I don't see why it should become an issue."

No one picked up that topic, but Raz saw Jane watching Claire, her eyes alert.

"When I was growing up," Claire began again, "No one was rude at meals. It simply wasn't allowed. We treated each other with respect, and there was a lot of joy at that table."

Raz was impervious to Claire's lectures on manners, but the others looked abashed. Jane was silent, biting her lips. He began to eat faster, as if a storm warning had gone up.

Charlie refilled his glass again and looked around, his head wobbling slightly. "We have a lot of joy too, Mom," he said. "Ha! Ha! Ha! Isn't that joy?"

Claire's features seemed to gather in a knot on her face. "Oh Charlie," she said, "how can you make fun of me? We've all been trying so hard to make this a nice day for you!"

"For me?" said Charlie. "What have I got to do with it?" He sounded angry. Jane had become very pale.

"Now Mommy, don't get upset," said Ben. "We all know how hard you've worked, and we appreciate it very much. This turkey is fantastic! I can't believe you cooked it so easily. It came out just perfect."

"No, it didn't," said Claire. "You all think I poisoned it. But I was only trying to save myself some work. You have no idea how hard it is for me to clean that oven. Bent over. Down on my knees. You're all here to eat the dinner, but who's going to be here later? Who's going to help me then? No one. It's all up to me."

"Oh Mom, the turkey's fine," said Charlie. "Don't get all wound up."

"Right, it's great Mom. You don't even need to cut it with a knife," said Tom.

Claire gave him a dark look. "Well, next year, I'm not doing this again, believe me. We'll just go to a restaurant. Raz's family always went to a restaurant, didn't you?"

"After my mother died," he said evenly.

"Well, maybe I'll be dead by next year, and you can all go wherever you want."

"Come on, Mom. Let's talk about something else. Remember, we were on joy," said Jane. "Yesterday I asked my students what they were thankful for, and do you know what they said?"

No one knew, but Claire was not about to give up center stage to Jane.

"I know I'm grateful to have my children around me," said Claire, "and I hope some day you all have children of your own to give you the joy you've given me." Then she burst into tears, stood up abruptly, and left the room.

There was complete silence after she was gone. Raz tried to catch Jane's eye, but she sat frozen, staring at her plate. What a wasted day, he thought and began eating again.

Eventually the plinking of knives and forks resumed, but no one spoke until Charlie shook his head and said "Wow. Was that a blessing or a curse?"

Raz had to restrain himself from laughing.

"This time of year is very busy for Mommy. Her business takes a lot of time, but she still wants to do everything to make the holidays just the way they used to be," said Ben, calmly buttering a roll.

Jane pushed away her plate. She'd hardly eaten a thing.

"What was all that about making it a nice day for me?" said Charlie, refilling his wine glass.

"Oh Charlie, don't be dense. You know," said Jane. "Because of Maura and Chris."

"Well, she sure has a funny way of making the day nice."

"She feels bad, Charlie, OK? Don't fucking criticize her for it," said Tom.

"I'm the one who got dumped. I'm the one who lost my child. I don't see how that ends up being about her and her feelings," said Charlie. He threw down his napkin.

"I think we should have had some music," said Jane.

"I need some air," said Charlie, pushing back his chair.

"Oh, come on, Charlie, don't leave. I'll go get Mom. Shouldn't I go get her?" said Jane, appealing to her father.

"She's all right. She'll come back in a few minutes. Everyone sit down and enjoy your dinner," said Ben. "Doesn't anyone want seconds?"

Charlie stood unsteadily and ran his hands back through his hair. "I'm going for a walk," he said.

"Now? You're going for a walk? In the middle of dinner?" asked Jane.

"Hey, I'm not responsible for this," said Charlie and started for the door. The dogs stood up uncertainly, and, with quick longing glances back at the table, ran after him.

There was another silence. Jane sat fiddling with her paper turkey until all of its feathers fell off.

"I think this turkey is really excellent, don't you, Raz?" said Ben. "Have you ever had it prepared this way?"

"No," said Raz. "I haven't." He was the only one who'd eaten everything on his plate.

"Why don't you have some more? There's plenty more."

"I think I'm full now," he said.

"Jane? Have some more. You're not eating enough."

"No thanks, Dad, I'm saving room for pie."

"All right then," he said. "I guess I'll be the only one."

Jane got up to begin clearing the table. Tom stared at his whiskey, while Ben carefully picked one piece of turkey after another off the platter and ate it.

Claire's plate was still on the table when she reappeared. She had applied fresh lipstick and sat down with a composed air.

"Where's Charlie?" she asked, picking up her fork. She began to eat again as if she had never left.

"He took the dogs out for a little air," said Ben.

"That's nice," said Claire. "I think it's snowing again. Charlie has always liked to walk in the snow."

Jane passed through the dining room to the living room without saying a word. A moment later, her favorite Bach concerto came on. It was music Raz always thought of as mournful, but now it flowed over them like the foam used to put out fires.

14

Sheila didn't turn up after all, but Charlie came back. Raz had done his best to end the holiday well: He had eaten two pieces of pie with ice cream, helped Jane clean up the whole kitchen, and listened to Charlie play his 12-string. Now it was eight o'clock. Time to hit the road.

When he went upstairs to pack his duffel bag, Jane followed him with an irritatingly forlorn and resentful expression. "So, you're really going," she said, leaning against the doorframe. As if to block his way.

"This is not a surprise, Jane. I've told you three times."

"I thought you might change your mind because of the snow."

"No."

"Last night was so nice."

"It was very nice. But I'd rather have those times at home. You know it's hard for me to be around all this drinking."

"So what are you saying? That we won't be able to spend holidays here anymore? I mean what about Christmas? Are you going to leave on Christmas night too?"

What he wanted to say was: Do you really want to be here for Christmas after today? But he didn't. That was beside the point.

"I don't know. It's not Christmas yet remember? It's today. Today I've had enough."

Jane moved across the room to her desk, and sat down in the chair backwards, with her arms folded across the chair back. She didn't say anything, but she looked sulky and her eyes slowly became glassy with tears.

Raz saw what was coming, but he kept on packing. "This is not about you, so don't try to make it that. It's not even about your family. It's about me and alcohol. What I need to do to stay sober. Do you understand that?"

"I do, Raz, but you know I'm sick of hearing about alcohol. It's like everywhere I turn. I thought I was going to get you back when you stopped drinking. That we would be able to go forward with our lives.

"Today I was thinking. Wouldn't it be great if we'd conceived a baby last night? Right here and now it would be starting. A new beginning for us with our own family."

Raz concentrated on zipping his duffel bag. He never understood why the same clothes took up more space when you were headed home than they did when you were leaving.

He didn't want to look at Jane, but, when he realized she'd fallen silent, he couldn't help himself. Her face was very pale.

"Are you listening to me? Did you hear what I just said?" she asked.

"Yes, but I don't think this is right time for that conversation. It's getting late."

"You know whenever I say anything about the future you get this frozen look in your eyes like a jacked deer."

Raz hoisted the duffel bag onto his shoulder. "You're probably right. I don't know anything about the future. I'm trying to learn to live one day at a time."

"That is such bullshit, Raz, and you know it. You might have to live one day at a time, but you can't only think one day at time. You're not fucking Arthur, for God's sake. You're just hiding behind this one day at a time crap because you don't believe we have a future."

Raz couldn't think what to say, so he moved toward the door. The silence had lasted only a split second before, like a clap of thunder after lightning,

Jane rose from her chair, crossed the room, and grabbed his arm.

"Don't you dare leave without answering me," she said.

"You didn't ask me a question, Jane," he said.

"Well, I am asking you one now. Are you planning to leave me? After all we've been through? You are, aren't you!" she cried and threw herself across her bed, sobbing.

"Jane," he said, going to her side. "Jane, listen to me, please." All his life, he thought, he would remember this moment: how soft her sweater was when he put his hand on her back and the heat of her body underneath it. The shadowy room of her childhood around them.

"Remember how you used to say you fell in love with me because I was so clear about what I believed and what I wanted to do with my life? Well, we both know I lost that sense of direction, and I have to find it again, whatever it takes, or I might as well be drunk. So my life is going to change, and I'm going to change, but that's not saying I'm planning to leave you." On the whole, he was proud of this speech. It felt true.

Jane stopped crying and lay still, but when she turned her swollen face from the pillow and looked at him, he could tell right away she hadn't appreciated what he said.

"That is so fucking typical of you, Raz Carter. I ask you a question about us, and everything you say is about you. You and your life. What you want. What you need. Well, guess what, I have a life too."

"I know," said Raz. "And maybe you'll decide you don't want me."

Now she looked like the deer in the headlights. "Don't sound so hopeful. If I didn't want you I would have left a long time ago, but I thought we were going to go the distance, Raz.

"I thought that's what this was all about. But at the moment, what I would really like, speaking just for myself, is for you to get the hell out of my house and leave me alone!"

15

Raz left his bag in the hall and crossed the silent dining room. It smelled of blown-out candles, and Jane's turkeys lay scattered across the snowy surface of the table as if there'd been a disaster in the barnyard. Sheila's clean place setting was still there, ready in case she showed up late.

The family had gathered in the back kitchen by the fire. Ben and Tom were watching television, while Claire knitted something green. Charlie sat cross-legged on the bench strumming his guitar quietly. The dogs were sprawled in front of the fire, asleep.

"Oh, Raz. Are you leaving now?" Claire asked.

"That's right. I have to get started."

She set down her knitting, all awkward politeness, and stood up to give him a hug. "Well, thank you for all the wonderful firewood. We'll think of you every time we build a fire."

"Yes, so good to see you again," said Ben.

"Hey, Raz—" said Tom reaching up over his head to shake hands. "Stay cool."

"Do you have snow tires, Raz? It looks pretty slippery out there," said Ben.

"Yes, I'll be fine."

Charlie got up, hitching up his pants. His pupils were dilated and his wool shirt smelled of pot. "Let's get together sometime," he said. "Why don't you guys come and spend the weekend? I'm working on a solo act. Maybe you could come and hear me."

Raz nodded. "That would be awesome."

Charlie offered his hand, but Raz pulled him into a hug. It felt like an ending, more than a goodbye. He didn't know that for sure, of course. He didn't know anything for sure.

Jane was sitting on the staircase in the front hall when he came back. She followed him out to the car without speaking. Her face still looked puffy, but she was calm.

Raz loaded his bag into the back seat. It was snowing hard. In the porch light the flakes shone in Jane's hair.

"OK, I'm off," he said, pulling her quickly to him. She turned her face away, so he kissed her cheek. "I'll see you Saturday."

She nodded, but she wouldn't meet his eyes.

"Jane," he said, taking her face in his hands. "I want this to work out for both of us."

Jane pulled away and wrapped her arms around herself. Snowflakes dotted her sweater and disappeared. "I have no idea what you think that means."

"Well, maybe we can find out together." He smiled, hoping for a smile back. He hated to leave with her standing there like a gargoyle on the porch, but she didn't say anything and she didn't move, so he got into the car, and, with a little wave, he left.

16

When Jane came back into the house, she found Tom in the hall, lacing up his boots.

"Where are you going?" she asked.

"I'm meeting Sheila for a drink," he said, and Jane noticed immediately that something had shifted in his eyes. He looked awake. Excited.

"I thought she was coming over here."

"I told her not to come."

"I can't imagine why. We've been having so much fun."

"Right." He stamped his feet like a horse and grabbed a long scarf off the hall seat.

"So where are you meeting?"

"Hope's."

"At Hope's? Everyone in the village will know by midnight."

"Everyone in the village has always known about Sheila and me."

"So why doesn't Joey know then?"

He wrapped the scarf around his neck twice and pulled on his gloves. Tom never wore anything more than a tweed jacket unless it was 20 below.

"Husbands and wives only notice what they want to notice," he said. "I should think you'd know that by now, little sis."

Jane ignored this attempt to deflect her. "Did they have Thanksgiving together?"

"They did. And, over pumpkin pie, Sheila told him that she loved me and always had. You can imagine what happened next." His expression told Jane that he could read every sign of her own fight with Raz on her face.

Self-consciously she ran her fingers through her hair. "I don't think I want to. So are you coming back here? Afterward?"

"I hope not. I plan to stop by my house, turn up the heat, and make sure I made the bed the last time I was there. But I can't predict the future. Can you?"

"No."

He smiled and tossed the ends of his scarf back. It was a gesture that once made the Dipstickers' girl gang scream.

"Personally I think that's the best thing about it," he said. Then he too kissed her and was gone.

17

"Where's Charlie?" Jane asked when she returned to the back kitchen. Her parents were sitting there alone, having a drink. Even the dogs had gone.

"He went to bed," said Claire. "You know he has to get off at five to be home by the time his store opens."

"Oh," said Jane, feeling desolate. The holiday seemed to have come to an end while she wasn't looking. A weekend alone with her parents was certainly not what she'd had in mind.

"Would you like a drink?" Ben asked. "We're having brandy."

"Sure, Dad," said Jane. Now that Raz was gone, she might as well.

She took the glass he offered and sat on the hearth with her back to the fire. It had been a long time since she'd had a drink. Usually alcohol made her dizzy and sick to her stomach. Tonight she wished she could get drunk the way other people did. Maybe she'd forget the feeling she had of not belonging anywhere any more—not here and not with Raz either.

"It's too bad Raz had to go back tonight," said Ben, sitting down again. He had a big armchair that only he sat in. When he was out of town it remained unused: Dad's chair. "He seemed awfully wound up though," he added.

"I know," said Claire, "that business with the wine glass at dinner. That was so odd. All Tom wanted was to make it possible for him to join in the toast, and he was so rude about it."

Jane twisted the stem of her brandy snifter between her fingers. The fumes from the brandy were strong enough to make her high without even drinking a drop.

"Please don't talk about Raz in front of me," she said. "You know I don't like it."

"We're not criticizing, dear. We're only trying to understand."

"But you don't. That's just the point."

"Of course we understand," said Ben. "Lots of young men run into a little trouble with alcohol, but as long as they stay away from drugs, they straighten out eventually. That was the problem with Branwell. If he'd stuck to alcohol—if he hadn't gotten mixed up with opium—he would have been fine."

"Daddy, Branwell was an alcoholic. That's a plenty big enough problem to kill you all on its own."

"I think I probably know more about Branwell than you do, Jane."

"Fine. Let's change the subject. All right? I'm sick of alcoholism. It's all I ever hear about."

"All we were trying to say is that we're glad things are working out better for you and Raz, honey," said Claire. "You're such a beautiful girl with so much talent and energy. All we want is for you to be happy. You deserve the best that life has to offer."

"Thanks, Mom," said Jane. She took a big swallow of the brandy and it burned going down, like the compliment.

"Tomorrow you can help me in the shop for a while, if you'd like. I want you to see those wreaths, and you know there's a new knitting shop in the village. They have some beautiful yarns."

"All right. That sounds good."

Jane drank some more, and the brandy still burned, but this time she liked it. She might be sitting quietly by the fire with her parents, watching logs collapse into embers, but inside she was replaying the scene with Raz. Watching her life collapse around her. The brandy helped stop the shock. Cauterized the wounds. She drank it all down and then said: "I need to go to bed too."

"Of course you do, darling. It's been a long day, and you worked very hard," said Claire.

Jane stood up from the hearth and felt a rush of blood leave her head. When she bent down to give her mother a kiss, she lost her balance and fell into her lap. Claire put her arms around her and hugged her. They all laughed, but Jane didn't get up. It felt good to be in her mother's arms.

"Look, Daddy," said Claire. "I still have one baby I can cuddle with. Isn't that nice?"

18

Upstairs Jane saw a strip of light under Charlie's door. She tapped on it and said: "Charlie? Can I come in?"

There was no answer, but she heard the scrabble of dog claws on the hardwood floor, so she opened the door, and the dogs swarmed around her. Charlie himself was oblivious, lying on his bed with his eyes closed and headphones on. The air in the room was thick with marijuana smoke.

"Hey," she said, grabbing his foot and shaking it. "What're you listening to?"

He opened his eyes, blushed, and took off the headphones. "The Dipstickers," he said. "Tom had that demo we made in '67 transferred to cassette."

"Oh my God. I remember when you made that. Is it good?"

He shrugged, fluffed up the pillows under his head, and moved over so Jane could lie down next to him. Then he handed her the headphones and pressed "Play" on the cassette player.

The first thing she heard was the whine of Charlie's Fender and the wild thump, thump, thumping of Ricky on drums. Then Tom came in singing "Paint It Black" with an anger that pounded through the song, never letting up from beginning to end.

"Wow," she said, taking off the headphones. "I'd forgotten how intense Tom's singing was."

"Yeah. Then he was intense about music. Now he's intense about everything. Or nothing. I'm never sure which."

"Me either. Did you know Sheila told Joey about them and now he thinks they're finally going to get together again? He's even planning to move back home."

Charlie shook his head. "I don't think women are the answer to what ails Tom."

"What do you mean? Sheila's the love of his life."

He gave her a look and took a joint out of his shirt pocket. After he'd lit it and had taken a toke, he offered it to Jane, who took one too. Between the brandy and the dope, she was beginning to feel like her body was made of soft warm clay.

"I can't believe you still think in those terms," he said.

"Well, I can't believe you're turning into one of those women-are-the-root-of-all-evil guys."

"I'm not," he said.

"Good. I should hope not," she said, fixing the pillows more comfortably on her side of the bed. She was happy to be with Charlie, just the two of them. It was cozy to lie in the circle of lamplight created by the pin-up reading lamp, passing the joint back and forth, and listening to the snow beat against the window.

The rest of the room was shadowy and neat, except for Charlie's clothes thrown over a chair and an old blanket on the floor where the dogs had settled down in a heap. His desk was bare, but the bookshelves still held old favorites like Sherlock Holmes and H.G. Wells and his college philosophy texts.

Crammed in next to them was a row of battered folders that Jane recognized as his research for conscientious objector status. She supposed he kept them as a souvenir—a declaration of his intentions—since he had never had to file; by the time he was 18, the draft lottery had started, and he drew a high number.

When she put the headphones back on Tom was singing "In My Room." Another Beach Boys young, lost, and lonely favorite—but this one reminded her of the room next door that her mother kept clean and Tom never entered, so she gave the headphones back to Charlie.

"I'd rather listen to you," she said. "I'm so happy you've started playing again."

"It's not like before. It's just because I love it. I don't expect anything," said Charlie, but he switched off the cassette player and picked up the 12-string. When he strummed across the strings with a pick, the sound was big and warm. Jane turned on her side, propping her head on her hand.

"What do you want to hear?" he asked.

"Moby Grape. 'Someday'."

"As always," he said, but he adjusted his tuning and slowly began to pick out the wistful melody that she loved. To Jane, the song always seemed like a prayer, and her voice was barely more than a whisper as she sang along.

When it came to an end, they were both silent for a while. Then she said, "You know, I played that song over and over the day Tom left for Vietnam, as if it could make me less scared that I'd never see him again."

"Yeah, well, in some ways we never have," said Charlie.

"I know what you mean. He was always the leader before, you know. Ahead of us. But after that something stopped."

Charlie lit another joint and passed it to Jane. She was already stoned, but she took a toke anyway.

"You think Sheila will get him started again?"

Jane poked him with her elbow. "Maybe, anyway it's not a joke. You know what Mom said to me today? That we should've had more respect for Tom's decision to go in the Army. Like somehow the way things have turned out for him is our fault."

"That sounds like something she would come up with."

"I was so floored I couldn't even think what to say."

"I respected that it was his decision, but I thought he was nuts."

"I don't know what I thought. Mostly I was so surprised. I just assumed we were all on the same side."

"Well, we weren't. Anyway, as much as anything else I think he hoped the Army would get him straight."

"What do you mean?"

"He was freaked out by how things were going. The band. The drugs. The drinking. All of it. He was looking for a way to slam on the brakes."

"Wow, that was an idea that bombed."

"Right."

"I'll never forget the look in his eyes when we met him at the airport. Like he knew in a split second from our faces that we were all so far removed from what he'd been through there was no getting back to us."

"I'm sure all he was thinking about was how glad he was to have gotten home alive."

"Well, you weren't there, and that's the way I remember it. Even after all these years. Suddenly we were strangers to him."

"That always happens. I mean, think of all he'd seen and been through. Shit, I'm not the same person I was the last time you saw me, and nothing actually happened to me. Just a quick, bloodless amputation."

"God," said Jane rolling over to sit on the edge of the bed with her head in her hands. "Everything is so fucked up." She was beginning to have a severe headache.

Charlie got up too and put his guitar back in its case.

"C," she said hesitantly, as he flipped the latches shut. "Was it really like that? I mean did Maura really leave without giving you any reason?"

"No, I know the reason," he said.

When it was clear he wasn't going to add anything else, Jane said, "But you really don't know where they went?"

"Right."

Jane looked into his sad eyes and sighed.

"Well, whatever happened, I will always love you. For whatever that's worth," she said.

"Thanks, J," he said. "I love you too."

"I wish you didn't have to go back tomorrow. If you stayed, we could hang out together for a while. Everyone's rushed away this year, and now I'll be stuck with Mom and Dad."

"That's your choice, Janer. Sticking with Raz is your choice too."

"Oh, I know," she said. She stood up, and the sudden change made her feel dizzy. She needed some air. "Everyone always says that, but it never seems that simple to me."

19

Charlie said he had to get to bed, so Jane went downstairs and, in the silent hallway, prepared to go out. It was still snowing, but the wind had dropped.

She was glad that she'd had the foresight to bring a pack of cigarettes from home. As she crossed the front yard, she took one out and lit it. The smoke burned her throat in the cold air, but it felt good. Really good. She didn't know why she'd ever thought of stopping.

She walked briskly away from the house, following the same route she and Raz had taken only the night before. Then the neighboring houses had been dark, but tonight everyone was celebrating. Lights blazed, and smoke curled from every chimney.

Jane hurried past them, heading for the pond in the woods at the end of the street. It was only a small pond, not deep or clear enough for swimming, but a great place to skate. She wanted to see if it was frozen yet. Skate-ready, Tom used to called it when they were young.

The air bit her face and hands, but she didn't want to turn back. She wanted to be cold; it distracted her from thinking about Raz and Tom and Charlie. About Maura and Chrissy and her parents. She used to believe her family would always be there at the center of her life, but now she couldn't begin to picture where any of them were going. Where they would be this time next year?

She hadn't been kidding when she told Raz she had no idea what it would be like to be on her own. Twelve years ago, she had stepped right from her parents' front door into his arms. All the times she had thought of leaving, it had been about him. It had never been about her. What she wanted. Who she was.

When she reached the thin band of woods, she could see the pond, and she crunched through the snow, frozen sticks, and leaves to the bank. Someone must have been there earlier in the day because the snow had been cleared away, and the ice gleamed in the moonlight.

She had never skated there alone at night before, but the ice looked solid. She tapped the surface with her boot and listened hard. Then she stepped out onto the frozen pond, pushed off with one foot, and let herself begin to slide.

20

Raz had begun to feel better the minute the Percys' house was out of sight. Snow flew straight into his headlights, so that all he could see ahead were its mesmerizing patterns. The surface of the road was slick, but the heavy car pounded along undeterred.

He made good time getting through Syracuse and out into the countryside. Almost no one else was on the road and he liked that. He knew he was driving faster than was safe, but he didn't care.

I'm on my path, he thought. I can go anywhere.

Then he remembered what his father used to say when they went hiking in the woods. "Sometimes you have to stand still to see which way your compass is pointing."

1993: Leaving Vietnam

1993: Leaving Vietnam

1

The night before I left Chicago, I put on an old Army t-shirt of Walter's, opened a bottle of Wild Turkey, and watched *Full Metal Jacket* and *Woodstock* back to back. I didn't run this gauntlet to stir up old memories. They had already been stirred up.

Ever since the Pearse Foundation called to offer me an assignment documenting their first projects in Vietnam, I had hardly thought about anything else. Over the past few years, freelancing as a photographer in Asia had become my specialty, and my assignments had taken me to some of its most remote areas, but Vietnam had always been off limits. Closed behind the doors that slammed shut to the West in 1975.

The Foundation sent me reports so that I could I prepare for the trip, but pages of dry prose and statistics couldn't tell me what, after all these years, I still burned to know. When I finally fell into bed that night, my bags packed and standing ready by the door, my dreams were filled with exploding bombs, anti-aircraft fire, Richie Havens singing "Freedom," and Country Joe McDonald inciting 400,000 people to shout, not "Peace now!" but "Fuck! Fuck! Fuck!"

Three days later I was on a plane circling the luminous green rice paddies and twisting rivers of the Red River delta. Its serene beauty surprised me, and my heartbeat quickened as houses and trees became visible, then cars winding along threadlike roads, and the dark shapes of water buffalo. Finer and finer details gathered before my eyes like a developing photograph as we rushed toward the ground. This was the world as Walter last glimpsed it.

I closed my eyes and clutched the arms of my seat as if the old Vietnam Airlines plane might suddenly blow apart, but it didn't. We bounced as we hit the ground, shuddered, then bounced again. The engines roared, and the brakes squealed, but we landed in one piece and, finally, slowed to a stop.

I opened my eyes and saw Henry Berenger looking at me curiously.

"You're completely white, Sarah," he said. He was already waiting to disembark, computer bag in hand, unruffled and professional, but Henry is English. To him this was just another arrival in a third-world country—one of many we'd shared working together over the years.

"Are you sure you're ready for this?" he asked.

I looked out the window at the squat concrete building marked: Noi Bai International Airport—Hanoi.

"Which this do you mean?" I asked, but the line of passengers had pushed him down the narrow aisle between the seats, and he didn't hear me.

I hurried after him and, at the door of the plane, hit a wall of heat hotter than Chicago at its worst. The heavy air smelled of exhaust and rotting fruit, and it was so humid, it dragged like water around my arms and legs. When I finally touched down in Vietnam, the sizzling pavement burned my feet with every step.

Inside the crowded terminal, overhead fans stirred the air without cooling it, and the sound of chattering voices echoed off the ceiling. Like most communist country airports, it had a Spartan look. The gray walls were unadorned except for a single advertisement: a large color poster for the newly reopened Metropole Hotel. This was no doubt a sign of *doi moi*—Vietnam's move toward a market economy and the West—because it showed rooms lavishly decorated with antiques and a garden restaurant full of Western and Asian customers. It looked completely out of place, but then, in that crowd of Thai, Vietnamese, and Chinese travelers, so did Henry and I. We were too tall, too pale, and too gaudy with our Anglo-Saxon blond and red hair.

Soldiers stood at intervals along the wall watching the crowd, as we waited in one line after another. There was a time in my life when I enjoyed provoking soldiers and policemen. I liked to try to break through their stolid composure and force them to see me. Deal with me and my opinions. It was a technique that had landed me in jail a few times, but I was proud of that. If they were law, I wanted to be outlaw.

I had a Minox "spy" camera left over from those days, and I wished it were in my pocket, as Henry and I waited for a uniformed clerk to stamp our visas. My fingers itched to photograph those soldiers, so clean and neat, with stiff smooth cheeks, and starchy brown uniforms. They had never crawled through the jungle, driven by patriotism, pride, and terror like their fathers and grandfathers. Their eyes moved over us as calmly and methodically as surveillance cameras. Already you could see in their faces, the bureaucrats they would become.

Henry turned to me and said: "I hope you're not thinking what I think you're thinking." He believed you should never even look at soldiers because it encouraged them to notice you and what you were doing.

I smiled. "There's no harm in thinking, is there?"

"I'm not so sure about that," he said.

"That's because you're a writer," I said.

He laughed, and for a moment our eyes met and sparked, but then he turned away.

In any case, the Minox was in my luggage, so I occupied myself with fixing my hair: twisting it into a clip so it was up and off my sweating neck. As I waited, I studied the familiar landscape of Henry's broad, but slender, shoulders and wondered if it had been a mistake to combine the old problem of Walter with the new problem of Henry on this trip. Fuck.

Fuck! Fuck! Fuck!

2

Outside the terminal a mob of luggage carriers, vendors, taxi drivers, and passengers vied for each other's attention. We scanned the crowd for our driver and found him at the edge of the sidewalk holding a printed card that said "Pearse Foundation". With a flash of silver teeth, he welcomed us to Vietnam.

By the time we had loaded our bags into the car and settled ourselves in the back seat, Henry had begun to try out his phrase-book Vietnamese on the driver, Han, who answered every question in English, but always with the same three words: "Very good, sir." Henry was more comfortable than I was with such vestigial remains of colonialism, so I let him do the talking and concentrated on looking out the window.

The first time I ever plunged out into the streets of Bangkok with my camera, I fell in love with Asia—the noise, the faces, the smells, the color, the ancient and classical tumbled together with the tawdry and new. I don't know why I felt so at home there. I grew up in one of those all-white Chicago suburbs where the lawns were never allowed to get more than two inches long and a living room never looked like anyone lived in it. Yet I did feel at home, and I'd fallen in love with every other country I'd worked in too—eventually. With some, like India and Nepal, it was love at first sight; but with others, like China, the attraction grew and deepened slowly; and, with still others, like Bangladesh, love mixed with frustration, irritation, and regret.

But I first traveled to those places with an open mind. No big preconceptions. Here that was impossible. Vietnam had burst into my consciousness when I was in high school with monks on fire in the street, blood-stained banners, shouting men, and arguments about the domino theory and the range of presidential power. It was a TV series, starring Walter Cronkite and Dan Rather, LBJ and Ho Chi Minh, Abbie Hoffman and J. Edgar Hoover. It was my brother Walter, changed overnight from a boy into a soldier, and then, within months, gone. "Ashes, ashes, we all fall down." Nothing in my life was ever the same again.

So what struck me first were the familiar, ordinary things. The blueness of the sky. The heavy heat and the scratchiness of the worn car seat. My own sweat on my skin. The breeze blowing loose hairs back from my face. The cacophony of traffic noise.

The edge of the road was bordered by new box-like concrete houses, but beyond I could glimpse the landscape that I'd seen from the air: the centuries-old tableau of farmers in conical straw hats tilling their rice paddies with plows drawn by water buffalo.

Closer to the city, the noise and crowds grew more intense, and Han barreled along, honking his horn continually at the vehicles, people, and animals all determined to own the road. Rice paddies gave way to ramshackle tin-roofed houses and concrete buildings that rose from bamboo scaffolding to mingle with dilapidated temples and the molding yellow stucco mansions of the French.

Where we ended up was a neighborhood that looked like a cross between Asia and New Orleans. Trees thick with bright orange flowers arched over the roads to create a shady, almost peaceful, atmosphere. Rows of once-elegant 19th-century houses with tile roofs and filigreed iron balconies had become festooned with sagging electrical wires, TV antennae, and laundry.

We entered a walled compound with a gravel drive that encircled a dry neglected fountain. The main building—white stucco with tall arched windows and wooden shutters—looked deserted, and Han delivered us at the front door of a newer annex—square and concrete like all the recent architecture seemed to be. He piled our bags on the steps and then with a salute and a spray of gravel, left us.

By the time we had registered and climbed three flights of hot dimly lit stairs to our rooms, we were both dripping with sweat. On our last few trips we had requested adjoining rooms, but this time we were only neighbors. I dropped my bags outside my door, waiting to see if Henry would invite me in, but he didn't. All he said was: "Shall we have a look around in about an hour?"

and then he shut his door behind him before I could answer.

In my room, the air was hot and damp as an incubator, although an air-conditioner wheezed and dripped water in a steady stream down the wall. I left my bags in a heap and sat down on the low wooden palette that served as a bed. My body felt like a bag of sand, and I was suddenly tired almost to the point of hallucinating.

From the next room I could hear Henry moving around, unpacking, and then the rush of water as he turned on the shower. I knew I should be unpacking too, but I didn't get up. It felt good to sit still—to begin to put the long trip behind me.

The urge to lie down became irresistible, and my head hit the pillow as if it had been thrown in one long arc half way around the world. This time, no bombs, no music, not even Walter, disturbed my sudden damp dark sleep.

The sound of knocking came from far away at first. I thought I said "Just a minute" but maybe I only dreamed that I did, because the knocking continued, and, when I finally opened the door, Henry had his credit card out, ready to force my lock. He shoved it quickly into his pocket, looking embarrassed, took in my rumpled bed and said, "You'll regret that."

"I couldn't help it," I said, trying to rub the grogginess out of my eyes. "This is all a little overwhelming for me."

"Which this?" he asked, and I gave him a look.

Without thinking, I began to strip off my clothes then noticed the cornered-dog expression on his face and grabbed a change of clothes to take with me into the bathroom.

"Sorry," I said, but fatigue made me resentful. I wanted things to be easy between us, not a constant dance to avoid hurt feelings. I thought he might leave, but, when I came out, damp and hot, he was still there, standing with his arms crossed tightly, scowling at the television.

I recognized the music instantly, but it was hard to identify the lurid pink blurs on the screen. "Is that really Mick Jagger?" I asked.

"Himself," said Henry, but this was not the Jagger who first demanded "Satisfaction" when we were young. This was a glittery Jagger, slathered with make up, who gyrated back and forth across the stage, still whining after all these years.

"God, that's weird," I said and sat down on the hard bed. "I never imagined *doi moi* as The Rolling Stones and the Metropole Hotel. I mean, that's great. Real progress. After all, what more does a struggling country need?"

"Us," said Henry, snapping off the TV. "Don't forget, we're *doi moi* too."

3

I had been surprised when the Pearse Foundation told me Henry agreed to be the writer for this job.

"I know you like to work together," the communications director told me, "and the chairman loved the annual report you guys did for the India projects last year."

"Great," I said, but what I really meant was "Oh, great."

I usually make a point of not getting involved with men I work with, so Henry was either an exception or a mistake, depending on how you looked at it. We had become lovers on a trip to Japan three years ago, and, in my opinion, sex had added an enjoyable dimension to our professional collaborations. Everything went well until the trip to India for that annual report, when Henry upped the ante by asking me if I would consider moving to London to live with him, and I said no.

Our relationship had frozen solid ever since, and, beyond the communication required to complete our assignment, I had never heard from him at all.

Now, as we walked along the shady streets of Hanoi, I felt the change sharply. I wanted to go slow, let the place seep into me, but Henry's pace was quick, a little impatient, and he kept his hands in his pockets, elbows out like protective gear.

"Are we rushing to get somewhere, Henry?" I finally asked him.

He pretended to be surprised. "I thought you wanted to eat."

"I do, but I'm not in danger of starving in the next half hour."

"I think we should get our bearings while it's still light," he said and set off again at a speed only fractionally slower than before.

Dusk had begun to close in, and, as if someone were turning dials, the light faded, the pounding heat eased, and a rackety chorus of tree frogs and crickets grew so loud it nearly drowned out the traffic noise. The sidewalks became crowded with women cooking dinner over small propane stoves, so we had to take to the street with the other pedestrians, dodging bicycles, cyclos, and cars.

I didn't hurry myself. Even though the distance between us sometimes stretched half a block or more, there was no danger that I would lose sight of Henry. We didn't see any other Westerners, and his white shirt and fair hair glowed in the dim light like a beacon before me.

Everywhere the influence of the French occupation was evident, but I could see no sign of the Americans and their heavy bombing. In fact, it was hard to imagine that time, walking along the languid, peaceful streets. We ended up at Hoan Kiem Lake, one of several large lakes in the city. There, light from storefront shops and art galleries spilled into the street, and the park at the lake's edge was crowded with people out to enjoy the embracing warmth of the evening.

The cozy domesticity of our neighborhood had impressed me, but I was really surprised to discover that Hanoi was a city of painters, as well as soldiers and bureaucrats. Even Henry's pace was slowed down by the number of galleries, and I caught up with him in one dusty shop, gazing up at rows of paintings that were hung all the way to the ceiling.

"Did you know about this?" I asked him.

He squatted down to peer at a street scene hung low on the wall. "I read something," he said, "but I had no idea."

"Look at this one," I said. Fingering through bins full of watercolors and woodcuts, I'd found a large watercolor that perfectly captured the light at dusk, the tiny glow of cooking fires, the gathering of families on the street. You could almost hear the frogs and crickets.

We wandered in and out of several galleries, and a profusion of street scenes and landscapes told the same story over and over. Of green rice paddies. The farmer watering his land by hand. The boy and the water buffalo. The bicycle-filled street. No Guernica there, but the accumulation—the repetition—of images also had a power to convey the message: "Remember this."

By the time we finally stopped to eat, Henry's elbows had relaxed a little, and we were talking gingerly about what we'd been doing for the past six months. He had been cloistered in London with the phone unplugged, he said, working on a history of tuberculosis. I said the winter had been slow for me. A patchwork of small, uninteresting jobs.

"I almost took a wedding job, and you know things have to be really bad for me to consider that," I said.

"I thought I'd go mad if I spent another day in my flat," he said.

For dinner, we picked a *pho* stand by the lake with three child-sized tables on the sidewalk. The menu was a blackboard; the kitchen, a battered kettle full of soup steaming over a coal fire. A toothless old woman ladled out two bowls of *pho ga*—a fragrant chicken soup—and set them down in front of us.

Henry began to eat right away, expertly pulling up noodles with his chopsticks. I was reminded of the first time we ate together—how surprised I was that someone so blond, so public-school-looking, could eat so fast with chopsticks. I sat watching him, until he said: "I thought you were hungry."

"I am," I said, and picked up my own bowl. We ate in silence for a while then I asked him "Is that why you took this job then? To get out of your flat?"

He looked at me over the rim of his bowl. "Partly. Why?"

"I don't know. I guess I was a little surprised."

He shrugged. "It's a good job, and I wanted to see Vietnam. I suppose you came because of your brother."

"Yes," I said, "and the job."

"I have no intention of reopening old questions, if that's what you're really asking." His face suddenly became as frozen and angry as when we parted in Bombay.

The sharpness of his emotion was like a sudden elbow jab. "No, I didn't imagine that you did," I said.

"Good. Then we understand each other," he said.

Possibly this was his idea of a joke.

4

Back at the hotel, we said good night at arm's length. Then I was alone again in my room, exhausted but wide awake. Outside the cricket and frog chorus had reached a new pitch. Inside the air smelled of insecticide.

I don't mind being alone. I live alone all through the school year, while my daughter Wendy is in San Francisco with her father, and, for the most part, I like it that way. I'm free to travel and work whatever hours I need or want to. In the summer, when Wendy comes to Chicago, it always takes us a week or so to get used to each other again, but the time is special and we enjoy it.

These were only a few of the reasons I gave Henry for doubting that I could adjust to living with him. The problem wasn't with him. The problem was Wendy. The problem was me.

Still, I had missed him, and I especially missed him now when he was right next door. I had gotten used to the casual intimacy of living together in hotels, the seamless transitions from work to pleasure and back again. I had forgotten how unforgivingly solitary a hotel room can make you feel.

But I wasn't whinging, as Henry would say. I hung my clothes in the meager closet and set out the few personal things I bring with me on every trip—a square of red embroidered cloth from my first trip to Thailand, a photograph of Wendy, another of Walter and me at a swim meet when we were children, and a small bronze statue of Ganesh—the Hindu god who governs luck and guides new adventures. That done I had made the place my own.

Then I sat cross-legged on the bed to check over my equipment: my Nikon and the Minox, which I carried more like a rabbit's foot than a camera, and also another camera that I'd brought with me this time. A Rollei 35 box camera that my parents gave Walter for his 18th birthday.

I couldn't even look at the Rollei without recalling Walter's excitement that day. The way his dark hair flopped over when he bent to look through the viewfinder. The concentration in his fingers as he adjusted the settings. The grin when he'd completed a shot.

He had brought the camera here with him, and, after he was killed, it was sent back with his other things. Two years went by before my father had the courage to develop the pictures he'd taken. I don't know what he expected to find, but the film had degraded, and all that was left were some blurred shots of Army tents and soldiers and one close up of a thin, frightened brown dog.

Even after I became a professional photographer, my father wouldn't let me have the Rollei. It was the closest he ever came to telling me that he couldn't forgive the way I had abandoned my parents and all they stood for in the wake of Walter's death.

It didn't matter now. He and my mother both died in the 1980s and I, the prodigal daughter, had inherited everything. The house with the perfect lawn. The untouched living room. The studio portraits that lined the stairs of a pink-cheeked boy and a red-haired girl—who looked like Disneyland versions of us even at the time they were taken.

I had still never touched the Rollei, but I planned to give it to Wendy for her 18th birthday later in the summer—a kind of present from the uncle she'd never had a chance to know—so I'd had it cleaned and serviced. This seemed like the right time and place to test it out.

It was after 2 a.m. when I decided I had to at least try to sleep. I lay down and turned off the light, but instead of becoming more sleepy I felt more alert than ever. It was very hot and the unfamiliar bed provided a selection of uncomfortable places to lie. In one, I thought about what I'd seen that day and the unexpected beauty of Vietnam. In another, I worried about the work ahead that week and whether the distance between Henry and me could ever be bridged. Rolling onto my back brought me to my 19-year-old brother, arriving here with 13 months of war ahead of him. And me at home, sending him letters and messages from everyone in the neighborhood, including the cats and dogs, sending music, sending food, trying with all my might to hold onto him, and failing. Utterly failing. In a burst of fire and falling debris, he had left us.

After a while, I got up. Our rooms opened onto a corridor that was like a verandah overlooking the compound. The cement floor was still warm under my bare feet. I listened at Henry's door for any sign that he was awake and heard nothing.

Down below, a guard sat at the gate, smoking. The old white stucco building with its elegant arched windows stood like a sad ghost in the moonlight. The crickets and frogs had at last gone to sleep, leaving the starry night hot and silent.

5

Sometimes work is the only thing that makes sense to me. That's why when Henry knocked on my door the next morning I had been sitting on the edge of my bed, fully dressed, for more than an hour. I needed to work.

"How are you?" he asked.

"I feel lousy," I said. "But at least it's morning." I picked up my camera bag.

"Shall we go then?" he replied, matching my abrupt tone. The corridor was narrow, and he moved quickly ahead of me. Giving me his back.

We shared a silent breakfast in the hotel dining room. As I picked at some greasy tasteless eggs, I reviewed all the reasons why making this trip had been a bad idea and calmed myself by counting the days until I could go home. Finally I pushed my plate aside and gulped down a cup of tea so bitter even milk and sugar couldn't sweeten it.

In the over-air-conditioned lobby I rechecked my camera bag for film and spare batteries while Henry stared into a large tank of koi fish that stared back at him. A sour-looking woman in a green uniform stood behind the reception desk, speaking rapidly in Vietnamese into a telephone. The air outside was so hot that moisture condensed on the inside of the windows, turning the view of the courtyard into a green blur. I stood near the door, as if that would summon the car.

At last an aging black sedan drove in, and a young man in a grey suit jumped out. "Good morning!" he said in English as he shook each of us by the hand. He had a round pleasant face and a firm grip. "I'm so sorry to keep you waiting. Our traffic gets more terrible every day," he said, his tone full of pride over this dubious result of progress.

He introduced himself as Mr. Hoang, an employee of the Ministry of Health and explained that he would be our escort and translator as he ushered us to the car. Han was our driver again, and, when we attempted to say good morning in Vietnamese, he replied "Very good, sir," threw the car into gear, and charged out of the compound into the street.

My spirits began to lift as soon as we were on our way. Nothing makes me happier than knowing I am going to spend the day taking photographs. Especially in a new place, and especially a new place in Asia. Early in our relationship Henry remarked that he thought photographers used cameras to insulate themselves from life, and I disagreed. A camera slows you down. You see whole layers of expression, color, light, shape, relationship, and meaning that you might otherwise miss, caught between living in your head and rushing through the outside world.

"You're put off because you're on the other side of the tool," I said. "It's like looking at a diver in a face mask. You can't see him well, so you think he can't see you, but you're wrong. I never forget a place or a person I have photographed."

He was not convinced until we did an experiment that contributed to our best work together. We went for a walk—me with my camera, and Henry with the little notebook he carries—and we recorded what we saw. Later we compared the results: What we had both seen, as well as what we had each missed, and the eloquence and efficiency of our separate media. The synchronicities between us were surprising. Inspiring.

I would not have guessed that our vision would match so well. Henry gave off the impression of a well-brought up, educated Englishman—all good posture and clean fingernails. He was the kind of man who looks like he carries a comb, but he doesn't. His hair just knows how to stay neat, no matter what. I, on the other hand, was born wrinkled, curly, and uncontrolled. The camera focused me as much as I focused it; and words forced Henry to reveal the man behind that well-schooled facade.

This morning Henry looked starched. As we crossed the city, passing through lush parks and crowded street markets, we sat side by side like two pillars and listened to Mr. Hoang tell us in clipped English about the places we were to visit that day. I wondered how the work was going to go—whether or not we would be able to recapture that rhythm of working together when we were so out of rhythm ourselves.

The Pearse Foundation, which was funded by the fortune the Pearse family made in rubber and tea, specializes in supporting health care and education in Southeast Asia. Our first stop was a storefront clinic near the Red River. The Foundation provided aid for several such clinics, but this one was still only about as big and as well equipped as an ice cream stand. A line of people waited in the hot morning sun to see the doctor on duty. They stood or squatted on the pavement, catching shade where they could.

Mr. Hoang introduced us to the doctor, a frail harried man with a deep scar on his cheek. He showed us his meager store of drugs and the tiny area where a lab worker sat hunched over a microscope. "This is most excellent," pronounced Mr. Hoang, but the doctor, shifting his eyes from us to the waiting patients, failed to smile on cue.

I photographed him at that moment, when he would look caught and exposed by the camera, but that was the old newshound in me, not the person hired to document the Pearse Foundation's success. What Pearse wanted me to see was a flash of hope in the doctor's eyes, not the fatigue and worry that drained the color from his face. What I wanted was to capture both. For me, that's where the story was, and I concentrated on finding that balance point.

As Henry interviewed the doctor, with Mr. Hoang translating, I moved on to photograph some of the patients and then took the required shot of Mr. Hoang and the doctor standing on the front stoop. Mr. Hoang smiled broadly, his shoulders thrown back and squared, but the doctor still looked uncomfortable and anxious for us to be gone.

From the clinic, we went to a slum neighborhood where a vaccination program was being held in a school. A large crowd of mothers with babies and young children had shown up, but nothing was happening because the people with the drugs hadn't arrived. Everyone was bored with waiting, so my camera and I provided a welcome distraction. Mothers held up their babies to be photographed, and the older children giggled and stared at me. It was hard to say which they found more fascinating, my curly red hair or the tiny image I showed them in the viewfinder.

The heat and humidity increased hourly, and my clothes became soaked with sweat, but I didn't mind. It felt good, the way it feels good to sweat when you're exercising hard. I was happy to see that Henry had become more relaxed too, asking the children their names and amusing them with his attempts to speak Vietnamese. When the health workers finally showed up, there were tears and howls of outrage over being vaccinated, but at least part of the morning had been fun.

After a quick lunch, we moved on to a large hospital where we were met at the door by a delegation of white-coated doctors and health workers. They welcomed us in the impersonal, but effusive way people greet you when you represent money. The hospital director, Dr. Nguyen, was middle-aged and full of energy and confidence. His manner was almost triumphal as he led us on a tour of the hospital complex, originally built by and for the French. The imposing stucco buildings formed a quadrangle around a grassy space where tall palm trees grew and a Vietnamese flag slashed scarlet and yellow against the blue sky.

Whatever the hospital had once been, the stairs were now cracked and worn, and the cavernous hallways lit only by the occasional bare bulb hanging from the ceiling. On each ward, thirty or more iron beds lined the walls with a single sink at the end. A fan slowly turned the air coming in from the open windows. Patients slept on straw mats laid over the wooden planks that served as their mattresses. Their meager possessions—a red plastic bowl, straw slippers, a spare shirt—were bundled together on the floor under their beds. Compared to a hospital in the United States, it was a bleak scene, but it was by no means the worst hospital Henry and I had ever visited.

We went to work dogged by Dr. Nguyen who spoke good English and so offered commentary on everything. Did we understand that they were saving hundreds of children who, a few years ago, would have died? Did we see that his lab had new equipment? This was an important innovation made possible by the Pearse Foundation. Did we notice how clean everything was?

How could I miss it, I wanted to say—the disinfectant fumes made my eyes water so much that I could hardly see what I was doing—but I didn't say anything, and I tried not to find him irritating. He was fighting for his hospital as he had once, no doubt, fought for his country. From all sides. And with persistence.

When I stopped to photograph an emaciated woman who sat at a table swallowing a stack of pills one by one, Dr. Nguyen startled me by grabbing my arm and announcing: "She is receiving here exactly the same tuberculosis treatment that Bill Clinton would get."

I looked up from my lens and said, "That's marvelous. You're really doing an amazing job here." There was a pause during which he weighed my sincerity then he nodded curtly and let go of my arm.

After the tour, we sat in a conference room around a long table, drinking tea out of little battered china cups and listening to presentations by the head of surgery, the lab director, and others. They spoke in spurts, waiting for Mr. Hoang to translate, and their faces grew shiny with the effort to convey to us the importance of what they were doing and the help The Pearse Foundation was giving them.

The painstaking progress they were making against disease, poverty, and population growth was charted on carefully drawn graphs. "We are a poor country," they said over and over, but their pride—in the clean, but dilapidated building, in their ancient equipment, in the tidy shelves of battered patient files—nearly overruled the meaning of the phrase.

Their voices droned on in the muggy heat. Henry's head nodded and then jerked up as he wrote, and I stood up to take some photos so that I wouldn't fall asleep myself.

Years ago, when I worked for Make Peace and graduated from mimeographing anti-war flyers to taking pictures for their newspaper, I was determined to be on the front lines of change. By that I meant big dramatic change like revolution or the end of the war and nothing less would do.

Back then I would have thought taking pictures of doctors lined up in front of a hospital was a complete sell-out. But working in Asia I had learned that you had to look closely to see change. It took a careful eye, and I believed that, however mundane, my work contributed a thread to its fabric. So even though I was dizzy with heat and jet lag, I did not fidget. I listened. I watched. And I tried, with my camera, to capture what I saw.

6

Once I started to notice the war damage, I saw it everywhere. On our second day we became stuck in a gridlock of motorbikes on our way from one appointment to another. I was looking idly out the window thinking about when we would stop for lunch, when I realized that through a gap between market stalls I could see a long stretch of brick-strewn rubble. A whole block of buildings had once stood behind the newer haphazard structures.

I leaned forward and tapped Mr. Hoang on the arm, interrupting his conversation with Henry comparing Britain's National Health and Vietnam's communal health system.

"Excuse me," I said, "what is that place—behind the stalls?"

Mr. Hoang didn't even have to glance out the window to know what I was referring to. The dark eyes that met mine were carefully expressionless. "That was Kham Thien."

"Kham Thien?" The name sounded familiar, and then I remembered. "The street that was bombed by mistake in 1972?"

I could tell he was surprised I knew, but he just nodded, and we all fell silent regarding the vanished neighborhood. I was shocked, but Henry had grown up in post-war London. Bombed-out buildings were nothing new to him; so, after a pause to see if Mr. Hoang had anything further to say, he quietly resumed talking about the difficulty of keeping track of TB patients during their long treatment. Mr. Hoang relaxed visibly and picked up his end of the discussion.

I sat back in my seat, camera bag on my lap, a quiet, detached professional on the job, but what I was thinking about was the day we heard the news about the Christmas bombings. I had spent the holiday with my parents for the first time since Walter died and I left home. It had been a failure—everything my mother had done to recreate our family Christmases from the familiar ornaments on the tree to the sweet potatoes with marshmallows on top had made me want to scream "Wake up! That's over!" Despite my parents' protests, I had left right after dinner and gone to the offices of Make Peace to work. There was always something to do there, and the rhythmic thumping of the mimeograph machines comforted me more than watching *It's a Wonderful Life*.

We hadn't expected the bombings anymore than the Vietnamese had, but Nixon was impatient to get the communists back to the conference table in Paris. I guess he thought bombing Hanoi and Haiphong was the way to do it. We hadn't bombed the capital directly before and, at Make Peace, we went right to work putting out a special issue of our newspaper about it.

I joined a candlelight vigil that night, but even though I shivered in the frigid wind and chanted about peace until my lips were blue, I couldn't come close to understanding what happened here. The night raked with the noise of jets. The sudden collapse of building after building. The fire. The heat. The confusion. Pain. And death.

The motorbikes finally moved and we continued on, but suddenly the traces of war became visible to me everywhere. Blocks of buildings all bearing post-war construction dates. The twenty-year-old heaps of rubble. White stupas commemorating the war dead. They were as much a part of the fabric of the city as the French colonial architecture, and life flowed on around them. Like a plane bouncing as it lands, with each sighting I became more fully present. Connecting a past, seen only in black and white, with the technicolor present.

Mr. Hoang had described the law school we were going to visit as "very distinguished," so I was surprised when we pulled into a dusty driveway between two battered high rises. We got out of the car, blinking in the bright sun. Mr. Hoang looked excited and straightened his tie as a diminutive man in a rumpled black suit came out to meet us.

"This is Professor Ly," he said, "Director of the college. Professor Ly, Ms. Shepherd and Mr. Berenger of The Pearse Foundation."

Prof. Ly greeted us in English with a grave courtesy, and Henry made an effort not to appear to be stooping as he shook his hand.

No classes were scheduled that day, so our footsteps sounded loud as we toured an empty building. Prof. Ly showed us every floor, but it didn't take long to get the picture. The future leaders of Vietnam were being educated in buildings with broken windows and walls buckling from mildew. I photographed one room where a single computer sat on a desk, covered with dust, its cables dangling in the air.

Prof. Ly was unapologetic about the state of the college. In the kind of quiet voice that commands attention, he told us, "Students from all over the country compete for the privilege of coming here."

As we walked across to the other building, he said: "I know what it is like at your great universities. Here we have no fine buildings. No green lawns. Only students and teachers. Your help," he said, with a quick, almost unwilling smile, "will provide us with the only other thing we must have. Books."

He opened the door and showed us into the library, a long room crowded with students, even though it was a holiday. In fact the students appeared to outnumber the books on the shelves, and some of them studied from a shared text.

"You see my point," said Prof. Ly.

I walked around quietly taking a few shots; then he asked a couple of students to come outside and talk to us. Prof. Ly introduced them as Kim and Danh, the leaders of the student government. Kim was about twenty, very thin with wide-set eyes, lank black hair, and a small defiant mouth. She hugged her arms to her narrow flat chest, but Danh held himself very straight and shook hands briskly as if he had practiced for just such a meeting.

"It's a pleasure to meet you," he said in English.

Henry explained the purpose of our visit, and the students listened with expressions that varied from excitement to suspicion. They reminded me of Wendy—how sometimes she had to define herself by not approving of a single thing I said or did. On the other hand, why shouldn't these young people be suspicious? The last time American advisors began to show up in Vietnam, they presaged the beginning of 20 years of war.

When Mr. Hoang explained that the Pearse Foundation had given money to buy books for the library, Danh nodded enthusiastically. "We need to know the laws of other countries, because we will write the laws that will shape our country's future."

I concentrated on my light meter to avoid smiling. He already talked more like an ambassador than a college student.

"Where are you from?" Mr. Hoang asked, encouraging Danh to tell his story, and translated when the boy switched back to Vietnamese to describe how he came from a family of farmers in a small village. He was the youngest of six children and the first to obtain a college education.

"Unlike in the West, here a great man may still come from nothing," he said.

I could tell Kim was irritated by Danh. She wanted her share of attention, but he talked on and on about his heroic journey from village boy to law student. Finally she mastered her shyness and spoke up, dropping her hands into small clenched fists. "In Vietnam," she said, "we are taught that we can overcome any obstacle." Her eyes flashed from him to us. I took her photograph, which made her blush, but she stood up to me, glaring at the camera, and I shot several more pictures of her. A small defiant figure against the crumbling facade of her college. I was sure they would turn out better than the ones of Danh, the boy diplomat.

Prof. Ly had to leave for a meeting, but he had asked one of his law professors to join us for lunch. Prof. Ngo was a pockmarked, sharp-eyed man, who been involved in writing Vietnam's constitution. We crowded around a table in a small restaurant, where a young man lay sleeping on the table next to us. The food was delicious though—soup fragrant with mushrooms and spring onions, platters of small baked crabs, salt-and-pepper chicken, eel in a thick spicy sauce, paper-thin pancakes, and mounds of fresh greens, including basil and cilantro and other varieties that I didn't recognize.

Henry and I sat opposite Prof. Ngo and Mr. Hoang. At first, I imagined this was going to be something like lunching with Thomas Jefferson, but the Moscow-educated lawyer was not a pleasant man. He treated Mr. Hoang like a servant, disregarded me, and sized up Henry with an arrogant, disdainful look.

Henry was unfazed. He'd read history at Oxford, and he'd learned how to handle arrogance and disdain from the best of them. He also was more familiar with the Vietnamese constitution than Prof. Ngo expected.

Like Kim, I did not take being ignored lightly, so I also peppered him with questions about the state of the country and the effect *doi moi* was having.

"You Westerners always think democracy is the answer to every problem," Prof. Ngo said in a patronizing tone. "But you do not understand the Confucian mind. We are used to a single voice of authority. That's why communism is the best form of government for us. It is the dual party system that is alien, not our own."

"We will not make the same mistakes as Eastern Europe. We will succeed where other communist countries have failed in combining our form of government with a market economy."

"How?" I asked, and he looked at me with an expression that said: You, of all people, should know we are indomitable. A flood of words followed that were certainly pompous and aggressive, but in my opinion, he never did answer the question, and I was relieved when the waiter brought the check.

On the way back to the hotel, we became stuck in traffic again—this time opposite the gates to the Temple of Literature. After about ten minutes of waiting to move, I said, "I think I'll get out and walk back from here. Can I leave my equipment with you?"

Henry looked surprised, but he agreed, so with a quick goodbye to Mr. Hoang and Han, I grabbed the Minox from my camera bag and jumped out of the car.

The heat outside was blistering, but as my body began to adjust to the temperature, I felt my spirits begin to rebalance too. I needed to shake off the oppressive energy of people who had all the answers and recover my own vision. Two things always did this for me: solitude and taking pictures.

I hurried from the bustling sidewalk into the shady courtyard in front of the temple gate. Instantly not only the level of light, but also the level of noise dropped. Only a few people sat as still as lizards on the low benches that lined the walk. Even the children were subdued or lulled to sleep by the heat.

The Temple of Literature was once a university—the seat of the Confucian philosophy and power that Prof. Ngo so admired. More than 900 years ago, silk-coated mandarins began coming there to study, but now it was a deserted ruin. An attendant, seated under the elaborately carved red and gold temple gate, roused herself from her torpor to take my entrance fee and hand me a description of the place in Vietnamese.

I walked through the gate and wandered around the extensive gardens. There were no guides and no signs in Vietnamese, much less in English. This was not a tourist destination for Westerners—at least not yet—and I was glad that it wasn't.

I peered into empty pavilions where statues of Confucius sat still and silent and walked along paths lined with rows of stone stellae. Mounted on the backs of stone tortoises, these pillars were carved with the names of the mandarins who studied there from the 15th to the 18th century.

I took photographs until the sweat running into my eyes made it hard to focus. Then I sat down on a bench in the shade overlooking a mucky pool and listened to the buzz of insects and the distant sounds from the street.

I tried to imagine Vietnam before the war. Before the invasions of the French and the Japanese. Before the 1,000-year domination of the Chinese.

The mandarins were trained here to uphold a tradition that stretched back centuries. A very different role than the shabby students I'd met that morning would play. They were going to be involved in making something new. A new government. A new economy. A new society that even a founding member like Prof. Ngo could not describe. No wonder they didn't care about broken windows.

My mother and father couldn't believe I would rather live in the slums of Chicago with a bunch of peace activists and angry veterans than in their clean, well-appointed home. They didn't understand. I couldn't go to high school. Walter was dead. The only way I could deal with that was to put every ounce of energy I had into ending the war. And beyond that, my goal had been nothing less than to save America. To launch a new, better world where there would be no such wars as Vietnam.

The arrogance of the Vietnamese we'd met was irritating, but we'd been arrogant too. Full of our mission. Convinced of our rightness. When I talked to my parents, I could see that they had no idea where the person inhabiting their daughter's body had come from, and I liked that. I thought the world they lived in was finished and good riddance.

I was wrong, of course. Nothing happens that simply. Not there and then and not even here and now.

7

When I arrived back at the hotel, my feet and ankles were gray with dust. I took a shower and changed into clean clothes, then knocked on Henry's door. I told myself I only wanted to pick up my equipment, but I was pleased when he invited me to come in.

He had been writing with his laptop set up on the narrow dressing table and his notebook propped against the mirror. The bench stood perpendicular to the table so he could sit on it like a horse.

"That looks comfy," I said, and he laughed.

"It's a bit dodgy actually. One leg is loose. I figure I'm less likely to fall sitting this way."

"How's the work going?"

"Brilliantly. I've already transcribed half of the interviews. You look better," he said, sizing me up.

"Clean," I said.

"Yes, but more than that." I don't know what change he saw in me, but under his scrutiny I suddenly felt embarrassed.

"I needed a walk. Some time alone," I said and immediately the brisk tone came back into his voice:

"Right," he said, turning back to his computer.

"Well, I didn't mean to interrupt. I only came by to get my stuff."

"I'll be done in a minute if you want to wait for tea."

"All right," I said, sitting down on a plastic chair. He had begun to type rapidly, while watching me in the mirror at the same time.

"The bed's more comfortable," he said.

I considered this invitation carefully. There was only one way that bed would be comfortable in my opinion, but I decided to play along and stretched out, plumping his pillow under my head.

I'm not sure what I expected—passionate reconnection, tearful forgiveness, renewed commitment—but what did happen was: nothing. The only sounds were the soft clicks of Henry's typing and the wheeze of the air conditioner.

I thought what I was ready for—what I wanted—was sex. I hadn't slept with anyone in months—in fact, I hadn't slept with anyone since we broke up. Instead, as I lay there, I found myself lowering slowly into his presence like a hot bath, and it surprised me to discover that my own resistance—as much as Henry's remoteness—was the surface tension I had to break through.

The only man I had ever lived with was Toby Woodruff—Wendy's father—a hippie veteran I met at an anti-war demonstration, who took me off to his commune of geodesic domes and tree houses in upstate New York. Fortunately for Wendy, although my relationship with Toby didn't last long, he grew up to be a very nice man and successful architect.

I told myself I didn't have time for complicated relationships with men. I had to work and take care of my daughter. These weren't empty excuses. After the war ended, I suddenly had both nothing to do and my hands full with a baby and my own life to start over. I had never held a job except for my work at Make Peace. I hadn't even finished high school. My parents helped—for Wendy's sake, if not for mine—but I found out quickly how hard you have to work to live in a safe neighborhood, even if you don't choose to live in the land of rolled green lawns and plastic-covered furniture.

The plan I had for my life—and Wendy's—was based entirely on what I did not want it to be. I pursued any pattern that didn't look like my mother's—that quiet steadfast monogamy and devotion to children that left her wide open to devastation. I can't explain why I let Wendy go in any other terms. When Toby married again and had another child, he offered to have her live with his new family during the school year, and I said yes. Better to lose her now, I thought, and get it over with. Whatever it was.

The first few years I drove her to California each fall because I couldn't bear the thought of plane crashes, and I would cry all the way back to Chicago. Just like my mother, I cried, but, unlike her, I was lucky. My daughter came back every summer.

Even when Wendy was away, the only men I let into my life were the ones who were fun to be with and easy to let go, and that had worked until Henry. Much to my surprise, our relationship lasted. Where the others slid away, he stuck. The one time he came to Chicago and met Wendy, she said, "He's a good partner for you, Mom," and I thought she was talking about the work, but she wasn't.

I enjoyed Henry as a partner in work and in bed, but as a partner in life?

In India, after I'd said I wouldn't move in with him, we tried to carry on as before, but it was impossible. On the last night, he stopped in the middle of making love, and said: "I can't do this any more." Our stomachs made a sweaty, sucking noise as he pulled himself up and looked into my face. "I love you, Sarah. I want to love you. And this isn't enough."

My reaction had been to get angry. I told myself he had everything of me there was to have. If that wasn't enough, that was his tough luck. "I can't help you," was all I said aloud, as if the problem were all his.

He slipped out of me without another word and got up to dress. I remembered vividly the pale glow of his skin from the streetlight through the window. It would have made a beautiful photograph. In the morning, when I awoke, I found he had already left for the airport.

I wondered now why he was willing to let me get close to him again. He continued to work and the sound of his typing was soothing like rain on a roof in summer. I didn't move from the bed, and he didn't turn around, but there was an intimacy in our silence. I felt touched by the sight of his leather slippers, crushed at the heels, on the floor. His blue chambray shirt hung over the chair. The collection of Vietnamese poetry he'd been reading that lay on his bedside table. His reading glasses. A crumpled Kleenex.

I have always liked to photograph people's possessions. Their capacity to reflect the person who used them fascinated me, and I have also found that they retain a peculiarly lasting power to comfort. Certainly that's why I kept

Wendy's toothbrush hanging in the bathroom through all the months when she was in San Francisco, and why wearing an old sweater of Walter's or drinking tea made in my mother's teapot still warmed me more than anything else on some winter nights.

I dozed off and woke up to find Henry reading the newspaper in the chair next to the bed. A cup of tea steamed on the table beside him. I didn't move, wanting to extend the moment as long as possible, but finally he looked up and knew I was awake.

"You finished?" I asked.

"A while ago," he said, sipping his tea. The sight of his lips touching the cup, warmed by it, filled me with warmth too. The desire to be kissed.

"I feel like everything that's happened since we arrived has been one giant hallucination. Now I'm really awake."

"That's an illusion too," he said.

I laughed. "You may be right."

"Of course I'm right," he said sounding very Oxford, but in his smile I glimpsed a shadow of his old smile.

8

How could I have forgotten that smile? It made you feel like you've just caught sight of yourself in a mirror and discovered that you look like the person you most want yourself to be. I have never been ashamed of my body, but only through the pleasure I'd seen in Henry's eyes have I ever felt myself to be truly beautiful.

He didn't make a move though. The seduction scene began and ended with that fleeting smile. He made me a cup of tea, and I drank it, feeling every second more awkward about being there, on his bed.

We talked in a desultory way about the work we were doing until at last I said: "I need to do some things before dinner."

"All right," said Henry, getting up from his chair to make room for me to leave.

"Thanks for the tea."

He pushed his hair back with one hand and smiled again, but it was the absent everyday smile, not the one that made me feel like someone had just sent gas to my pilot light.

I didn't really have anything to do, but I put away my equipment, then wasted a good hour changing my clothes and making refinements to my hair—a twist, a bun, a braid, loose. When I finally decided I was ready, it was held up with a silver clasp, and I wore a turquoise silk blouse that we'd bought together at the Weekend Market in Bangkok with slim black slacks and sandals.

I twisted this way and that to make sure every part of me was in order, and, from the bureau, Walter grinned at me. His was a different kind of smile though. The smile of someone who could and would always see through all of my disguises.

The only edge I gave Walter without a fight was the fact that he was three years older. I never let his being a boy stop me from competing with him. He was the hero of my childhood and whatever he did, I wanted to do too. Read. Ride a two-wheeled bike. Play the piano. Do a back dive.

I am nothing if not persistent, so I kept up pretty well, and in swimming we found a shared passion. For years we practiced together, went to each other's meets, and cheered each other on. Then Walter turned fifteen, and overnight, it seemed, biology and society divided us. We still swam, and some other interests could bring us together—the White Sox, Monopoly, a fresh snowfall—but he had begun to move away from me in ways I couldn't understand no matter how hard I tried.

He was there all through high school, of course. Growing tall, listening to the radio, fudging his homework, talking about cars, and falling in love with girls he never spoke to. When I compare my memory of him with Wendy, he seems painfully immature and sheltered, but then we all were—my whole family at that time.

Walter lived the way he drove—one handed and with very little forethought. My parents didn't seem to worry much about him. They didn't push him toward college when he said he wasn't ready to go, and they didn't try to protect him from the draft. They were proud that he was willing to go into the Army, and they believed that the president knew what was best for the country, even if to us some of his decisions were hard to understand. Disasters like the 1968 Democratic Convention in Chicago shocked my parents, but they made them cling even harder to what they thought of as "the right thing" and what I came later to think of simply as "the right." As for Walter, I'm not sure he formed that much of an opinion about these issues until he was already on his way to Vietnam, and then it was too late.

When Henry and I met for dinner, I could tell from his expression that he recognized the blouse, but he didn't say anything other than, "You dressed up." An inscrutable compliment, if there ever was one. He was preoccupied, and

I tried not to take it personally, but this was obviously not, as I had begun to imagine, a date.

We were dining with a German doctor who was advising The Pearse Foundation on projects to fund. Dr. Weidig had a long pedigree; he had worked in Asia for a number of different organizations, and I had heard his name in connection with several previous clients, but I had never met him.

He had invited us to eat with him in the dining room of the hotel where he lived, which turned out to be a dim shabby place with the air of waiting for guests who would never arrive. We found him already seated in the large empty dining room, quite drunk and bent on getting drunker.

He stood up to greet me with a heavy-jowled leer—apparently my costume made more of an impression on him than it had on Henry—and waved his hand for a waiter to bring more beer. Our seats placed us under a noisy fan that whirled the air around our faces and ruffled the paper placemats on the stained white tablecloth. Bored waiters in tight purple jackets hovered with nothing to do, and a bartender lounged at the empty bar across the room.

We exchanged introductory news about various people we knew in common, while the waiter laid on a sad-looking spread of greasy spring rolls, watery curry, and stale-looking rice. If this was what Weidig ate every day, it was no wonder he drank instead. Or maybe he never noticed the food, since he didn't bother to serve himself anything but a bowl of rice.

In addition to learning how various Pearse projects were going, Henry wanted Weidig's perspective on how Vietnam was doing. Weidig knocked back another beer and said, "The Vietnamese think getting loans from the World Bank is going to help them, but the World Bank is really the Americans coming back to finish the them off. They couldn't defeat the Vietnamese with their bombs, so they're going to do it economically."

"The Vietnamese we've met sound very eager to engage with the U.S.," I said.

"Yes," added Henry. "They seem know exactly what they want."

"They may know what they want, but they don't know what they're going to get," said Weidig, pounding his fist on the table. "You must know what it's all about," he said, leering at me again. "You must know how the Americans feel about this country."

Before I could answer, his expression suddenly changed, and he leaned across the table waving a finger at Henry.

"Henry Berenger," he said. "Did you write a book about malaria?"

"Yes, I did," said Henry. He had pushed aside his dinner plate and taken out his notebook. Weidig ignored this signal that he intended to take notes.

"Are you a doctor?"

"No, I'm a more of historian."

"History!" And then he was off on another story about the World Bank screwing somebody. Or was it everybody.

When he paused for breath, Henry gave up and signaled for the check.

"You haven't listened to a word I've said," Weidig roared. "But you'll see. I'm right. The Americans want revenge, and they'll get it."

"Perhaps you're right," Henry said ambiguously and held out his hand to say goodbye.

"Jesus," I said, as soon as we were outside. The night air was warm and refreshing after the stale cold air in the dining room. We walked away quickly, distancing ourselves from Weidig's rage and headed toward Hoan Kiem Lake. "I wonder if the foundation has any idea what kind of shape he's in."

"I doubt it," said Henry, walking briskly with his hands in his pockets. "But he's probably all right when he isn't pissed."

"You must be kidding. He's probably an asshole, drunk or sober, but he's right about one thing. A lot of Americans do want revenge—and not only against the communists. They want revenge against the people who protested the war too."

"Now you sound as paranoid as he does," said Henry. "Let's stop for an ice."

We were outside a crowded cafe where families were eating dishes of multi-colored ice cream topped with candied fruit.

"OK," I said. "I'm starving. That dinner was a nightmare in every way."

We took a table on the sidewalk and ordered from a menu in French and Vietnamese. With its striped awning and round metal tables, the cafe had a decidedly European air. But it was more than that: the cheerful sound of the talk, the polite little children, the sharp smell of coffee, and the twinkling lights on the water made me think of Paris too.

After we'd had ice cream and a glass of strong sweet Vietnamese coffee, the ranting of Dr. Weidig gradually subsided in my head. We browsed through the galleries again and talked about the possibility of buying paintings.

"You know if I bought one of these I'd have to sneak it into the U.S.," I said. "Otherwise I'd be breaking the Trading with the Enemy Act."

Henry looked surprised. "And you are going to abide by this law?"

I laughed. We had both done our fair share of personal smuggling. "Maybe. Maybe not."

"Well, if your conscience gets the better of you, I can always take something for you. You can pick it up in London the next time you come."

I smiled, more pleased that he imagined we'd be meeting again than at the thought of buying a painting.

When we finally headed back to the hotel, a sprinkling rain had begun that was so light you could feel each drop kiss your skin.

"I can't decide what to make of this place," I said to Henry, as we passed through the gate and crunched across the gravel of our hotel compound. A light showed for the first time from behind one of the tall arched windows of the old building. Music was playing, and we could hear laughter.

"You love it," he said.

"What do you mean?"

"You have ended up loving every place we've ever been. No matter how awful."

"Have I?" I asked, but I knew he was right.

"Yes. You always love places. It's people you have a hard time with."

"That's what you think?"

"It is."

I felt disappointed and didn't know what to say. I had hoped we'd end the night in his bed, but it was clear from his tone that I was out of luck. We climbed the stairs, not speaking. At his door, Henry said good night as if neither of us had ever ripped off a button in our haste to be together, and that was that.

9

The Americans never occupied the north of Vietnam, so unlike in the south, there were no abandoned camps, munitions, roads, or airports, and no half-American children either. In the north were signs of the war being lost, not won. The shadowy presence of spies and prisoners. This struck me hard when we crossed the Chuong Duong Bridge over the Red River to visit a communal health post in the suburbs of Hanoi.

Chuong Duong was a post-war bridge that ran parallel to the much-older Long Bien Bridge. I had heard of Long Bien Bridge because it had often been in the news during the war. It was a major transportation link between Hanoi and the coast—and it was bombed frequently until the Vietnamese had the clever idea of making American POWs do the repair work. After that it wasn't touched, so it had never fallen, but the girders looked ominously black against the sky as if they had been burned over and over and over. Which in fact I guess they had. No longer strong enough for cars, it was still used by pedestrians and bicyclists, and from Chuong Duong we could see them crossing the undefeated bridge in a steady stream.

For the first time since our arrival we were back in the flat, lush countryside. The air was fresher, although equally hot, and we opened the car windows to let in the breeze. There is no green in the world like the green of a rice paddy, and no film that can quite do it justice, but I asked Han to pull over so I could take some photos of the farmers at work. Like the painters, I could not resist the lone man with his beast and his plow suspended between the blue sky and the green field. Why did the image suggest peace, steadiness, and purpose, rather than heat, struggle, and desperate odds? That is the beauty of distance.

Our destination turned out to be a compound of low brick buildings where several young men lounged in the shade of the eaves and doorways. The atmosphere was peaceful. Sleepy. We seemed to be the only piece of the landscape in motion until the usual health workers in white coats emerged from the building and the scene came to life. The young men melted away, and we went to work.

We had come to visit the tuberculosis unit, a small building isolated from the rest of the communal hospital, where patients lay on their palettes struggling for breath in the heavy air. They stared at us with glassy eyes and reacted to being photographed as if it were an unpleasant, uncalled-for, medical procedure. The last straw in lives that had too much straw already. Or was it too little? At any rate, I finished as quickly as I could.

After the tour, we crowded into a small conference room, where Dr. Thuy and Dr. Phan, the physicians who ran the unit, gave us the statistics on TB. Although the unit was small and did not look crowded, they said these patients represented a troubling sign. A few years before TB had been in decline; now it was starting to make a comeback. And not only that. They were worried about the risk of drug-resistant TB and the looming danger posed by the HIV/AIDS epidemic. In light of these possibilities, the contribution of The Pearse Foundation seemed frighteningly inadequate. Not even close to a finger in the dike.

The doctors were very interested in Henry's book and what he had learned about the spread of TB in other countries. Mr. Hoang was kept very busy translating a discussion that began in the conference room and continued at lunch.

We ate in the hospital cafeteria, a large room with long tables. At one end of the room, there was a television set surrounded by empty chairs that was showing a documentary on the war in black and white. The soundtrack was in Vietnamese, but there was no mistaking the content. I suppose it was there to educate the generation that had grown up in peace, for whom the long struggle for independence had become a history lesson. Something the older people went on about. Ho Chi Minh talked rapidly and bombs exploded in my peripheral vision as I tried to make small talk with my neighbor, a nurse who wanted to try out her few words of English. No one else seemed to even notice the film.

They were busy passing around heavy brown glass bottles of beer, urging us, and each other, to drink. Then everyone helped themselves to food from the serving dishes at the center of the table. The prize dish was a curried snake, and I took some hoping I could get away with not actually eating it. There was no rice, but instead warm baguettes, sweet butter, and soft cheese. Some people ate their bread folded over hunks of cheese, while others buttered it and sprinkled on a thick layer of sugar—a treat Walter and I had enjoyed when we were little. As we all ate, the beer circulated freely and people became more adventurous about speaking English.

"Are you English?" asked Dr. Thuy, who sat on my left. He was about my age and handsome with a smooth dark complexion.

"No," I said, "American."

"But your husband is English?"

"Henry is not my husband. He's my colleague. But you're right. He's English."

The news that Henry and I were not married encouraged him to shift his chair closer to mine. He leaned toward me confidentially, and I could smell the beer on his breath as he said: "The Americans used to be our enemies. But now we like them very much."

He leaned back in his chair and raised his voice, stopping other conversations in mid-sentence as he addressed the whole table.

"Isn't this true? We love America now," he said with a loud laugh. "But before, most definitely not!" Then he turned in his chair, lifted his right leg into the air, and pulled up his pant leg, revealing the long dark scars that scored his skin.

"In the war, there was shelling all the time! Boom! Boom! Boom! All day! All night!" He waved his leg up and down drunkenly, then turned with a lightning quick movement to Dr. Phan and rapped him on the head.

"Dr. Phan likes Americans too. He thanks them for his metal skull!"

Despite—or maybe because of—Dr. Phan's obvious displeasure, all the Vietnamese tittered. I felt my own face stiffen with embarrassment. I didn't know what to say and when I tried to catch Henry's eye instead I saw footage of the fall of Saigon. The departing heliocopters. The looters. The panicked people left behind.

I forced myself to turn to back to Dr. Thuy, who was now leaning his arm possessively on the back of my chair. "The war was terrible," I said. "I'm glad you both survived."

He laughed again. "Me too!" he said then translated my remark to the others at the table, and they nodded their approval. Survival was something to be celebrated at any time and place, so the beer went around again for a toast.

I already felt queasy from the heat and the greasy aftertaste of snake, but I joined in as the beer went round and round, and more hands reached out for bread, butter, and sugar. Then finally, a hot bitter tea was served, and lunch was over.

10

We had the rest of the day free, and I needed it. I thought I might take a nap, but, when Henry invited me to join him in his room, I said I'd love to. I didn't really want to be alone with the sound of "Boom! Boom! Boom!" going through my head.

I found him curled at one end of his bed, reading the small English-language newspaper, *Viet Nam News*. He was wearing a faded "God Save Queen" t-shirt and shorts. That t-shirt had traveled everywhere with him, but the first time I ever saw him in it, I was shocked. Henry and Queen struck me as a very unlikely combination. I had him pegged as a baroque music type, who listened to Bach sonatas in his book-lined tomb in London. I don't know why I pictured him that way. He had lived all over the world.

The last time I'd seen the shirt was in Bombay. We'd gone for a walk on Chowpatty Beach, and Henry had bought me a garland of jasmine flowers from a ragged girl. I could still remember the way the fragrance encircled my head.

"Would you like to read the paper?" he asked, as he swept aside the books and papers scattered on the bed to make room for me.

"Sure," I said, taking the four-page tabloid. I settled myself facing him, cross-legged, at the far end, and tried to banish the scent of flowers and the other memories inspired by the nearness of his golden-haired knees.

I started to read, but the very first story stopped me dead.

"Shit!" I said. "Did you read this? About Clinton being booed during his

Memorial Day speech at the Vietnam Veterans Memorial?"

"Was that news?" said Henry, totally English. "In Parliament, it happens to the PM all the time."

"Well, here it practically caused a riot."

"Why? What did he say?"

"It wasn't because of what he said, Henry. It was because of what he did. Or I should say didn't do. He was against the war. He didn't fight in it. That still makes Americans crazy. I don't know why you don't get that." I tossed the paper at his feet.

"At least they didn't shoot him. But I never knew you had so much respect for presidents. I thought you were a bomb-throwing radical."

"I wasn't the one with the bombs," I said, surprising myself with my own anger.

He lifted one eyebrow. His Oxford don look.

"Make Peace was into civil disobedience, not violence. And anyway, you're missing the point. The point is it's twenty years later, and people who were against the war are still being vilified. Marginalized. As if that redresses the wrong the country did to the boys who went."

"But now everyone admits the war was a mistake. That means the ones who supported it have lost face. You lot were right, so now you need to be gracious to those who weren't, and move on."

"That's a joke. Nobody has moved on."

"Nobody?" said Henry. He picked up the paper again and began to fold it neatly.

"What's that supposed to mean?"

"Nothing."

"Don't nothing me, Henry." I tapped his knee with my foot.

"All right. I think a lot of people have moved on, but you haven't. You're as stuck in the past as any of those angry veterans. Forgiveness on both sides would not go amiss."

This remark hit home like a dart, and I felt my face flush. "The fact that I don't forget what's important to me and try to live by it does not make me stuck," I said.

His cool expression made it clear that he knew I was ignoring what he said, and I saw him slipping away from me again. This time it would be final, but I couldn't care less.

"Fuck you, Henry," I said. "This is not history, this is my life we're talking about, and you don't know a fucking thing about it." With that, I struggled clumsily to my feet, stormed out of his room, and ran down the stairs.

I emerged, blinking, into the bright hot compound, where the guard dozed on his stool by the gate and no breeze stirred the foliage. I had nothing with me, only my room key in my pocket, but it seemed impossible to go back inside. To sit in my room with Henry and his judgment on this other side of the wall. So instead I plunged into the crowded streets, bumping and brushing against people as if that could dislodge the memory of what he had said.

I had always told myself I spent those years trying to end the war to avenge Walter's death. To prevent more American boys from being killed for such a doomed, unworthy cause. And I had.

But there was also another side to my anger that I did not like to admit, and that was directed at Walter. It was true that he was drafted, but Walter had been willing to serve in the Army. To do what was expected of him and go to war. I could never understand that. He was a peaceable, easygoing boy. A swimmer. A photographer. And somehow that very likable nature had set him up to become cannon fodder.

How could he have let this happen to himself? How could our parents? They claimed they were proud of him and that he was safer in the airborne division than on the ground, but there is no safe place in a war.

In those days, I had a map of the world in my room with two pins and a string between Chicago and Vietnam. I liked to think that, as long as the string was there, Walter and I remained connected. But the string broke long before he died, and I didn't want to admit it. Whatever Walter thought or felt about his life and the decisions he made were completely beyond my power of imagination. Like the other boys who went to war, he had been irrevocably changed.

I walked furiously past Hoan Kiem Lake, through markets and neighborhoods I had never seen before, until I suddenly found myself in front of an imposing stone building with the words Maison Centrale carved over its arched doorway. There was something familiar about the name, and, when I realized what it was, my skin grew cold under its coating of sweat and dust. Maison Centrale was the French name for the Hoa Lo Prison. Better known at home as the "Hanoi Hilton."

I had to sit down, and the only place was the curb.

In that moment, huddled in the heat radiating from those massive stone-walls, I had my first and only flash of gratitude that, if Walter had to die here, he had died instantly and not in a place like this.

There may be something more unforgiving than a prison wall, but it's hard to imagine what it would be. The only windows were narrow and barred, in case you could reach them, which you couldn't. The prison was empty now, and there was no movement or sound from within, but it was a silence resonant with the memories, prayers, and nightmares of the prisoners who had been held there.

Looking up at those windows, I thought about the American POWs. Brothers and boyfriends. Husbands and sons. Imprisoned. Tortured. Utterly cut off from the world they knew, day after day, month after month, year after year, while on the other side of the wall, the crickets sang and the life of the city went on as usual. What bravery and faith they must have had to have to stay alive.

When I first joined the anti-war movement, some people claimed that it was undermining the war effort. The dissent in America gave Ho Chi Minh hope that we would give up and made it harder for the boys who were fighting the war. They were certainly caught in the middle, but, as the war went on and on, many people in the military became equally vocal, angry and disillusioned. It was as if the government wasn't listening to anyone.

Standing by the Hoa Lo Prison, sweat streaming, I hoped for Walter's sake that he believed in what he was doing when he went up in that plane that day. I hoped he didn't think his faith in freedom and democracy had been squandered as well as his life.

I got up from the curb and went over to touch the wall. It was so hot, the stone burned my fingertips, but I couldn't take my hand away. I had rejected my parents' religion along with everything else in my teens, so when I made a prayer then for the souls of the living and the dead, I didn't get on my knees. Instead I walked, trailing my hand along the scorching stone, the way you walk around a Buddhist temple spinning the prayer wheels as you go.

At first I didn't notice the man squatting on the sidewalk. I was preoccupied with my thoughts. But a flash of sun on steel caught my attention, and I looked to see what had caused it.

The man was thin and ragged with stumps for legs and crouched beside his wares: a crude wooden tray filled with rows and rows of American Zippo lighters. They were lined up like little tombstones and each engraved with a message:

"Gloria and Archie forever"

"Get me home alive!"

"Billy, Tuy Hoa 10/1/67-10/31/68"

"My country right or wrong"

The voices of the boys who had owned them spoke across the years, and I wondered: Were those lighters lost in bars, hotels and whorehouses? Or had they been collected in the field from the wounded and the dead?

"Nice souvenir, miss?" the man asked. He held out "My country right or wrong" on his flat brown palm. I could see from his expression that the slogan didn't mean a thing to him, but I turned and fled.

11

The pre-dawn hours, when a city is tousled and vulnerable, are my favorite time to be out walking, and the next morning I sought the solace of that peaceful atmosphere to overcome a night of dark thoughts and bad dreams.

The crunching of my feet on the gravel drive sounded very loud in the early morning quiet. The air was damp and fragrant. A sleepy guard waved me through the gate into the street, where a scattering of cyclo drivers dozed in their carts and women squatted on the sidewalk making breakfast. An occasional bicyclist went by.

As I approached Hoan Kiem Lake, the light grew stronger, and I discovered that I was far from the only person out enjoying the fresh air of the early hour. A few men and women practiced tai chi's slow stately moves, but more were playing badminton in courts painted onto the sidewalks. The players were not all young people either—some of the most enthusiastic were gray-haired men and women who laughed and leapt after the shuttlecock as it sailed through the air. On the grass surrounding the lake, young men dressed only in ragged shorts were doing pushups and, on the lake path, old ladies walked briskly pumping their arms, and schoolgirls in plastic sandals jogged side by side, their black braids bouncing on their shoulders.

I had seen morning calisthenics in China, where rows of people gather in the squares to perform their ritual exercises. That was an impressive sight—a demonstration of unity, discipline, and obedience that you would never see among civilians in the West. But this was completely different. It was varied and individual. Full of laughter and exhilaration.

As I studied the people through the lens of my camera, I had the feeling that this was what peace meant. The right to enjoy your city without foreign domination. The right to get up and play badminton if you want to. The Vietnamese had fought decades, against all odds, for this simple pleasure, but they had made it. No wonder that nearly twenty years later it still felt like there was a block party going on.

My spirits lifted as I watched, and I took so many pictures that I became as hot as if I had been playing badminton myself. I had high hopes for one sequence of two little gray-haired ladies who looked very demure until they lifted her rackets and went into action.

As the temperature rose, the activity shifted from play to work. Shops and market stands began to open, and the badminton players gradually melted away. I had started back to the hotel when I caught sight of a familiar figure on a bench in the shade of an orange-blossomed flame tree. With his elbows hooked over the back of the bench and his legs stretched out, Henry was the picture of indolence, but I knew better. This was his protective coloration and later he would be able to write down everything he had observed in remarkable detail.

I hoped I could get past him without being noticed, but he looked up, saw me, and waved.

I couldn't ignore him. We were supposed to begin work in an hour and spend the whole day together. My present and future livelihood depended on doing this well, so I went over to his bench and dropped down next to him.

"You look knackered, and the day hasn't even started yet," he said, as his eyes slowly lost their dreamy look of concentration and focused on me.

I pinched the front of my damp shirt and waved it to create a breeze inside. "I got up early," I said, "but I'm glad I did. It's been very nice. Extraordinary."

He nodded. "So you're feeling better?"

"Yes, but I need breakfast," I said, standing up, "and preferably not from the hotel."

Henry looked at his watch. "OK, if we push along, we ought to be able to find something."

I expected him to set off at his usual fast pace, but he didn't. We walked more or less side by side, not touching, but keeping together. Maybe he was thinking of his livelihood too—the days of work ahead.

We left the lakeside, winding down narrow streets lined with shops and market stalls selling everything from eggs to engine parts, toys to tombstones. Finally we settled on a spot—little more than a doorway containing a glass case full of pastries and small baguettes with a table on the sidewalk in front. I ordered Vietnamese coffee over ice and a baguette stuffed with fried eggs, both of which turned out to be excellent. Henry drank two hot coffees and, once I was finished eating, he lit a cigarette.

"I'm sorry I upset you yesterday," he said, exhaling smoke in a slow curl. "I actually had hoped this trip might give me a chance to understand your war better."

"Really. You didn't go about it in a very good way."

"No."

"So what did you want to know?" Even I could hear the edginess in my voice.

Henry shrugged. "I have a sister. I think the world of her, but I don't carry around her photo."

"Well, she probably lives in Cheltenham with her husband and three blond children. She wasn't blown to smithereens when she was nineteen years old."

"Point taken. But still."

"Walter wasn't special, if that's what you're asking. He was just a boy like every other boy who died here—he didn't deserve to have his life snatched away because the United States government was too fucking proud to admit it had made a mistake."

"You know, as a historian, I would have to point out that to some extent that's true about the boys and men who've fought in every war through all the centuries. Also that it's what society raises boys to do."

"That's unconscionable."

"But it's a fact."

"Just because it's a fact doesn't make it right." I put my money down on the tiny table and picked up my camera. "I thought we were supposed to be aspiring to something better."

12

Back at the hotel, Henry and I stood side by side waiting for the car like negotiators at a peace conference that had reached a delicate stage. I could feel the pounds per square inch of air between us, and each time one of us shifted slightly, the other did too, so as to maintain the equilibrium of that space. We had ceased hostilities, at least for the moment, but the road to a lasting peace promised to be a rough one.

Maybe, I thought, that was because I didn't want to take that route after all. It would be so much easier to go home, back to my life, and accept that Henry was a mistake: I never should mix work and relationships.

When Han finally arrived, I think we were both relieved. Today he was not in the sedan but in an old Land Rover, which he drove up to the hotel entrance with a flourish of flying gravel. To my further surprise, instead of Mr. Hoang, a heavyset man with small twinkling eyes, unruly wisps of gray hair, and several silver teeth clambered out of the car to greet us. He was dressed, not in a suit, but in hospital whites, and announced, "I am Dr. Tran," as he vigorously shook first my hand, then Henry's.

"Mr. Hoang had other duties today, so I was asked to come in his place," he explained. "I am retired, with, as you say, time on my hands. I hope you will find that my English is not too hard to understand." He grinned, sizing us up in a bold but reasonably friendly way.

"Not at all. It's brilliant," said Henry. "We're delighted you could come."

The Land Rover appeared to be a step up from the cars we'd been traveling in. As Henry and I stowed our gear and settled ourselves at opposite ends of the wide back seat, I thought this might not be such a grueling day after all. We were scheduled to go to a village about two hours away, but getting out of Hanoi would take an hour, so we had a good six hours in the car to look forward to.

It took only a few minutes to realize that I was wrong. The seat was about as comfortable as a buckboard, and the air conditioning didn't work. We lurched along, stopping and starting, as the traffic inched across town and, Han, who had acquired a red baseball cap, exercised his new status as a Land Rover driver by honking continually at every real or imagined obstacle.

None of this appeared to faze Dr. Tran. Looking as pleased as if we were speeding along a six-lane highway in a stretch limo, he lit a cigarette and leaned toward us with his arm over the back of the front seat, ready to chat. "So, how do you like my city?" he asked, with a flourish of his cigarette.

"It's very beautiful," I said. "I love the different architectures and all the lakes."

Dr. Tran nodded approvingly. "Yes, it is lovely, isn't it? Everyone who has tried to take us over has left their mark, but the result is still somehow entirely our own. I've seen Paris, Moscow, and Beijing—but, to my eyes, none of them have that special character.

"Of course, everyone thinks his homeland is special. You have 'this sceptre'd isle'," he said to Henry, "and for you, it's the 'amber waves of grain'. This is as it should be. It's very important to love the place you were born."

Once we reached the outskirts of the city, the traffic grew lighter. The road that headed north shrank to a pitted two-lane blacktop. The countryside was exquisite though, and I could understand why Vietnamese painters never tired of it. The flat green rice paddies of the river delta gradually gave way to hillier ground and in the distance we could see mountains that rose in the spectacularly irregular shapes caused by limestone formations.

Dr. Tran pointed out sites along the way as cheerfully as a tour guide, and every one, it emerged, had a connection to war. Passing a small town, he told us:

"This is where the Americans spent one million dollars bombing the same tire plant over and over, and it only produced twenty tires a week." Crossing a river: "Here's where three sisters died, one after the other, attempting to keep a ferry running." In a lovely wooded valley: "This is where I lived in the woods for three years—but that was a different era—we were fighting the French then, not the Americans." He chuckled with satisfaction at the memory of his guerrilla days as he gazed out the window.

Henry sat with his back to the door and his notebook in his lap taking notes in a desultory way. I listened to this running commentary without saying anything until curiosity drove me ask if he had fought in the battle of Dien Bien Phu. The legendary battle that had brought down the French regime in 1954.

"No," he said ruefully. "I was captured right before it and ended up in prison for two years. You know, the one your soldiers called the 'Hanoi Hilton'? That's where I was." He said this in the same tone a person might use to say that he had spent two years in graduate school.

"I've seen it," I said. "And I don't see how anyone survived there."

"It wasn't easy," he admitted, "but you want to live, so, if you possibly can, you do.

Dr. Tran's enthusiasm carried us like a wave through our visit to a remote commune of traditional brick houses and the newer concrete structures nestled among palm trees. We toured the Pearse-supported communal health clinic, where people came from as far away as ten miles on foot and by bicycle for health care, and the doctor and health workers flushed with pleasure at his praise.

Where Mr. Hoang always maintained a polite and official manner, Dr. Tran was warm and gregarious. He chatted with everyone, interrupted presentations, told stories and asked questions, then boiled down the fast-paced dialogue to a summary in English for us.

He wasn't content to sit in the conference room and look at charts. He wanted to see everything. Everyone. After the presentations were over, he asked to meet some of the patients being treated through a pilot home-care program. The doctor looked flustered, conferred quickly with his assistants, and then agreed to take us.

Dr. Tran strode happily along the muddy village paths trailed by the clinic staff, children, dogs, and us. He was a one-man photo op, and he hammed for the camera in the nicest possible way, giving me some of the liveliest shots of this trip.

In the work Henry and I did we saw people in profoundly intimate circumstances—the poor, the ill, the dying, and the dead—but we didn't usually see them in their homes. That day we visited several people, including two who were part of Vietnam's small but growing middle class—a mild-mannered old gentleman who served us tea in his living room, where one wall was covered medals and plaques from Ho Chi Minh, and a teenaged Madonna fan, who had obviously worked very hard to produce her big hair.

Everywhere Dr. Tran was greeted with respect—almost reverence—and the entourage from the clinic cheered up as they realized they were gaining prestige from the association.

"Do you come here often?" I asked him, when we were walking back to the clinic. "Everyone seems to know you."

He shook his head. "No, but I came here a few times to help during the war, so I have many old comrades in this neighborhood. We're a small country in many ways, and we have a long memory. When people fight together for something and suffer losses, as well as achieve victories, it binds them together and makes them strong."

"Here there are also people who lost the war though," I said.

"Yes. These wounds take a long time to heal. Look at your Civil War. Those who still wave their own flag."

On the way back to Hanoi, Dr. Tran told Han to stop at a restaurant along the side of the road. It was in a squat ramshackle building, but the owner—another old friend—greeted us enthusiastically and led us to a table on a patio in the back. The patio was shaded by a canvas awning and surrounded by a hedge of huge poinsettia bushes covered with the red blooms I associated only with Christmas.

The owner, a small man in fresh white clothes, brought us bottled water and tea and laid the table, while Dr. Tran quizzed us about what we liked to eat. Then he and his friend talked for several minutes in rapid Vietnamese, and Han's eyes began to shine with anticipation. We were going to have a good dinner on the Pearse Foundation.

The dishes that arrived were the best we'd had in Vietnam: a gingery soup, glistening prawns, delicately fried crab, green papaya salad, shredded pork with noodles, sautéed fresh greens, and more. All of us were hungry, but Dr. Tran probably ate as much as Henry and Han put together, even though he talked continually at the same time. His chopsticks never stopped moving until the plates were bare.

He wanted to know all about us: where we were from, how we met, what we enjoyed about our work, and what we didn't. Henry and I reminisced under

Dr. Tran's warm, approving gaze and after awhile we were talking more easily than we had all week.

"We hit it off immediately on our first job together," I told him.

"I beg to differ," said Henry, pushing aside his plate and lighting a cigarette. "I was a last-minute substitute, and you made it very clear that my writing had better be up to your mark."

"Well, maybe it did take a day or two. But we discovered that we care about the same things. We notice the same kind of details, and that has made our work go very well."

"It's true," said Henry. "I can hear a good story and write it down, but Sarah sees the picture that captures the same idea."

Dr. Tran nodded. "I could see that there is something special between you. You are very lucky. I had a partner like that once. We ran a clinic together, and it was marvelous to work with someone who understands how you think and knows what you would do even before you have said it aloud. Unfortunately, he was killed a long time ago. Early in the war."

"And you never found another colleague like that?" I asked.

"No," he said with a wistful expression. "And sometimes it is better to just accept that a situation was unique."

I knew at that moment he was right, and how much I had probably gambled away by my attitude toward Henry, who had lit another cigarette and was looking off through the poinsettias at the growing dusk.

Dr. Tran signaled for coffee and sweets. With his coffee in front of him, he lit a cigarette, threw back his head, and blew smoke into the air—the picture of contentment.

"Yes, you are lucky," he said. "But I've had my share of luck too. There was a time when I did not know how I would ever get enough rice to feed my family. Now, we are still poor, but we know we will have rice, and that is a very wonderful thing.

"We progress. It is good that your foundation is helping us, because Vietnam still has many, many needs, but our progress is our own. This no one can give you."

He looked directly at me. "You know, I have always liked Americans. I don't have any quarrel with you. Your boys, when they came here, they had a job to do. It was shoot or be shot. For me it was the same with the French. For my son, it was the Chinese. That's the way wars are. You have to fight, so you do, but when it's over, you must let it be over. Otherwise there is never peace. Only war.

"What I don't understand is the American obsession—" he lifted his hands and waved his fingers as if he were feeling his way along something invisible and, before he even spoke, I knew what he was referring to. "Fifty-eight thousand names."

"The Wall," I said. The story of the angry veterans flashed into my head.

"Yes, The Wall," he nodded. "Have you seen this place?"

"No, but people are very moved by it."

"No doubt, but, you know, here we lost more than three million people in the war. My family alone lost twelve members. No wall could be big enough for the individual names. That's why the only way we can honor them is to progress."

He shook his head and took a sip of coffee. "As a doctor, I have spent my whole life worrying about whether I might make a mistake and cost a life. But politicians? They make a mistake, and three million die. Those are the people that I get angry at. Nevertheless, we, as individuals, can be friends. Am I right?"

He smiled, his warm engaging smile, and Henry said "Of course."

In the past, I would have treated them to a rant on how you can't separate the two. That individuals have to take responsibility for what their politicians do. But maybe I have progressed a little too, because this didn't seem the right time or place to say that, so I let the subject go and said only, "Thank you. It's an honor to be your friend."

13

On the trip back to Hanoi, Henry and Dr. Tran fell asleep, but I remained awake, watching the dark landscape flicker by. Han had turned the radio on very low, adding a murmur of voices to the comforting hum of the engine.

As village after village went by, I thought about governments going to war, and the individuals on both sides who lose their lives as a result. They each had a story about what they hoped their life would be, but wasn't. They all had family and friends who loved them and suffered from their loss. That is a body count that is never tallied.

After Walter's death, my mother cried all night for weeks until my father had to move out of their bedroom to sleep. She told me she dreamed the same dream over and over about holding Walter as a baby in her arms. She'd be looking down at his tiny face, and then he'd be gone. Vanished. She could never find him. Mothers all over the world must dream that dream.

There were no remains. Walter's corporeal self was incinerated when his plane exploded, so he had, in fact, vanished. I don't know what my parents buried in the family plot—I refused to go to the funeral—but it wasn't Walter.

I saw his grave for the first time when my father died and again, a year later, after my mother's death. Since then I have been out to the cemetery a few times, but it gives me a strange, untethered feeling to see their three stones lined up side by side. Their togetherness is an illusion like the illusory togetherness families create when they pose by the fireplace for the annual Christmas card photo, because Walter is not there. Walter is here. In Vietnam.

Wendy wanted me to go to The Wall with her, when her senior class took a trip to Washington. She was excited about seeing her uncle's name carved there and wanted to learn more about the war that had so affected her family.

I thanked her, but I said I couldn't go; I had too much work to do. She knows me well, so she accepted this explanation, but she sent me a postcard of the White House that said "Missed you here!" and later a packet of photos.

On the day of her visit, it snowed and the landscape was somber, monochromatic. She recorded the usual images of people laying flowers and making rubbings, but she also had a friend take her picture, and, amazingly, I realized for the first time that I could see not just me and Toby, but something of Walter too, in the leggy teen-ager she had become.

I was glad she went and found a connection with him there, and, maybe it was wrong of me, but I didn't want to be fobbed off by seeing Walter's name on a wall. Not even to please her.

I wanted more than a monument.

I wanted a humble, direct apology, including a confession that it was pride and greed—not any ideals about human rights and government—that had cost those 58,000 lives and bitterly divided the country.

Dr. Tran's stories struck me not only because they illustrated the hardships of the war years, but also because he had come out of them with so much faith that things were getting better. Yesterday he didn't know if he would be able to eat. Today he was confident about feeding his family. In all the comparative abundance and privilege of my life as an American, I could not remember how long it had been since I believed anything was getting better or ever would.

14

When Han dropped us off, I followed Henry up the stairs to our rooms wearily, for once, thinking only of sleep. He looked exhausted too and was still fumbling for his key when I said good night and closed my door.

I threw off my clothes, hastily washed the dust and sweat from my face and hands, then collapsed on my bed. Nothing, I thought, could keep me awake tonight, but I was wrong. My body felt like it was made of cement, but my mind kept flitting restlessly from the past to the present and back again.

I would have said I had not slept at all, but I must have, because a thump against my door startled me into full awareness. Suddenly every nerve was alert as I listened to the silence that followed.

Then I thought I heard a voice whisper "Sar-ah," and a shiver ran over my skin. The room was completely dark, but I was sure my eyes were open. I really was awake.

"Sar-ah," the voice whispered again, and I was on my feet, opening the door, almost before the syllables hissed away.

If I had believed that the ghost of Walter could come and haunt me, I would have been relieved to discover it was only Henry. But I didn't and I wasn't. The sight of him huddled against the door, quite alive but deadly pale, was alarming enough.

"Henry, my God, you look literally green. What's the matter?" I asked, as I helped him to get up and stumble across the room to my bed.

He lay back on the palette and said with great effort, "I'm out of water," then closed his eyes.

I hurried to the bathroom, filled a glass with bottled water, and came back, but, in those few seconds, he had fallen asleep.

He was only asleep, I assured myself, not unconscious. There was a difference, surely, but his uneven breathing frightened me. I stood there holding the water and didn't know what to do.

"Henry," I said, touching his shoulder. "Here's the water. Let me help you drink it."

His eyes opened briefly at the sound of my voice, though he didn't really appear to see me. I tried to lift him up enough to drink, but he groaned so loudly that I gave up.

Instead I sat down by the bed, watching him breathe until I realized that I was hardly breathing myself. Then I opened the door and stepped out into the corridor.

The night was warm and sweet and peaceful, but, behind me, Henry groaned again, and I went back inside. "Henry!" I shook him. "You've got to drink some water."

His eyes fluttered open, and the total vulnerability I saw there shook me almost more than the dead weight of his body.

"Try to drink this," I said, lifting him up. "You're getting dehydrated."

Obediently he took a few sips then he slipped back into sleep.

I ran through a list of all the things that might be wrong with him—food poisoning, meningitis, encephalitis, malaria, the flu—calculated the number of hours until Dr. Tran would arrive in the morning—and found the list too long and the hours too many. I considered asking the stoic and uncomprehending hotel staff for assistance and knew that we were completely alone.

I went back to the bathroom and soaked my towel in cold water, but when I tried to lay it across his forehead, he flinched and pushed the cloth violently away.

"Henry —" I whispered, "I've got to do something!"

He surprised me by answering, without opening his eyes.

"Turn out the light."

For a moment, I almost laughed. It was such a relief to hear him speak.

"All right," I said, but first I rummaged in my bag for my flashlight.

With the lights out, the room was once again completely dark, except for the glimmer of light from the open door, but now I had no thought of sleep. I pulled my chair up to the bed so that I could see the outline of his body clearly and settled myself to watch and wait.

Huddled there with my whole attention fixed on Henry, I remembered the women I had seen that week in hospitals and clinics, crouched on the floor, waiting dutifully to serve their sick husbands and children.

I had never in my life been like that—a dutiful wife. During my marriage to Toby, it had been almost a point of honor not to be dutiful in any way. To assert my independence by being unreliable, unfaithful, and self-centered. Since then, although I had become a reasonably dutiful mother—part time—I had never given anyone else the opportunity to expect such behavior from me.

And what had I gained by that?

Freedom, I thought. Freedom from the ties that bind and cut your flesh.

Henry called this freedom from love, but his history was littered with would-be long-term relationships that had gone belly up: a wife who became pregnant by another man, a married woman who decided not to leave her husband, and others.

When I teased him about his bad choices, he said loving someone wasn't a choice. It happened, and you either went with it or you resisted.

As I gently rubbed him down with the damp cloth, touching him as I had longed to all week, I knew that this was a kind of intimacy that I had only had with Wendy when she was a child, never with a man.

It was strange. I prided myself on going with my feelings—not holding back ever—but that had mostly meant sleeping with anyone I wanted and leaving whenever I chose.

Henry had once referred to this as my deprived existence.

"You mean depraved, don't you?" I'd asked.

"No, I mean deprived," he said, and I laughed because we were in bed together when he said it, and I thought he was so peculiar.

"OK. What am I deprived of?"

I was joking, but what he said stuck with me because I didn't understand it.

Now I saw that, although I had been deprived of my brother through no fault of my own, the scorched earth way that I had lived my life ever since had created a kind of deprivation that I had imposed on myself.

Throughout the night, as I cooled him down and helped him drink, I saw a trusting look in his eyes that amazed me. How could he still not know he had chosen the wrong person to trust? I had been a runner all my life, and I liked to be alone.

At dawn I opened the door, and the sun flooded the room with rose-colored light. His breathing finally grew lighter and more even, and I knew he was going to be all right. He sighed, a soft sweet sound, and shifted his position. I covered him with the thin blanket so that he wouldn't get chilled and went outside.

A cigarette would taste really good and I knew where Henry kept his supply, but instead I crouched down on the cement floor and put my head down on my folded arms. I was beyond tired, and, as the sun rose higher, sunlight warmed me, and I began to cry. For relief and fear and for years of grief. For Henry, whom I was sure to disappoint, and for Walter who had died young and alone, far from home. For my parents, who lost their children; and for Wendy, whose mother had been afraid to love her too much.

I cried because I knew I had been wrong, not right, about practically everything, and I needed all of them to forgive me and also to forgive.

When the sun was high overhead, sweat replaced my tears, and I went back inside to take a shower. Henry slept on, snoring softly, as I dressed, made tea, and puttered around tidying the room. I liked having him sprawled across my bed as if he had been there his whole life.

Slowly his color improved, and I was just wondering how long I would have to wait for him to wake up, when his eyes opened. Clear and blue.

"Hey," I said. "Are you feeling better?"

He nodded. "Thanks to you," he said, reaching for my hand.

"So you think I have potential as a nurse?"

"Among other things you'd never expect. Come here," he said, moving over to make room for me, and I didn't require any further coaxing to do what he said.

15

We were nearly late for our appointment with Dr. Tran, who had planned a fast-paced day of visits to several noisy primary schools that I would hardly remember except for seeing them recorded on film. I was more interested in Henry, who was still a little shaky. My own fatigue was offset by relief and anticipation. The tension between us was gone, and every glance promised that we would be together again that night.

Dr. Tran observed us with avuncular good humor and, when Henry was out of earshot, he said: "International relations seem to have improved," and I laughed.

When it was time to say goodbye, I hugged him and said, "I hope life will continue to get better and better for you and your family."

He looked surprised, but smiled broadly, his silver teeth twinkling. "For you too," he said. "And you," he added, as he shook Henry's hand.

That night, Henry and I did sleep together in his room, and this time, he did not get up and leave me. I was the one who slipped quietly out to sit on the warm floor of the open corridor and watch the stars fade into morning.

Then I dressed, loaded the Rollei with film, and went out. I had been meaning to use it all week, and this was my last chance.

I handled the unfamiliar camera with extra care because it had once been Walter's and now would be my daughter's, but I knew how I wanted to use it: to bring Vietnam to Wendy. The flowering trees and stucco houses. The grand old opera house. The temples. The glittering lakes and crowded markets. The tiny cafes and patisseries. The bustling colorful streets. I wanted her to know that Vietnam was much more than a war, and that, in the end, there was peace.

My parents always said Walter gave his life for his country, and they didn't question the right or wrong of it. Now I could see, there wasn't any point in debating this any longer, and the only way his life was really wasted was if there was never any peace for us at home.

As I sat by the lake, watching the glittering patterns of sun on the water, I promised him that I would work as tirelessly for that as I had once worked to end the war.

I also promised myself that I would come back to Vietnam someday to see how they progressed. How I progressed.

Acknowledgments

Many people supported and encouraged me as I moved from Connecticut to New York to New Hampshire to Maine to California to England and finally to France during the writing of this book. A few who need to be especially remembered are Maria Aragon, Lorraine Archacki, Janet Basu, Peter T. Bennett, N.M. Bodecker, Kathryn Chetkovich, Martha Conway, Christine Davidson, Michelle Dionetti, Sue Duffy, Marianne Faithfull, Debra Feiner, Mark Fishman, Marion Gibbons, Hank Humphrey, Ann Hill, Diane Johnson, Margaret Jones, John Murray, Seamus O'Connor, Edward R. Sammis, Carol Sanford, Victoria Schultz, Elizabeth Knies Storm, John Strassburger, Lindy Strauss, Katie Supinski, Diane Tanzi; and, of course, my husband, parents, and brothers, Jim Mullins and Howard, Helen, Lea and David Boatwright.

I would also like to thank the UC Berkeley Professional Development Program for two grants that supported my work, and the Djerassi Resident Artists Program and Hedgebrook for the residencies that afforded me uninterrupted time to write in idyllic settings.

Finally, very special thanks to Robert Colley of Standing Stone Books for his vision and commitment.